VIGILANTE JUSTICE

W.D. FROLICK

Author: W.D. FROLICK
ISBN 978-1-7751958-6-3
Published by WDF Publishing
(www.wdfpublishing.com)

Copyright © 2020 by W.D. Frolick. All rights reserved.

No part of this book may be reproduced in any form or by electronic or mechanical means, including information storage and retrieval systems, without permission in writing from the publisher, except by a reviewer who may quote brief passages in a review.

This book is a work of fiction. Names, characters, places, and incidents are the product of the author's imagination or are used fictitiously. Any similarity to persons living or dead is purely coincidental and not intended by the author.

ACKNOWLEDGMENTS

I want to thank beta-reader **Peggy McGrady** for her constructive suggestions after reading my first draft.

Thank you, **Lieutenant Partick Taylor, of the Metropolitan Nashville Police Department (MNPD),** for your help.

Editing by **Allister Thompson Editorial**.

Cover design and formatting by **bookdesign.ca**

CHAPTER 1

For the first time in a long time, Homicide Detective Michael John McMahon's six-foot-two body felt relaxed and stress-free. He was stretched out on his well-worn recliner with *Goldfinger*, one of his favorite James Bond films, playing on his large-screen TV. Just as the movie was about to reach the climax, his cell phone began to dance on the coffee table. McMahon smiled and glanced at his watch—11:17 p.m. *It must be Suzanne.* Suzanne Taylor, his fiancée, was a fast-rising country music artist, currently on tour for her Nashville record label. Mike paused the movie, picked up the phone, and checked the screen. His smile quickly faded into a frown, and alarm bells started ringing in his head.

"Detective McMahon," he said without any enthusiasm.

"Hi, Detective, it's Sergeant Harding. Sorry for calling so late on such a miserable night. You've got a new case. We've had three murders in the past few weeks with similar MOs. The chief believes we're dealing with a serial killer, and he's assigning the case to you and Detective Sergeant Goodwin. I just sent a text to you and your partner with the address of the crime scene. Your boss, Lieutenant Foster, has also been informed."

"Okay. Thanks, Sergeant."

McMahon had just read the text when his cell phone began to vibrate in his hand. This time it was his partner.

"Hey, Rose."

"Hey, McMahon. Have you heard the good news?"

"Yeah, Harding just called. You sound like you're still half asleep."

"I was dead to the world and having a nice dream when that damn phone woke me up. As soon as I splash some cold water on my face and get dressed, I'll be on my way."

"Okay. See you there."

By the time Mike arrived at the parking lot behind a two-story gray brick building on 17th Avenue in the heart of Music Row, a light rain had begun to fall. He removed his umbrella from the back seat, walked over to the security officer, logged in, and ducked under the crime scene tape. The CSU team was already hard at work. He headed straight toward forensic pathologist Dr. Tony Capino, who was on his knees examining the body. In his late forties, short and stout, Capino had a full head of dark hair and a round, wrinkle-free, clean-shaven face. The ME looked up and smiled. "Hey, Mike. Nice of you to join us on such a lovely evening. Where's your partner in crime?"

"I'm here," Rose said, walking up behind them. Goodwin, a pretty African-American in her early forties, had a slim, athletic build. She had sparkling blackish-brown eyes, a radiant smile, and an afro-style hairdo that made her appear taller than her five feet, four inches.

"Do we have any idea who the victim is, Doc?" McMahon asked.

"The person who found him told me his name is Steven Starr. I just checked the victim's wallet, and his driver's license confirms his full name is Steven William Starr."

"That name rings a bell," Rose said.

"I know who he is," Mike said. "He's the president, CEO, and majority shareholder in Star Gazer Records and Shooting Star Music."

"And how do you know that?" Capino asked.

"My fiancée interviewed with him before she accepted the Frozen North deal. Suzanne got a bad vibe from Starr and didn't think she could trust him."

To get a closer look at the victim, like two baseball catchers, Mike and Rose squatted next to Capino. Starr lay face up on the pavement. He appeared to be in his late forties, with a full head of dark brown hair and a clean-shaven face. A pool of blood surrounded his bashed-in skull. A golf club driver lay in Starr's lifeless right hand, and a red golf ball sat in his mouth. The killer had meticulously staged the crime scene.

"Do we have a serial killer on our hands, Doc?" Goodwin asked.

"It looks that way. The MO at this murder matches the two previous homicides. Everything looks similar. He's left the same Taylor Made M-4 club at each crime scene. It must be his favorite driver."

"Yeah, the guy must be a golfer and likes the way that particular club feels in his hands when he swings it hard. It looks like he got a hole in one," Mike said, pointing to the golf ball.

"Give me a break," Rose said, pretending to be disgusted at McMahon's attempt to lighten the mood with a little morbid cop humor.

Not to be outdone, Capino said, "I think he's teed off about something. I'm guessing the red golf ball represents the blood he spills."

"Serial killers are a weird breed. He's using the red golf ball as his calling card," Goodwin said. "Have you found any prints at any of the crime scenes, Tony?"

"Not even one. The killer must have worn gloves and made sure the clubs and the golf balls were wiped clean."

"It's obvious the perp knows what he's doing," Mike said, running his fingers through his thick black hair.

"Based on the condition of the body, do you have an estimate of the time of death?" Goodwin asked.

"I'd say Starr has been dead for about three hours." Glancing at his watch, Capino continued, "That would place the TOD at about 9:00 p.m."

"Who found the body?" Mike asked.

"He's the guy standing over there, the one smoking a cigarette," the ME said, pointing behind them.

Mike and Rose walked over to the man with balding, gray hair who looked to be about sixty.

"Hello, sir, I'm Detective Sergeant Goodwin, and this is my partner Detective McMahon. Are you the person who found the body?"

"Yes, Detective, I am," he said, throwing his cigarette to the ground and crushing it out with his shoe.

"Who are you, and how did you come to be in this parking lot?" Rose asked.

"My name is Greg Moore; I work in this building. I'm Mr. Starr's janitor and handyman. I come in at ten until 6:00 a.m."

"What time did you discover Mr. Starr's body?" Mike asked.

"I always come to work a little early. I think it was around nine forty-five when I pulled into the parking lot. As I got out of my car, I noticed Mr. Starr lying on the ground. I rushed over to see if I could help, but it was too late. He was already dead, so I called 911."

"The ME estimates the time of death was around 9:00 p.m. Do you have any idea why Starr would be here so late?" asked Rose.

"Mr. Starr was a workaholic. He often stayed late. He said he could get a lot of work done after the staff went home when it's quiet, and there aren't any interruptions."

After writing down Moore's statement and contact information, Goodwin handed him her card and said, "If you think of anything else that could help our investigation, Mr. Moore, please give me a call."

"I will, Detective."

It was almost 3:00 a.m. by the time the crime scene wrapped up.

"Before you leave, Detectives, I'll be doing Starr's autopsy today at two."

"We'll be there, Tony," Rose said.

Glancing at his watch, McMahon said, "Let's meet in the squad room around nine."

"If we're lucky, we might get two or three hours of sleep. I think we're gonna need a gallon of black coffee to get us through the day," Rose said, trying to stifle a yawn.

CHAPTER 2

At nine that same morning, bleary-eyed and exhausted, Mike and Rose had just begun to discuss their new case when their boss, Lieutenant Foster, summoned them into his office.

A career cop, Foster had been with the MNPD for thirty-five years. The little bit of hair on his head was white stubble. He had a salt-and-pepper mustache under a pug nose, and his face always seemed to have a five o'clock shadow. Over the years, his job had taken its toll. Foster's brown eyes had lost their sparkle, and the vein on his forehead pulsed from time to time during stress-filled situations. His sense of humor was on the dry side, and most of the time, it was hard to tell if he was serious or joking.

"Good morning, Detectives."

"Good morning," Mike said.

"Good morning, Lieutenant," Goodwin said.

Foster popped a couple of antacid tablets into his mouth and swallowed them with a sip of coffee, hoping they would ease the pain radiating from his stomach ulcer.

"Catch the Golf Club Killer yet?"

"Golf Club Killer? Is that what we're calling him?" Mike said.

"No. That's the name, Jeff Stone, gave him in our telephone conversation this morning."

Mike and Jeff Stone, Investigative Reporter for the *Nashville Star Daily*, didn't care for one another. They had had several run-ins in the past, and Mike wasn't looking forward to reading his column on this case.

"Stone called you this morning?" McMahon asked.

"Yes, he did. He asked me if we have another serial killer on our hands."

"And what did you tell him?" Rose asked.

"The usual bullshit. I told Stone we're just starting our investigation, and it's too early to tell."

"And what was his response?" asked Mike.

"He wasn't too happy. He said that, as usual, I'm giving him the run-around. I told him I'm sorry he felt that way, but we would be issuing a press release and holding a press conference when the timing is right."

"What did he say to that?" Rose asked.

"Nothing. he hung up on me."

"That sounds like him," Mike said. "If Stone doesn't get his way, he acts like a spoiled kid who takes his ball and runs home."

"Let's not worry about Stone. What's up with the latest murder?"

"So far, the killer hasn't left even one clue at any of the crime scenes. No fingerprints and no DNA," Rose said.

"It looks like he knows what he's doing," Foster said.

"I agree," Mike said. "Whoever he is, he's no dummy. I don't think it's a coincidence that there aren't any security cameras at or near the crime scenes."

As Rose tried to hold back a yawn, Foster said, "I presume you didn't get much sleep last night."

"A few hours," Rose said.

"What do we know about the latest victim?"

"We know he's Steven William Starr, the majority shareholder, president, and CEO of Star Gazer Records and Shooting Star Music," Mike replied.

"Do you have any idea why our unsub might have targeted him?" Foster asked.

"If the killer is staying true to form, I'd say it's because Starr did something that pissed him off," Goodwin said.

"You're right," McMahon said. "Starr was on TV news last week and in the local newspapers denying that he stole a song from a young female songwriter named Sally Vasser. The songwriter claims that she left the lyrics and a demo of the song with Starr a few months ago. He said he'd get back to her. A few weeks ago, Vasser said her song was recorded by Jesse Jenkins, Starr's top female recording artist, on Star Gazer Records. The songwriter said that Starr made a few minor changes to the lyrics and put his name on her song. Vasser was in the process of suing Starr for stealing her song. The Golf Club Killer murdered him before the case could go to court."

"I seldom watch TV news or read the newspaper anymore," Foster said. "I get enough bad news on the job."

"Well, at least we now have a motive for Starr's murder," Rose said. "It looks like the killer must've read the story or watched Starr's interview on TV and decided to take the law into his own hands. A little vigilante justice."

"That seems like 'overkill' for the theft of a song. Pun intended," Foster said with a slight grin.

"Could be, but who knows how these nut jobs think," McMahon said.

"Maybe the songwriter decided to get even by killing Starr herself," Foster suggested.

"With all due respect, Lieutenant, that doesn't make sense," Rose said. "I don't think Sally Vasser would have had a motive to kill the other victims. The MOs were all the same."

"Unless she read about the other murders and decided to do a copycat version," Foster said.

"I guess anything's possible," Mike said.

"To be sure, I think we should interview Sally Vasser to see if she has an alibi for the time of Starr's murder," Rose said.

"Good idea," Lieutenant Foster said. "By the way, the Central Precinct, who caught the first two murders, is sending the files over after lunch. When they arrive, I'll leave them on your desk, Detective Sergeant. I'd like you to study each file carefully. Look for anything that the victims might have had in common. What's your plan for the rest of the day?"

"We have to complete a few reports, and after lunch, we're heading to Starr's autopsy. After that, we'll track down Sally Vasser and have a little chat with her," Rose said.

"Okay, keep me informed," Foster said as he picked up his ringing phone.

CHAPTER 3

At noon, the two detectives headed to the Songwriter's Bar & Grill. After lunch, they attended the two o'clock autopsy of Steven Starr. Nothing unusual turned up. The overwhelming conclusion by ME Dr. Tony Capino was that Starr had died from blunt force trauma to his head caused by repeated blows from the golf club left at the murder scene.

After leaving the Steven Starr autopsy, Mike and Rose headed to the Nashville Songwriters Guild International (NSGI) building located in the heart of Music Row. They were expecting to see Rita Thompson, a young lady they had dealt with previously in another case. Goodwin and McMahon identified themselves to the receptionist whose name was Carol Stewart.

"Does NSGI have a member named Sally Vasser?" Rose asked.

"Yes, we do," Carol confirmed.

"Does Rita Thompson still work at the reception desk?" asked Mike.

"Yes, but not as much as she used to."

"Carol, could you please give us the address and any phone numbers you have on file for Sally Vasser?" Goodwin asked.

"Just a minute, please," Carol said as she typed the name on her keyboard. "Ah, here it is."

She wrote the information down on a sticky note and handed it to Goodwin.

"Thank you," Rose said. "We appreciate your help."

"If you wish to talk to her, Sally's in a songwriting session just down the hall."

"Yes, we'd like to speak with her," Mike said.

"Okay. I'll go get Sally."

It didn't take long before Carol returned with a petite young woman with short red hair and a freckled face.

"This is Sally Vasser," Carol said.

"Hi, Sally," Rose said, extending her hand. "I'm Detective Sergeant Goodwin, and this is my partner, Detective McMahon."

"Pleased to meet you," Sally said, looking confused. "What's this about?"

"Is there someplace we can talk privately?" Mike asked.

"We can go back to the writing room. I'll ask my co-writers to take a break."

"Thank you, Sally," Rose said.

After the two co-writers had departed, Rose said, "Sally, we understand that you are suing Steven Starr, claiming he stole one of your songs. Is that correct?"

"Yes, that's right. I dropped off a demo of my song, 'Hotter Than Hell,' about two months ago and left Starr a copy of the lyrics. Two weeks ago, my song was recorded by Jessee Jenkins and released on Star Gazer Records. I wasn't surprised when I found out Starr changed a few lyrics and put his name on my song."

"I bet that made you angry," Mike said.

"It sure did. That's why I'm suing Mr. Starr. He's nothing but a smooth-talking crook."

"Did it make you angry enough to kill him?" Rose asked.

Surprise registered on Vasser's face. Her mouth opened, but nothing came out. Finally, she asked, "What? Is Mr. Starr dead?"

"Yes," Mike said. "An employee found his body in the parking lot behind his building last night."

"And you think I killed him?"

"I didn't say that," Rose said. "We have to check everyone who knew Starr, especially anyone who might have had a run-in with him. You happen to fall into that category."

"Where were you last evening between eight and ten?" Mike asked.

"Well, I sure wasn't killing Mr. Starr. I was doing a show at the Songwriter's Bar & Grill. Frank Fulton, the owner, his staff, and a full house of customers can confirm I was there."

"Okay," Rose said. "We'll talk with Mr. Fulton. Thank you for your time, Ms. Vasser. Have a nice day."

CHAPTER 4

When they arrived back in the squad room, Rose found the files from the first two murders sitting on her desk. She thumbed through them while Mike called Frank Fulton to confirm Sally Vasser's alibi. As he hung up the phone, Mike said, "It looks like Sally Vasser's alibi checks out. Vasser was performing at the Songwriter's Bar & Grill, just as she said. That would eliminate her as a suspect unless she hired someone to kill him."

"I doubt that," Rose said.

"I see you received the files from the Central Precinct. Let's hear what they have to say."

"Having watched the news and read the newspapers, we both know who the first two victims were. I took a glance at the files while you were speaking with Frank Fulton. I'll skim through them and hit the highlights."

"Okay. I'm all ears."

"As you know, Mitch McConnell, the first victim, was a District 19 councilor. He had just gotten out of his car in the parking garage of his downtown condo building when the killer attacked him from behind. His attacker left a golf club in his right hand and a red golf ball in McConnell's mouth. Similar to what we saw last night at the Steven Starr murder scene. McConnell was not married, and he lived alone. No one witnessed the murder."

Before Rose could continue, Mike said, "I met McConnell at a party about two years ago, before I hooked up with Suzanne. He was the kind of guy who thought he was God's gift to women."

"Yeah, I know the type. There's a newspaper article from the *Nashville Star Daily* by Jeff Stone, attached to McConnell's file."

"What's the article about?"

"It says to secure his support, McConnell may have accepted bribes from the second victim, Anthony Garanti of Garanti Developments Inc. of Chicago. McConnell was instrumental in lobbying to have the zoning changed on the Church Street Park site. The veteran highrise developer planned to build a 60-story, 750-foot-tall residential tower containing 300 units on the location across from the main library. Citizens who opposed the zoning change said that homeless people used the park and the adjacent Nashville Main Library as a refuge during inclement weather. The critics of the deal stated that the condo development was exclusively for wealthy buyers with units expected to start at over one million dollars."

"Very interesting," Mike said. "Go on."

"Linda Middleton, a former Metro Council Member, sharply criticized the development while stressing the importance of the park for the homeless. Reverend Donald Matthews of a nearby Methodist Church criticized the project noting that the homeless desperately need green space and housing."

"Garanti got approval for the zoning change, so most councilors must've supported the development," McMahon said.

"You're right. The deal's supporters listed several positive benefits: They said the tower would generate much-needed tax revenue for the city and that it would yield improvements to Anne Dallas Dudley Boulevard. Another benefit was that the development would provide a park for the homeless closer to a future social services building than the existing green space. Local developer Corey Sanderson said he had known Garanti for over thirty years and told reporters he favored the project. Nashville-based public relations spokesperson Beth Nelson, representing Mike Sherman, said the local real estate investor and developer favored the project as well. Sherman and Garanti recently partnered on a residential development north of Midtown."

"Since the developers are responsible for creating millions of tax dollars for the city, councilors don't want to kill the goose that lays golden eggs," Mike said.

"I'm sure you're right. I'd say the developers and city council are all in bed together. Garanti Developments Inc. is giving the city a parking lot on James Street as a replacement for the park to sweeten the deal. According to a recent appraisal, the projected value of the land is almost 3.5 million."

"What else is new," Mike said. "politicians and big business working hand in hand to screw the little guy."

"Sounds that way," Rose agreed.

Goodwin opened the second folder and began to read.

"It says Garanti was found dead in his hotel suite by a chambermaid. Garanti had ordered room service the previous evening. The cart with his uneaten food was sitting in the living room, and his body was on the floor staged the same way as McConnel's murder. It says the killer got into Garanti's room by disguising himself as a waiter."

"I wonder how he got the cart with Garanti's food?"

"The report says a hotel employee came across the real waiter in a supply storage room near the kitchen."

"Did the waiter get a look at his attacker?"

"Unfortunately, he didn't see a thing. He was knocked out from behind and dragged into the storage room, where his attacker bound his feet and wrists with duct tape and gagged him."

"What do these two murders tell you?" Mike asked.

"That, for some reason, our killer was seeking revenge for the homeless people. From what we know, a lot of people opposed the condo development. The list of suspects could be a long one."

"What about Steven Starr's killing? I don't see any connection to the McConnel or Garanti murders," Mike said.

"You're right. This case is going to be a tough one to solve. It's almost seven. Why don't we sleep on it and pick it up in the morning?" Rose said as she locked the files in her middle drawer.

CHAPTER 5

The killer smiled while reading the words "Golf Club Killer" in the article Jeff Stone had written about the murder of Steven Starr. He was about to put the newspaper down when another headline caught his attention.

ALLEGED DRUG DEALER ARRESTED BY MNPD

By Jeff Stone, Investigative Reporter

Alleged drug dealer Samson Smoke was arrested last Wednesday morning by an MNPD narcotics squad. When they raided his house on Douglas Avenue, the police seized a large quantity of the drug known as Bath Salts and two unregistered handguns. The estimated street value of the drugs was determined to be approximately two hundred thousand dollars.

Despite the name, Bath Salts have nothing in common with products used when taking a bath. They are designer drugs that recently became popular mainly because they are easily obtainable and hard to detect. These drugs are highly addictive, and they come in a crystalline powder that users swallow, inhale, or inject. Bath Salts are also known as Plant Food, Bloom, Cloud Nine, Ivory Wave, Lunar Wave, Scarface, Vanilla Sky, or White Lightning.

The drug contains a stimulant called cathinone, similar to amphetamines. These stimulants increase levels of dopamine, a brain chemical that can create feelings of euphoria.

Statistics show that twelve users overdosed and died from Bath Salts in the past two months. How many more deaths will result from Bath Salt overdoses? Your guess is as good as mine.

At his arraignment, well-known criminal defense attorney Timothy Barnes represented Smoke. After hearing arguments from the prosecutor, Assistant DA Karley Smithson, and Barnes, judge Harold Hudson set bail at $150,000.

When contacted, Police Chief Bradley Cummings said, "The arrest of Samson Smoke took place after months of surveillance and undercover work by narcotics squad detectives, Jack Bowman and Rico Costa. However, there is still a lot of work required. Drug dealers are like weeds. When you eliminate one, another pops up."

After reading the article, the "Gulf Club Killer" could barely contain his excitement. He had found his next target.

When Mike opened the door and stepped into his condo, he was surprised to hear the TV playing. He cautiously crept down the hallway and was about to draw his Glock when he saw a beautiful woman with long, wavy blonde hair and sparkling cat-like green eyes. She was sitting on the sofa in the living room with a glass of red wine in her hand. McMahon smiled. It was his fiancée, Suzanne Taylor.

"Hi, honey," Mike said as he entered the room. "I didn't expect you home for at least another day or two. How come you didn't call?"

"I thought I'd surprise you."

"You did surprise me. Now that you're here, I guess I'd better cancel the dancing girls. How come you made it home so soon?"

The dancing girls were a little joke between them. Every time Suzanne went on tour, Mike said he would bring in the dancing girls to keep him entertained while she was away.

"My last show got canceled due to an electrical problem. The bus got in around four, and one of the band members gave me a ride home. I've got three days off before we hit the road again."

Suzanne had been away on a two-week concert tour for her record label, Frozen North Records, owned by Canadian partners, Bill Ormond and Dave Franklin.

McMahon went over to Suzanne, gave her a warm welcome-home kiss, and sat down beside her.

"Are you ready for some food?" Mike asked.

"I'm starting to get a little bit hungry. I've just been chilling out with some wine waiting for you to get home."

"How about I take you out, and we can catch up over dinner."

"If you don't mind, I'm exhausted from the tour. I want to stay in tonight and relax."

"Okay, sounds good. I've had a crazy day and didn't get much sleep last night."

"Oh, what happened?"

"We've got a new serial killer case. This time the psycho is using a golf club instead of a guitar string." Mike went on to fill Suzanne in on the gruesome details.

When he had finished, Suzanne said, "I'm not surprised by Steven Starr's murder. When I met him, I didn't get good vibes from the man. I don't doubt he stole a song from a young songwriter. He's probably stolen a lot of songs over the past several years from naive songwriters. I'm glad I didn't leave him any of my songs or sign with him."

"Let's not talk shop. How about we order in some Chinese?"

"That works for me."

"After we eat, maybe we can find a good movie on TV and veg out with a few drinks," Mike said.

"Or, instead of a movie, why don't we find something more exciting to do?"

"What do you have in mind, Ms. Taylor?" Mike asked, a broad smile lighting up his face.

"Do I have to draw you a picture, Detective?" Suzanne said, breaking into a mischievous grin. "For God's sake, use your imagination."

CHAPTER 6

Without waking Suzanne, McMahon was shaved and showered by seven. Before leaving, he wrote a note and placed it on the kitchen table. It read:

Good morning, my dear. I hope you had a good rest. Have a relaxing day.

See you tonight.

Love,

Mike

McMahon arrived in the squad room at 7:45. He put the coffee he had picked up on the way on his desk and began to think about the case. He was deep in thought when Rose came through the door and sat down at her desk next to him.

"Good morning," she chirped.

"Good morning. You sound cheery this morning."

"I'm in a good mood. I slept well last night. It's amazing what a little sleep can do for your disposition. How did you sleep?"

"I slept soundly. Suzanne's last concert got canceled due to an electrical problem. She was waiting for me when I got home."

"With Suzanne home, I'm surprised you got any sleep at all," Rose said, a silly grin on her face.

Changing the subject, Mike said, "Have you thought about our serial killer? Any ideas as to who we're dealing with?"

"If I had to guess from the information gathered so far, I'd say we're dealing with someone who's between forty and fifty years of age. I'm sure our killer isn't some young pup in his twenties. He strikes me as highly organized, disciplined, meticulous, and very clever. Like Dexter on TV, he's creating a form of vigilante justice. It looks like he doesn't trust the system and has decided to become judge, jury, and executioner. I'm sure he thinks he's doing society a big favor by eliminating these people."

"You could be right," Mike said. "The killer is probably a psychopath who thinks the system is failing to do the job. Maybe he's had a loved one injured or murdered by someone who has never been caught and brought to justice."

"That makes sense. Now, all we have to do is figure out who the killer is and arrest him."

Mike grinned. "Piece of cake. We should have this case wrapped up in a day or two."

"Yeah, piece of cake." They both laughed.

Just then, Lieutenant Foster appeared, his face flushed, and the vein on his forehead was pulsing rapidly. In a stern voice, he said, "I don't know what you two think is so funny. We've got another murder on our hands. Come with me, please."

Rose looked at Mike, and Mike glanced at Rose. They both shrugged and followed the boss into his office.

As they sat down, Foster's phone rang. After glancing at the screen, he picked up the receiver. "Good morning, Chief." By the look on his face, he wasn't pleased with what he was hearing. He listened for a minute, then said, "They're with me now, Chief. Yes, sir, I'll tell them. Goodbye."

Foster hung up and shook out two antacid pills from the bottle on his desk. He gulped them down with coffee and cleared his throat. "As you heard, that was Chief Cummings. He's not in a good mood this morning. He said since the Golf Club Killer has struck again, a shit storm is brewing, and he wants this case solved fast. The mayor is on his back, and he said the media would be relentless until we find the killer. Finding the perp is your job, and I'll be jabbing your asses until this maniac is arrested and brought to justice. Speaking of which, you'd better get off your butts and get over to the crime scene."

The address on Douglas Avenue turned out to be a well-maintained, white frame bungalow built in the thirties. Two TV news crews and several newspaper reporters were hounding two officers who kept them away from the crime scene. When Mike and Rose arrived, they hurried past the media, ignoring all their questions, logged in, and headed toward the CSU crew.

Lying on the pavement next to a gray BMW SUV, the body looked similar to the previous victims. A bloody golf club driver lay in the victim's right hand, and a red golf ball protruded from his mouth.

As the detectives approached, Tony Capino looked up from examining the victim and smiled. "Hello, detectives. It's good to see you again. I'd rather meet in a bar over a drink instead of at a crime scene over a dead body."

"You and me both, Doc," Mike said. "It looks like our vigilante friend doesn't get much sleep."

"Yeah, he's into the *swing* of things and is *driving* my team and me crazy. Hurry up and catch him, will you? I'm not getting much sleep these days."

"Neither are we," Rose said.

"Have you ID'd the body yet?" McMahon asked.

"Yes. The victim's name is Samson Smoke, an alleged drug dealer."

"Any idea when this happened?" Goodwin asked.

"Judging from the condition of the body, I'd say the victim died early this morning. Somewhere between three and four."

"It looks like our killer surprised Smoke as he got out of his vehicle," Mike said.

"That would be my guess," replied Capino.

"From the look of his skull, I'd say the killer *smoked* Smoke real good," Rose said, attempting a little cop humor of her own.

"The caved-in skull indicates that our killer hit Smoke several blows more than his other victims. To me, that indicates this murder was more personal," McMahon said.

"It looks that way," Rose agreed.

"Tony," Mike asked, "do you know who found the body?"

"Sorry, Mike, I was told the caller refused to identify himself. He said he had just killed Samson Smoke and gave the 911 operator this address. The operator's screen didn't show any caller ID. He must've used a burner phone. Don't hold your breath; this guy isn't stupid. So far, we haven't found a single print or clue at any of the crime scenes."

"It doesn't look as if anyone witnessed the murder," Goodwin said. "I'll go round up a few uniforms and have them canvass the street. Maybe a neighbor saw something that could give us a lead."

At that moment, a red Corvette pulled into a neighbor's driveway. An attractive African-American woman in her early thirties got out. She hurried across the lawn, heading toward the crime scene, side-stepping an officer who tried to intercept her.

Hot on her heels, the officer yelled, "Lady, this is a crime scene." He grabbed her by the arm and began to escort her away when Rose said, "Hold on, Officer, I'll handle it."

Turning to the woman, Rose held up her badge and said, "I'm Detective Sergeant Goodwin. "Who are you, and why are you here?"

"My name is Camile Blackmon. I'm Samson Smoke's girlfriend. Did something happen to Samson?" That's when she noticed a body bag on a gurney. "Oh, no. Is Samson in there?"

"Yes. I'm sorry to have to inform you, Mr. Smoke was murdered sometime during the early morning hours," Goodwin said.

"Oh, my God," she screamed. Tears began to flow, and Blackmon looked like she was about to faint.

Quickly, Mike stepped up to steady her before she collapsed. It took a moment before she was able to stand without his support. Once Blackmon had composed herself enough to speak, Mike asked, "Were you with Mr. Smoke last evening?"

"No. I went to visit a girlfriend and stayed overnight. Samson asked me to join him for breakfast this morning."

"Do you know where Mr. Smoke was last night? Rose asked.

"Samson was out with some friends at the bar he owns, celebrating his release from jail."

"And which bar would that be?" asked Mike.

"It's called The Snake Pit."

"I know the place," Rose said. "It's not in the best part of town."

"Do you have any idea who might have wanted Mr. Smoke dead?" Mike asked.

Blackmon hesitated briefly, then replied, "Not really. Although in his business, to put it bluntly, I'm sure there's a lot of people who weren't too fond of him."

"I'm sure you're right about that," Rose said.

After writing Camile Blackmon's address and phone numbers down in his notebook, Mike gave her his card and said, "If you think of anything that might help solve your boyfriend's murder, please give me a call. Thank you for your time. You have our sincere condolences for your loss."

"Thank you, Detective." Camile Blackmon turned and slowly walked back to her car.

Before leaving the scene, the officers reported back to Rose. As expected—everyone had been asleep. No one had witnessed Smoke's murder.

CHAPTER 7

The two detectives arrived at the Snake Pit at 1:15 p.m. As they walked through the door, it took a moment for their eyes to adjust to the dark, dingy atmosphere. The odor of spilled beer and the lingering sweet smell of reefer smoke hung in the air like an invisible fog. Two "ladies of the night" sat at the far end of the bar sipping fruity drinks while they carried on a quiet conversation.

As Mike and Rose approached, the hookers glanced in their direction. When they realized the detectives weren't potential customers, the women turned and continued talking.

The bartender looked to be in his early thirties. He was muscular with a shaved head and tree-trunk arms covered with tattoos. His back faced the two detectives while his eyes watched a baseball game on a large screen TV. He hadn't noticed the new arrivals.

"Are you the manager?" Rose asked.

No answer.

"Turn that damn TV down," Mike barked.

The man jumped, turned around, and scowled. "What the fuck …"

They held up their badges.

"I'm Detective Sergeant Goodwin, and this is my partner, Detective McMahon," Rose said.

When the bartender realized they were cops, his attitude changed. He picked up the remote control and hit the off button.

"To what do I owe the pleasure, detectives," he said in a civil tone.

"Once more, Rose asked, "Are you the manager?"

"I guess you could say that. I'm the manager, bartender, bouncer, chief cook, and bottle washer all rolled into one. I even take out the trash."

"Do you have a name?" asked Mike.

"Yeah. My name is Tom, but everyone calls me Tank."

"Do you have a last name, Tank?" McMahon asked.

"It's Blackmon—Thomas Jefferson Blackmon."

"Blackmon," Mike repeated. "Would you happen to be related to a Camile Blackmon?"

"Yeah, Camile's my sister."

"We'd like to ask you a few questions," Goodwin said.

"What about?'

"About Samuel Smoke, the owner of this place," Rose said.

"What about him?"

"It sounds like you've already heard what happened," McMahon said.

"Yeah, I heard. My sister Camile pounded on the door around eleven screaming for me to let her in. When I opened the door, she was cryin' and shakin' like a leaf in a wind storm. I gave her a stiff drink to help settle her nerves. She told me what happened. We talked for a while, and she finally calmed down. When I opened for business at noon, she took off, sayin' she was goin' to her girlfriend's place."

"We understand that your sister was Smoke's girlfriend?" Mike said. "Is that correct?"

"Yeah, I guess you could call her that."

"Do you have any thoughts on who might have wanted to kill Smoke?" Rose asked.

Blackmon chuckled. "Hell, I'm sure there's a list as long as my arm or longer. Samson wasn't Mr. Nice Guy. He rubbed a lot of people the wrong way. There were times when I felt like killin' the bastard myself."

"Why do you say that?" Mike asked.

VIGILANTE JUSTICE

"Smoke treated all his employees like shit. He was never satisfied and was always givin' us hell about somethin'. And my poor sister, he treated her like she was his maid and sex slave. I don't know what Camile saw in that mean son of a bitch."

"We met your sister this morning at the crime scene. She said she was coming to meet Smoke for breakfast," Rose said.

"That cheap bastard wasn't taking her out for breakfast. Camile was goin' there to cook for him."

"Was Smoke here last night?" Mike asked.

"Yeah, he was. Samson came in around ten with a few of his asshole friends. They were celebratin' his release from jail."

"Do you remember what time he and his friends left?" Rose asked.

"Samson staggered out around two, but his friends stayed till I kicked them out at three."

All this time, Rose had been taking notes.

"Did you happen to see anyone suspicious who might have been watching Smoke, maybe followed him out when he left?" Mike asked.

"I was kept busy tendin' bar and dealin' with drunks. If there was anyone watchin' Smoke or followin' him when he left, I didn't notice."

"I see that you have several security cameras located throughout the place. Would you happen to have last night's activity on file?" Mike asked.

Blackmon laughed. "Sorry, Detective, we don't. The cameras are all fake. Smoke didn't want real cameras, if you know what I mean."

"Yeah, I get the drift," Mike said. "What time did you leave last night?"

"I left around four."

"Where do you live?" Mike asked.

"Upstairs. I rent the crappy cockroach-infested one-bedroom apartment. I was in bed by four fifteen and slept until ten."

"Okay, Mr. Blackmon," Rose said as she closed her notebook, "Thanks for your time. Here's my card. Please call if you think of anything that might help solve Mr. Smoke's murder."

"To tell the truth, Detective, I hope you never catch Smoke's killer. That guy did the world a favor. He deserves a medal."

CHAPTER 8

Before starting the car, Mike turned to Rose and asked, "Is Blackmon telling the truth? He wasn't upset about Smoke's murder. It's obvious he hated the man."

"You're right; Blackmon wasn't upset at all. He seemed happy that his boss was dead. But I don't think he had any involvement in Smoke's murder."

"You're probably right. So far, we don't have a clue who we're looking for."

When they arrived back at the station, as Mike sat down, his desk phone rang. The screen didn't display any caller ID. He picked up and said, "Homicide, Detective McMahon."

"I understand you're the detective in charge of the Golf Club Killer case. Is that right?" a deep, raspy voice said.

"Yes, I'm one of two detectives working the case. How can I help you, sir?"

"I think I saw Samson Smoke's killer last night."

"You what? Who are you, sir, and what did you see?'

"I prefer to remain anonymous. That's why I'm using a burner phone."

"Okay. Tell me what you saw."

"I was driving by when I saw a man running from a driveway on Douglas Street. When I watched the news this morning, I put two and two together and realized drug dealer, Samson Smoke, must've been killed by the man I saw fleeing the scene."

"Can you describe the man?"

"The guy was about six feet or slightly taller, average build, and dressed in black leather."

"Did you happen to see his face?"

"No, because he was wearing a motorcycle helmet with a tinted visor. In my rearview mirror, I saw the guy jump on a motorcycle and take off in the opposite direction."

"Can you tell me what type of motorcycle he was on?"

"I have no idea."

"I don't suppose you were able to get the plate number."

"Sorry, Detective, I didn't. It was dark, and I had driven past the house before I noticed the motorcycle."

"Sir, are you sure you won't reconsider and come in, identify yourself, and give us a written statement of what you witnessed?"

"Sorry, Detective, no can do. At first, I wasn't even going to call you. When I heard about Smoke, it didn't bother me at all. One less drug dealer makes this world a better place. I'm sure the drugs he peddled killed more people than we will ever know. As a law-abiding citizen, I thought it was my duty to let you know what I saw."

"As a law-abiding citizen, why don't you come in and complete that duty by identifying yourself and giving us a signed statement?"

The caller did not reply. He had hung up.

"What was that all about?" Rose asked.

"We may have just caught our first break in the case."

Mike proceeded to give Rose the details of the phone call. When he had finished, she smiled and said, "You're right; this could be the break we've been looking for."

Since Lieutenant Foster had left early for a doctor's appointment, their update would have to wait until the morning.

CHAPTER 9

Mike and Rose met with Lieutenant Foster at eight the next morning.

"It sounds like we may have caught a break in the case," Foster said after Mike had filled him in on the previous day's phone call.

"If the call was legit, at least we have an idea of where to start looking, Mike said."

"It's still going to be a daunting task trying to find this guy," Rose said. "There could be thousands of motorcycles registered in the Nashville area."

"You're right," Foster said. "Too bad he didn't get the plate number. It's like looking for a needle in a haystack. There's no way we can check out the owner of every motorcycle in Nashville. For all we know, the suspect may not even live in the city."

Rose glanced at Mike. "What are you thinking?"

At first, it appeared as if McMahon hadn't heard her question. Finally, he said, "Sorry, what did you say?"

"I asked, what are you thinking?"

"I've been tossing that call around in my head. I've come to the conclusion it wasn't from a concerned citizen; it came from the killer himself."

"What makes you say that?" asked Lieutenant Foster.

"It sounded rehearsed, plus it came from a burner phone, and the caller wouldn't identify himself. He said he was doing his civic duty by reporting what he saw. If he were truly doing his civic duty, he would come to the station and provided us with a signed statement.

That tells me the call came from the killer and not a legitimate witness. Besides, I don't think he used his normal voice."

"That makes sense," Rose agreed.

"I think the killer is deliberately trying to send us on a wild goose chase," McMahon said.

"I think you're right, Detective," Foster said. "You'd be wasting valuable time trying to find an imaginary suspect. I suggest you go back to the drawing board, do some brainstorming, and see what you can come up with."

At 1:00 p.m., they attended the autopsy of Samson Joseph Smoke. The results of the toxicology test would take a few days to complete. The ME suspected the results would confirm that Smoke had a high alcohol level in his blood when he died.

Shortly after returning to the station house, Lieutenant Foster called them into his office. He wanted to know how the autopsy went.

"Nothing unusual turned up," Rose said. "The tox test will take a few days. I'm sure the results will show Smoke had a high alcohol level in his blood at the time of his death."

"It looks like our vigilante doesn`t show any signs of stopping. He`s a relentless bastard. Do you think Smoke`s girlfriend knows more than she`s letting on?"

"I don't think so," Rose said. "She appeared to be genuinely distraught when she found out about Smoke's murder. As strange as it sounds, I truly believe that Camile Blackmon loved Samson Smoke."

"Or maybe she was putting on a good act," Foster said. "What's your next move?"

"We're going to review all the murders to see if there's anything we missed," Goodwin said.

"Okay. Keep at it," Foster said. "I'll see you tomorrow. I'm leaving early today. It's my wife's birthday. I'm taking her out to dinner and a movie."

"Give Doreen our best wishes for a happy birthday," Rose said.

"Will do."

As they left Foster's office, McMahon suggested they go somewhere quiet. A place where they could think without the distractions of people coming and going and the ringing of telephones. Neither detective had eaten since breakfast, so they picked up a pizza on the way. Forty minutes later, they were sitting in the living room of Mike's condo, sipping beer and devouring their food.

Gazing out the window, Rose said, "I've never been here before. The top of the AT&T tower does look like Batman's mask."

"Yeah, it does. That's why it's called the 'Bat' building."

"I guess I've never paid much attention to it before."

"Where should we start?" Mike asked.

"I think you should do a profile on our killer just like you did in the Guitar String Strangler case."

"I guess it can't hurt. You had a few good ideas the other day."

"Do you think so?"

"Yeah, you did, but we didn't write anything down. Why don't I tell you what I think, and you can take notes?".

"Okay," Rose agreed.

"For some unknown reason, our unsub targets people suspected of crimes. In his mind, they're guilty. He has decided to act as judge, jury, and executioner."

"What type of serial killer category does he fall into?" Rose asked.

"Our killer falls into the organized category. He's smart, plans his attacks carefully, and brings a weapon, the golf club, to each murder. He doesn't leave any clues behind. No fingerprints and no DNA. Our unsub knows how the system works."

Rose laughed. "You'd almost think our killer is a cop."

Mike jumped to his feet. "That's it," he yelled.

"What…what's it?"

"You're a genius. The killer's a cop, an ex-cop, a retired cop, or someone like a forensic expert who knows what we look for at crime scenes. That's why we haven't found any clues."

"Do you think so?"

"Yeah, I do."

"Maybe the guy's a cop who isn't happy with the justice system and wants to speed up the process. He could be an active cop, a fired cop, or a retired cop. Let's look into all these possibilities."

"It sounds like a good place to start," Mike said, glancing at his watch. "Let's call it a day and start fresh in the morning. Meet me in the squad room at eight. We can delve into MNPD records to see if any suspects turn up."

"Good idea. I'd better get moving. I promised myself I'd go to bed early and get a good night's rest for a change. I'm picking Jill up tomorrow after school. She's coming to stay for the weekend."

Jill, Rose's twelve-year-old daughter, lived with her ex, Paul Goodwin, a criminal defense attorney. At the time of their divorce, about a year ago, they mutually agreed that Jill would stay with Paul because of the crazy hours Rose worked as a detective. Paul had hired a full-time nanny so that their daughter would never be alone in the house.

After Goodwin had left, Mike grabbed another beer from the fridge, went back into the living room, and sank into his recliner. He picked up the phone from the side table and dialed a familiar number. Four rings later, he heard Suzanne's voice. "Hi, you've reached Suzanne. Sorry, I'm not available. Please leave a message, and I'll call you back as soon as possible."

"Hi, sweetie. I just thought I'd give you a call before tonight's concert. I hope your tour is going well. Talk soon. Love you."

Mentally exhausted, Mike closed his eyes. Half an hour later, the telephone rang. It was Suzanne. "Hi, honey. Sorry I missed your call. I'm just about to go on stage. I'll give you a ring after the concert."

"I'm bushed. I probably won't last until your concert's over. Can we talk tomorrow night?"

"Okay. I'll call you tomorrow. Love you."

"Love you, too."

CHAPTER 10

Mike was at his desk at 7:45 a.m. At precisely eight, Rose strolled in, humming a cheerful tune.

"Good morning, Detective McMahon," she said with a warm smile.

"Good morning, Detective Sergeant Goodwin. You sound and look rested this morning. I trust you slept well."

"Like a baby."

"Me too."

"Sounds like you're rarin' to go," Rose said.

"Yeah, I am. Let's get at it."

"Where do you want to start?"

"I think we should begin by checking MNPD internal records."

Mike turned on his computer, brought up the Records Department, and entered the password. He typed in MNPD cops terminated in the last five years. After a brief search, two names came up, along with a detailed report.

"Looks like we have a few possibilities," McMahon said as Goodwin peered over his shoulder.

The first report was about a cop who was suspended and then fired for police brutality. The record said that officer Russell David Scott, twenty-five, a three-year patrol officer, used excessive force when he arrested a suspected drug dealer last July. During the arrest, a street camera showed officer Scott, after handcuffing the suspect, a twenty-one-year-old African-American named Daryl Drew, punched and kicked the suspect several times. Drew spent three weeks in Nashville General Hospital with four cracked ribs, a broken nose, and severe lacerations to his face. After an assault conviction, the judge placed the fired officer on probation for two years, during which time he was to complete one hundred hours of community service. The judge also mandated Scott to complete an anger management course during his probationary period.

"It looks like Russell Scott could be a possible Golf Club Killer candidate. From the sound of the report, he had anger issues. Maybe he still does. I wonder where he is now?" Rose said.

"I'll find out in a minute."

The second report dated two years ago said that Joseph Anthony Russo, fifty-five, a narcotics detective, had been charged with stealing five thousand dollars from a drug bust. His partner, a fellow detective, witnessed the theft and turned him in. At his hearing, when Russo couldn't explain how a cash deposit of five thousand dollars ended up in his bank account, he confessed and was immediately dismissed from the MNPD. Russo was five years from retirement at the time of his firing.

"I don't think Russo is a candidate. He made one mistake that got him fired, but I don't think that would cause him to become a vigilante," Mike said.

"I agree. Let's keep Russo on the back burner for now," Rose said.

"I think we should visit Russell Scott. Let's find out where he lives." Mike typed in the name Russell Donald Scott on the DMV site, and a driver's license with a picture and address came up.

Thirty minutes later, they were knocking on the door of Scott's apartment. At first, there was no answer. Mike pounded harder and yelled, "Russell Scott, open up, MNPD. We need to talk to you."

"Maybe he's not home. He could be out or at work," Rose said.

Just as Mike was about to knock again, a sleepy voice shouted, "Hold on, I'm coming."

A moment later, dressed in a white terrycloth robe, a tall, muscular man with short, dark hair and a slim face with a five o'clock shadow opened the door.

"Russell Scott?" Mike asked.

"Yeah, I'm Russell Scott. What's this about?"

"I'm Detective McMahon, and this is my partner Detective Sergeant Goodwin." They held up their badges. "We'd like to ask you a few questions. May we come in?"

"Questions? About what?"

"We'll tell you when we're inside," Rose said.

"Be my guest," Scott said, stepping aside and waving them in.

When they were seated in the sparsely furnished living room, Rose asked, "Where were you three nights ago on the fourth?"

Scott paused for a moment, then said, "I was at work."

"At work? Where would that be?" Mike asked.

"At Music City Electronics. I work in security as a night watchman. I do a twelve-hour shift from seven till seven five days a week."

"Is there anyone who can verify you were there that night?" Rose asked.

"No. I work alone. But the video cameras have date stamps and will show me making my rounds every two hours. What the hell's going on? I won't answer any more questions until you tell me why you're here."

"I see a set of golf clubs in the far corner. Are you a golfer?" Mike asked.

"I'm more of a duffer than a golfer. I do eighteen holes a couple of times a year with a few of my friends. Why do you ask?"

"We're investigating the murder of a man named Samson Smoke. Have you heard of him?" Mike asked.

"Yeah, I've heard of him. I read about his murder in the paper and saw it on TV news. Just because I have a set of golf clubs doesn't make me the Golf Club Killer. Is that what you're thinking?"

"Are you the Golf Club Killer?" Goodwin asked.

Scott began to laugh. "I may hate drug dealers, but I'm not running around killing them. Although I do applaud whoever killed that Smoke guy."

"You were fired by the MNPD for police brutality and convicted of assault. You took the law into your own hands when you beat the shit out of Daryl Drew, a suspected drug dealer," Rose said.

"Yeah, I lost control that one time and I've been paying the price ever since. My wife divorced me. She was granted custody of our two-year-old son and moved back to Atlanta to live with her parents. I never see my kid, even though I pay her alimony and child support every month. Between my regular hours and some overtime, I can barely make ends meet. I've taken an anger management course, and now I'm a changed man."

"Glad to hear that," Rose said.

"To eliminate you from our suspect list, let's go to your place of work and view the videos you mentioned," Mike said.

Scott glanced at his watch. "You've got to be kidding. I don't leave for work for another three hours."

"Looks like you'll be going in early today," Goodwin said. "Go get dressed. I'll ride with you, and Detective McMahon will follow us."

Mumbling under his breath, Scott went to his bedroom to change.

The video proved Russell Scott was at work the night of Samson Smoke's murder, eliminating him as a suspect.

CHAPTER 11

Lieutenant Foster called Goodwin and McMahon into his office at nine. They were surprised to see Chief Bradley Cummings sitting behind Foster's desk. Foster sat in a chair to the chief's right, face crimson, and sweat beads on his forehead. He looked like a schoolboy on the verge of tears who had just been reprimanded by the principal.

Without smiling, in a frigid voice, Chief Cummings said, "Good morning, detectives. I hope you slept well last night. I haven't had a good night's sleep since this Golf Club Killer thing began. Are you making any progress?"

Before anyone could speak, Lieutenant Foster's phone rang. Checking the screen, he frowned as he picked up the receiver. "Lieutenant Foster. One moment, please. It's for you, Chief. It's the mayor."

"Good morning, Mr. Mayor." The chief listened briefly, then said, "That's what I'm doing. I'll call you when I'm back in my office. Goodbye, Mr. Mayor." He glared at Mike and Rose. "As you could hear, that was the mayor. He wants an update on the case. He's getting calls from the media, wanting to know what the MNPD is doing to catch the Golf Club Killer. He also said the business community is on edge. Hotel reservations are down, and entertainment venues are playing to sparse crowds. It's obvious that tourists have heard about the killings and are avoiding coming to Nashville like the plague. So, I'll ask you again, are you making any progress?"

"So far, Chief, we haven't been able to come up with any leads. The killer is smart. He hasn't left any clues at any of the crime scenes.

No fingerprints and no DNA. He has everyone baffled. We think we could be dealing with a cop or an ex-cop, but sooner or later, he's bound to make a mistake. Yesterday we checked out a cop who was fired recently for assault, but his alibi checked out," Rose said.

"I'm getting tired of saying 'no comment' to the media, especially that pesky reporter, Jeff Stone. I don't know how much longer I can stall before calling a press conference. What's your next move?"

"The killer uses the same make and model of golf club driver to kill his victims. He stages each crime scene by leaving a red golf ball in their mouth and the murder weapon in their hand. All the clubs appear to be new. Our next move is to visit every local golf retailer to see if they can recall selling red golf balls and one or more of the make and model club to anyone. It's a long shot, but we could get lucky," McMahon said.

"Let's hope you do get lucky, and your idea turns up a suspect. Lieutenant Foster will keep me informed as you update him."

After Chief Cummings had left, Foster said, "Since we don't have much to go on, your plan to visit sporting goods stores can't hurt. To save time, I suggest you make a list of all the stores that sell golf clubs in Nashville. Instead of going together, split the list in two. That way, you can cover all the outlets in half the time. Get another car from the garage. Good luck."

When Mike Googled golf stores in Nashville, thirty names came up. He printed two copies and handed one to Rose. They divided the city into two geographical sections and revised each list accordingly.

Nothing turned up at the first five stores Mike visited. At the sixth store, after showing his badge, when he asked the question, a clerk named Eddy said, "A few weeks ago, I remember a man came in asking for a Taylor Made M4 driver."

"Did you sell him one?" Mike asked.

"No, because we didn't have that model in stock. When I recommended another Taylor Made driver, he thanked me for my help and said he'd try another store. The guy was very polite, but he seemed a little weird."

"Do you have video surveillance that may have caught this guy?"

"We do have cameras throughout the store, but we erase them every forty-eight hours. Sorry, Detective."

"Do you remember what he looked like?"

Eddy paused and thought for a moment. "I'd say he was about six feet, in his early sixties, with a slim build and seemed fit for his age. The guy wore mirrored sunglasses and a Taylor Made golf cap. The cap covered his head, so I couldn't tell if he was bald or had hair. A bushy salt and pepper beard covered his face, but one thing caught my eye. The man had a strawberry-colored birthmark on his forehead similar to that former Russian president. I can't remember his name."

"Do you mean Mikhail Gorbachev?"

"Yeah, Gorbachev, that's the guy."

Mike wrote down the description in his notebook and handed the clerk his card, "If he comes in again or if you think of anything else, please give me a call immediately. Thanks for your time, Eddy."

"Do you think this guy's the Golf Club killer I've been reading about?"

McMahon ignored the question, turned, and left.

Back in the car, Mike pulled out his cell phone and dialed Rose.

When her phone rang, seeing McMahon's name, Goodwin asked, "Hey, Mike, what's up?"

"I think we may have a lead." Mike gave her the description that Eddy had provided.

"That's interesting. Maybe we're finally catching a break."

"Yeah, maybe. Have you had any luck?"

"Not so far. I'm almost halfway through my list. I have to go. I just arrived at another store."

"Okay. Good luck. See you later."

"See you."

Entering the golf department, Rose identified herself to a middle-aged salesman whose name tag read Rick. She asked, "Do you stock Taylor Made golf clubs?"

"We sure do, Detective," he replied.

"Do you carry the Taylor Made M4 driver?"

"Yes, we do. It's a very popular club. Would you like to try one?"

"No, but I'd like to know if you've sold any lately to an elderly man?"

"I'm not sure, Detective. Let me go and ask Sandra." A moment later, he returned with an athletic-looking young woman in her twenties and introduced her to Goodwin.

Rose gave Sandra the description of the man Mike had given to her over the phone.

Sandra's eyes lit up, and she said, "Yesterday, a man like you described came in and purchased two M4 drivers. I was curious, so I asked him why he needed two drivers. He laughed and said he was a duffer. The day before, he was teeing off on a long par five, and he wanted to hit the ball a mile. He said he took a full backswing and, on the way down, lost his balance, and the club hit the ground in front of the ball, and the shaft broke. He said that mistake cost him a hundred-dollar bet with his friends because he had to use his three wood to tee off the rest of the day. He said he was replacing the broken driver and decided to have a backup if it happened again."

"Did he use a debit or credit card to pay for the clubs?"

"Most customers pay with plastic these days, but not this guy. He paid by cash. As I recall, he pulled out a wad of hundred-dollar bills that could choke a horse. He didn't even want the receipt."

"Since it was a cash purchase, I suppose you didn't get his name," Goodwin said.

"Sorry, Detective, I don't have a name. But we may have caught him on video. Would you like me to check?"

"That would be great," Rose said enthusiastically.

"Please follow me, Detective."

Sandra led Goodwin into a room that contained a video surveillance monitor.

In less than five minutes, Rose was staring at a video of the man Mike had described.

"Is it possible for you to make a copy of this video?"

"No problem, Detective."

It didn't take long before Sandra handed Rose a thumb drive. "Thank you, Sandra, for your time and help. Here's my card. Please call if you think of anything else. If the same man comes in again, make an excuse to leave the room and call me immediately on my cell number. Stall him as long as you can. If he leaves before we arrive, if you can, follow him into the parking lot and try to get his plate number and a description of the vehicle he's driving."

"Okay, Detective, I'll do my best. I'm curious, does this have anything to do with the Golf Club Killer case?"

"Sorry, Sandra, I can't comment on that." Without another word, Goodwin turned and walked away.

By mid-afternoon the next day, Rose left the last store on her list and met Mike in the squad room at four. Comparing notes, three more retailers reported cash sales of the Taylor Made M4 driver to a man matching the description that Eddy and Sandra had provided. As Rose showed Mike the video, he couldn't contain his excitement. "Wow," he said. "Great work, partner."

They gave the description and video of the unsub to the department sketch artist. While waiting for the drawing, they discussed the case and compared ideas about who the killer might be. Half an hour later, with sketch in hand, Rose made several photocopies before knocking on Lieutenant Foster's door. He waved them in, and as they sat down, he asked, "Well, how did the golf store visits turn out?"

"It looks like we may have found a possible suspect," Goodwin said.

"That's good news. Tell me about it."

After giving the lieutenant a brief synopsis of their findings, Rose said, "Based on descriptions given to us by salespeople in five different locations, our sketch artist came up with this composite drawing of the suspect from a video I obtained at one of the stores." She handed Foster the memory stick.

Foster studied the sketch for a moment, then popped the flash drive into his computer. When the video ended, he said, "The sunglasses hid the guy's eyes. Knowing his eye color would help. However, the birthmark on his forehead is an excellent clue. Good work, detectives. The chief is planning on holding a press conference in a few days. He may want to release this composite and video to the media. Hopefully, someone will recognize the suspect and provide us with information that will help us catch the bastard."

"If the chief decides to release the composite and video, it could help identify the unsub, but it will also alert the killer that we're on to him. That may cause him to change his appearance or to go underground," Mike said.

"You're right, Detective, but it's up to the chief to weigh the pros and cons of releasing this information. I'll throw the ball in his court and let him decide. Leave it with me. Again, good work. That's it for now."

After the detectives were gone, Lieutenant Foster made a phone call. He informed Chief Cummings about the composite sketch and video. Not wanting to waste time, Cummings immediately scheduled a press conference for ten the next morning.

CHAPTER 12

"Good morning, everyone, and thank you for coming. Today's press conference will provide you with an update on the so-called Golf Club Killer investigation. Lieutenant Robert Foster and two of his most experienced homicide detectives, Detective Sergeant Goodwin, and her partner, Detective McMahon, are working on the case. With us today, the detectives have been burning the midnight oil trying to find this vicious serial killer. Finally, after long hours and devotion to the task, the detectives have found a person of interest that could be the suspect. Based on descriptions provided to our detectives, we have created a composite sketch of the person of interest that we wish to identify and question." The chief held up a copy of the composite drawing. "Also, we have obtained a video of the unsub from one of the sources the detectives visited. Before leaving, you will all receive a copy of this composite drawing, and TV stations will also receive a copy of the video for their newscasts. Should anyone recognize this individual, there is a telephone number in each package. If desired, the caller can remain anonymous. I will now open the floor to questions. Please raise your hand, identify yourself, the media you represent, and to whom your question is directed. Thank you."

The chief pointed to a woman in the first row.

"I'm Connie Myers from Fox News Channel 17. I'd like to know where the description of the suspect came from."

"I'm sorry, Connie, I can't give out that information. If the suspect knew who gave us his description, it could put that individual's life in jeopardy."

"You, sir," the chief said, pointing to Mike's favorite reporter.

"Good morning, Chief. I'm Jeff Stone, with *Nashville Star Daily*. My question is for Detective McMahon. Do you have any idea why the killer uses a golf club to kill his victims?"

Mike stood and looked directly at Stone, who had a smirk on his face. "I don't have a clue, Jeff. Maybe the killer doesn't own a gun. If you have any suggestions, I'd like to hear them."

"Sorry, Detective, I don't. That's your job. I hope you catch this guy quicker than it took you and your partner to catch the Guitar String Strangler."

Inside, McMahon was boiling. He wanted to say something nasty but kept his cool and said, "So do I, Jeff. So do I." Mike sat down and whispered to Rose, "That Stone is a real asshole. He couldn't leave well enough alone. He had to throw in a jab about our last serial killer case."

Rose whispered back, "He was trying to get you riled up. I'm proud of you. You didn't take the bait."

Mike grinned. "I guess my anger management course is paying off."

After several more questions were asked and answered, the chief called an end to the press conference.

The Golf Club Killer grabbed a beer from the fridge and headed to his recliner. He turned on Fox Channel 17 and sat back to watch the six o'clock news. He was about to take a sip, the bottle halfway to his mouth. The lead story showed a composite drawing of himself wearing his disguise. Then a video came on the screen showing him at the cash register holding two golf clubs and a clear bag of red golf balls. He turned the volume up as the announcer said, "This man is a person of interest and is wanted for questioning by the MNPD in a murder investigation. If you know the name and whereabouts of this individual, please call the number on your screen. If you wish, you can remain anonymous. An operator is standing by to take your call. Please call now." A few seconds later, the scene switched to an automobile accident. "In other news—"

The killer turned the TV off and sat in stunned silence. Then he began to laugh. *I don't need to worry. The cops will be spinning their wheels looking for a person who doesn't exist. I will create a new disguise that won't look anything like the composite sketch. I won't buy any more clubs in Nashville; I'll go to Knoxville or Chattanooga. I doubt the MNPD will be checking golf stores in those cities.*

CHAPTER 13

Two days after the press conference, Mike parked his car and entered the elevator in his condo building when someone yelled, "Hold the elevator, please." He put his hand out to stop the door from closing, and a few seconds later, a fit-looking gray-haired man in his late fifties or early sixties came trotting around the corner.

"Thanks," the man said as he entered the elevator.

"No problem. What floor?"

"Twenty-four, please."

McMahon punched twenty-two and twenty-four.

As the door started to close, Mike said, "You look familiar. Do I know you?"

"I don't think we ever met. I'm retired now. I was a detective in the West Precinct Homicide Unit."

"Of course. You're the legendary Detective Sergeant Patrick O'Connor. You were tenacious. You never gave up on a case. You and your partner solved a lot of difficult homicide cases that had other detectives stumped."

"Legendary? I've never heard that one before," O'Connor said with an embarrassed smile.

"You certainly are an MNPD legend. Pleased to meet you, Detective Sergeant O'Connor. I'm Detective Mike McMahon."

The two men shook hands.

"Now, I recognize you. I've seen you on TV, and I've read all about the cases you and Detective Sergeant Goodwin have been working. By the way, good job on the Guitar String Strangler case. I'm curious, how are you making out on the Golf Club Killer case?"

"You may have read the newspapers or watched it on TV. We have pictures of a possible unsub, but no one has come forward with information to help us identify this individual."

"Yeah, I saw the composite and video on TV last night. I hope you catch that madman soon."

"You and me both. I didn't know you live in this building. How long have you been here?"

"After retiring, we sold our house in the country, and my wife and I moved in here about two years ago. We thought it would be easier to travel if we lived in a condo. Unfortunately, that didn't work out the way we had planned."

That's when a news story flashed through McMahon's mind.

"I'm so sorry for your loss. I read about your wife's tragic death about a year ago. I can't even begin to imagine what you've been going through."

"Thank you, Detective. It's been hell, but I'm starting to get on with my life."

Just then, the elevator dinged as it stopped at Mike's floor.

"It's been a pleasure meeting you, Detective Sergeant O'Connor."

"Likewise, Detective McMahon. By the way, Pat, please call me Pat."

"Okay. Call me, Mike." McMahon held the door to prevent it from closing. "After eating, why don't you come down for a drink? If you don't mind, I'd like to get your perspective on the Golf Club Killer case. My number is 2225."

O'Connor paused for a moment, then said, "Okay, Mike, I'll see you in about an hour."

"Great!" McMahon said, releasing the door.

After a quick supper of warmed-up meatloaf, Mike decided to Google Patrick O'Connor. He found some interesting information. An article written at the time of his retirement said Sergeant O'Connor had been with the MNPD for over thirty years. He was a New Yorker, born and raised in Queens. Initially, he had applied to join the NYPD, but the waiting list was a mile long. While on vacation with his wife in Nashville, they fell in love with the city. O'Connor had always wanted to become a police officer. The MNPD was hiring, so he applied, got accepted, and he and his wife, Cindy, moved to Nashville. O'Connor was a patrol officer for seven years before being promoted to a homicide detective. The article went on to say that O'Connor had a photographic memory. He was able to remember minute details from crime scenes. Those details helped him and his partner, Joe Carson, solve over fifty homicide cases. The article didn't mention anything about the O'Connors having children.

McMahon was relaxing with a beer and *Dirty Work*, a Stuart Woods novel, when the doorbell chimed. Mike opened the door to a smiling Pat O'Connor, who handed him a cold six-pack of Coors Light.

"Thanks. You didn't have to bring any beer. I've got plenty on hand."

O'Connor laughed. "I wanted to bring them. Shut the fuck up and invite me in."

Surprised by O'Connor's sharp sense of humor, McMahon laughed. "Sorry, come in." Before putting the beer in the fridge, Mike gave one to O'Connor and kept one for himself. "Would you like a glass, Pat?"

"Don't dirty a glass. I prefer drinking from the bottle."

"Me too. Let's go into the living room."

Mike sat in his recliner while O'Conner took a seat on the sofa.

"As I said earlier, I'd appreciate your thoughts on the Golf Club Killer case."

"I don't know if I can be of much help. Since I retired, I'm probably a little rusty."

"I doubt that. Based on what I've read about your career, you and your partner, Joe Carson, solved several cases that had other detectives stymied."

"We got lucky on a few of those cases. There are many good detectives in the MNPD, including you and your partner, Sergeant

Goodwin. It comes down to never giving up on a case, no matter how long it takes. Hard work eventually pays off."

"Yeah, you were tenacious. You never gave up until the case was solved. I guess that's why other detectives gave you the nickname Bulldog."

O'Connor laughed. "I hope I didn't get that nickname because they thought I looked like a bulldog."

"I think you got that name because of your persistence. You'd sink your teeth into a case and never let go until it was solved. I read about a case that you and your partner solved that must've given you a great deal of satisfaction."

"Oh, which case was that?'

"It was the one where you collared a pedophile who raped and murdered a twelve-year-old girl."

"I hate those bastards. I remember that case like it was yesterday. Someone saw a suspected pedophile in the area where a little girl's body was found in a dumpster and gave us his description. We brought the suspect in for questioning, and, of course, he denied it. I could tell he was nervous by the way he was sweating. I offered him a bottle of water, which he gladly accepted. The guy had scratch marks on his neck. When I asked him how his neck got scratched, he said it was from his cat. After finishing the bottle of water, the dummy threw it into a wastebasket. We checked the skin particles under the girl's fingernails and the DNA from the water bottle, and they matched. The next day, we arrested him for second-degree murder. At his trial, he was found guilty and sentenced to life in prison without any chance of parole for twenty-five years. Six months later, the bastard was murdered in prison."

"How did you feel when you heard he was murdered?"

"I hate to say this, but I was glad to hear the news. That maniac got what he deserved. So, what do you want my thoughts on?"

"I'd like your best guess as to who the killer could be and why he's acting as a vigilante and taking the law into his own hands."

"That's a tough question, Mike. I wish I had a crystal ball so I could provide the correct answer. If I had to take a wild guess, I'd say the killer is someone who thinks our justice system isn't working. He's decided to help out by eliminating a few bad guys."

"That sounds logical. My partner and I were thinking the same thing."

"From what I've read, the killer hasn't left any evidence at the crime scenes. Is that correct?"

"That's right. The killer knows what he's doing. It's almost as if he's had experience processing crime scenes."

"Do you mean someone like an ex-homicide detective or a forensic specialist? Someone like me, for instance?"

McMahon chuckled. "Now that you mention it, yes, someone like you fits the profile. I hope you don't mind, Pat, but I wouldn't be doing my job if I didn't ask. Are you the Golf Club Killer?"

O'Connor grinned. "What do you think, Detective? Am I the guy you're looking for?"

"You could be, but I can't prove it, so you're off the hook for now."

"Thank God," O'Connor said, feigning relief by wiping his brow with the back of his hand. "I could use another beer. How about you, Mike?"

"That sounds like a good idea."

Before McMahon could get out of his chair, O'Connor was on his way to the kitchen. Seconds later, he handed Mike a beer and said, "Now, where were we?"

"You were giving me your thoughts on the Golf Club Killer case."

"Oh, yeah. I can sympathize with the killer to a certain degree. He's taking scumbags off the street and saving the state a lot of time and money for trials that may not get convictions. During my time as a homicide detective, we arrested murderer suspects who we knew were as guilty as sin, only to have a smart defense attorney find a loophole or a technicality that got them off. That frustrated me to no end seeing all our time and hard work go down the drain. I'm sure in your brief career, you and your partner have experienced similar frustrations."

"We certainly have."

"Don't get me wrong, Mike, I don't condone taking the law into your own hands. What this maniac is doing is wrong. Keep at it. You'll collar this guy sooner or later."

Mike laughed. "Sooner would be preferred. As you mentioned, hard work pays off. I guess we'll just have to work a little harder."

O'Connor looked around, took a sip of beer, and changed the subject. "Is your condo a two-bedroom unit?"

"Yeah, it is. That's all I need. How about your unit? Is it a two-bedroom as well?"

"Yes. My unit looks exactly like this one. Now that Cindy's gone, a one-bedroom would be big enough for me."

"Again, I'm so sorry about your wife. Are you able to talk about it?"

"It took a while for me to get my head around what happened. Looking back, I still can't believe she's gone. My wife was in the wrong place at the wrong time. We had booked a trip to Paris. A week before our flight, Cindy went shopping. She was having lunch in the food court at the Opry Mills Mall when a young man named Tyron Parker, twenty-one, spaced out on drugs, decided to shoot up the place. He shot and killed six innocent people, including my wife. Three others were seriously wounded but survived. Before the druggie could reload his pistol, two mall security guards tackled Parker, cuffed him, and held him until the police arrived."

"I can't remember. What happened to the guy? Was he ever convicted? Is he in prison?"

"That's what should have happened, but Parker's intelligent defense lawyer pleaded temporary insanity caused by the cocktail of opioids he had consumed. At his trial, so-called experts testified that the accused was in a drug-induced state and was not aware of what he was doing; therefore, he could not be held responsible for his actions. The jury swallowed the story hook, line, and sinker, and after deliberating for two hours, Parker was found not guilty. Instead of being sentenced to death or life in prison, he got sent to a country club rehab facility. Can you believe that?"

"My God, that's unbelievable,"

"You've got that right. So much for our justice system. That bastard could be released soon and be back on the streets, killing more people. Let's pray the Golf Club Killer finds him before that happens."

In his mind, Mike agreed. He hoped the Golf Club Killer did find the son of a bitch, but he kept his thoughts to himself. He decided to change the subject. "I'm curious, what do you do with yourself now that you're on your own?"

"I keep busy. That way, I don't have time to sit around, feeling sorry for myself. At my retirement party, the MNPD gave me a complete set of golf clubs. I take lessons, practice, and try to get out a few times a week with some of my retired cop friends. I'm even helping my former partner, Joe Carson, coach a little league baseball team. I work out regularly in the gym in our building and jog three or four times a week. All these activities keep me stress-free and my head clear."

"Good for you, Pat. Keeping busy is excellent therapy."

"Do you live alone, Mike?"

"No, I live with my fiancée, Suzanne Taylor."

"Suzanne Taylor? Why does that name ring a bell? Is she out this evening?"

"I guess you could say that. Shortly after we became engaged, Suzanne moved in with me. About a year ago, Frozen North Music signed her as a songwriter and a recording artist. Ever since she released her first album, Suzanne's been out on the road doing concerts. She comes home for a few days, charges her batteries, and then is gone again. We don't see much of each other these days. But if you want to survive in the music business, being on the road is necessary if you wish to further your career."

"I'm a big country music fan. I've heard Suzanne's duet single, 'Don't Throw Our Love Away,' several times on a local country station, and I've watched the video on CMT. Your fiancée is a beautiful woman."

"Yes, she is. I consider myself the luckiest man in the world."

"I've heard that Marven Jones, the guy she sings the song with, is from Canada."

"That's right. Marven was born in Timmins, Ontario. It's the same town that Shania Twain hails from."

"A lot of talent seems to be coming to Nashville from north of the border."

"You're right. The partners from Frozen North Music are also Canadians."

"Getting back to your case, Mike, I might be wrong, but I think your Golf Club Killer could be an active cop who has become fed up with the justice system."

"That's one possibility. Like in the TV show *Dexter*, the killer might even be a forensic person."

"You never know."

"Maybe someone will recognize him from the composite drawing and the video from the golf store. God knows we could use a break."

"I'm curious, Mike, what prompted you to become a cop?"

"I decided to become a cop because of what happened to my mother. When I was fifteen, my dad, a homicide detective on the Dearborn PD, took me to a Red Wings game. When we got home, my father found my mom in bed. Someone had broken into our home while my mother and my sister were sleeping. The cash from my mother's purse and her jewelry was missing. The police suspect my mom woke up during the robbery, the burglar panicked and smothered her with a pillow. Joanne, my ten-year-old sister, slept through the killing and was not harmed. Because my dad was emotionally involved, the Dearborn PD did not allow him to work the case. That drove my dad crazy. To this day, the murder has gone unsolved and is still an open cold case."

"Oh, my God. That's terrible, Mike. I'm so sorry. I can see why you decided to follow in your father's footsteps. Is your dad still with the Dearborn PD?"

"At the time, my dad took my mom's death extremely hard and blamed himself for not being there to protect her. He began to drink heavily and almost lost his job. A friend got him going to AA, and with the help of a shrink, he finally quit drinking. A few years ago, he retired, sold his house, and moved to Florida. Dad purchased a small bungalow on a canal in Fort Myers. He took up golf and met a nice widow on the golf course. I believe my dad is finally beginning to enjoy life again."

"That's good to hear. What about your sister? Is she still in Dearborn?"

"Joanne and her husband, who works for GM in Detroit, still live in the area. They have a couple of rug rats and are doing fine."

"McMahon…that's an Irish name. You probably got your blue eyes from your father's side, but I'm curious about your jet-black hair. I trust your mother wasn't of Irish ancestry."

"No, my mother's parents immigrated from Italy. Her maiden name was Ambrosi."

"Ah, that makes sense." O'Connor glanced at his watch. "It's past my bedtime. Six a.m. comes early."

"You get up at six every morning? That's early for someone who's retired. Stay and have another beer."

"Sorry, Mike, I can't. I've had my limit for today. Besides, too much alcohol fogs the brain. I want to go for an early morning run with a clear head."

"Okay, Pat. Thanks for stopping by. It was nice meeting you. I appreciate your thoughts on the case."

"No problem, Mike. I don't know how much help I've been. I'm glad I'm retired, and it's not my case to solve. Good luck to you and your partner. I hope you find your killer soon."

After O'Connor had left, Mike grabbed another beer and flopped back down in his recliner. His mind was rehashing their conversation. He couldn't help but think that Pat O'Connor had all the qualifications to be the Golf Club Killer, but so did many other people. Before going to bed, he decided to jot down the highlights of their conversation. Unlike Patrick O'Connor, Mike didn't have a photographic memory.

CHAPTER 14

The following day, Patrick O'Connor met Joe Carson, his former partner, Steve Larkin, and Fred Thomas, two other retired MNPD detective friends at the Richland Country Club, for their 1:00 p.m. tee-off time.

The first five holes went smoothly. Because of the water hazard, there was a backup at the par-three sixth hole. While waiting to tee off, Larkin asked, "Have any of you been following the Golf Club Killer story?"

"Yeah, last night, when I watched the TV news, I saw the composite drawing and video of the person of interest that the MNPD wants to interview," said Fred Thomas.

"I saw it, too," Patrick O'Connor said. "The guy looked familiar, but I didn't recognize him."

Steve and Fred agreed that the man in the news story looked familiar, but neither could determine if they had seen him before.

"How about you, Joe, are you following the case?" Steve asked.

"Yeah, I've been following it. I watched Channel 17 news last night. If that guy is the Golf Club Killer, all the more power to him."

"Why do you say that?" asked Thomas.

"Because he's doing the job our so-called justice system hasn't been able to do. He's getting slimeballs off our streets and making Nashville a better place without them."

"I don't agree," Fred said. "The guy's taking the law into his own hands. He's nothing but a vigilante. He's not any better than the people he's killing."

"Vigilante or not," said Steve, "I agree with Joe. He's doing us all a service. In all the years I was on the force, I witnessed criminals getting off for lack of evidence, screwed up search warrants, and technicalities discovered by clever lawyers."

"I can see both sides of the argument," O'Connor said. "We know our justice system isn't perfect, but it's all we've got. There's no justification for taking the law into your own hands."

"What about what happened to your wife?" Carson said. "Do you think our justice system worked back then?"

"Stop it, Joe," O'Connor snapped. "That subject is taboo. We're not here to solve the problems of the justice system. We're here to play golf."

"Sorry, Pat. I didn't mean to open old wounds. I wasn't thinking."

"Damn right, you weren't thinking. So shut the fuck up and tee up your ball."

The rest of the game went well. The Golf Club Killer case never came up again. O'Connor had the best net score and won seventy-five dollars. After a few beers at the nineteenth hole, the friends parted ways, agreeing to play another round the following week.

The morning after his conversation with Patrick O'Connor, Mike told Rose about their chance meeting. He described their conversation in detail. As he finished, Goodwin said, "I agree O'Connor fits the profile of the Golf Club Killer, but I doubt he's our man. Patrick O'Connor is a decorated legend, a cop like no other in the history of the MNPD. I can't believe he would retire and become a serial killer. It just doesn't make any sense."

"O'Connor is smart and knows what we look for at crime scenes. Maybe he snapped after his wife was murdered, and her killer was sent to a drug rehab facility instead of prison."

"I guess anything's possible, but I still don't think he's our killer. We're missing something. It must be someone else."

Without warning, the boss appeared and asked them to join him in his office. When they were all seated, Foster asked, "Have there been any new developments in the Golf Club Killer case?"

"Not really," Rose said.

"There might be," Mike said, ignoring the keep-your-mouth-shut stare from Goodwin.

Confused by the two different answers, Lieutenant Foster asked, "Are there or aren't there any new developments?"

McMahon went on to tell the story about his evening with Patrick O'Connor. As he concluded, Lieutenant Foster laughed and said, "You're barking up the wrong tree, Detective. I've known Pat O'Connor for a long time. There's no way he's our killer."

"But Lieutenant, he could've snapped after his wife's murder. A traumatic experience like that could've sent him off the deep end."

"I don't think so, Detective. I'd stake my life; it's not O'Connor. Now go out and find the real killer."

Back at their desks, Rose asked, "Why did you tell Foster you suspect O'Connor could be the Golf Club Killer?"

"Because I feel he's a legitimate suspect."

"Do you have any proof?"

"No, but that's what I intend to do, with or without your help."

Before getting into an argument, Goodwin decided to change the subject. "Let's go over every murder. Maybe we missed something."

"Okay, but I think we'll be wasting our time. We should be concentrating on O'Connor."

"Give it a rest, Mike."

Two hours later, after discussing every killing in detail, nothing new surfaced.

"Let's take a break and go eat," McMahon said, "I'm starving."

"Okay. We might think better on a full stomach."

The food didn't help. Frustration consumed the two detectives, and the investigation came to a grinding halt. Mayor Hardy and Chief Cummings were getting bombarded with questions from the media about the lack of progress in finding and arresting the Golf Club Killer. Jeff Stone called Mike and Rose almost every day looking for updates on the case. It got to the point whenever Stone called, they did not pick up, and his messages went unanswered.

The day after Stone's last call, as Mike read the *Nashville Star Daily*, he spotted a headline that drew his attention.

WHERE IS THE GOLF CLUB KILLER?

By Jeff Stone, Investigative Reporter

I'm sure we are all relieved that the Golf Club Killer has not murdered anyone in the past month. Has he left town? I don't think so. Maybe he hasn't found a new victim that meets his criteria, or he could be taking a vacation or laying low until the heat dies down.

The composite sketch and video of a possible suspect released to the media weeks ago did not produce any results. So far, no one has come forward identifying the unknown man.

Every time I try to get updates on the case, Police Chief Bradley Cummings says he has "no comment." Lieutenant Robert Foster, the two detectives' supervisor assigned to the investigation, tells me he has nothing new to report. I suspect Detective Sergeant Rose Goodwin and Detective Mike McMahon are spinning their wheels like a car stuck in the mud. Every time I have tried to contact Detective McMahon or Detective Sergeant Goodwin, they do not answer their phones, and my messages go unanswered. They are avoiding me like the plague. I'm sure it's because they are embarrassed by their lack of progress. Perhaps the MNPD should consider assigning new detectives to the case. My suggestion is to bring legendary homicide detective Sergeant Patrick O'Connor back from retirement. During his years with the MNPD, O'Connor and his partner, Detective Joe Carson, solved well over fifty murders. They were assigned cases that left other detectives baffled and scratching their heads. O'Connor and

Carson found clues others had missed leading them to catch and bring elusive killers to justice.

What do you think? Is it time for the "Bulldog" to return?

After Mike had finished reading the article, he handed the newspaper to Rose and said, "It looks like our friend, Jeff Stone, is trying to stir up a hornet's nest with his latest article."

Goodwin read the story, shook her head, and said, "He's trying to make the MNPD, and the two of us, look like bungling idiots."

"I'd say he's succeeding."

Rose laughed. "You've got that right. I'm sure as soon as Chief Cummings and Lieutenant Foster read Stone's article, there'll be hell to pay."

Before McMahon could reply, a red-faced Lieutenant Foster appeared. He growled, "Detectives, into my office. Now!"

As they followed Foster, Mike whispered to Rose, "Looks like the shit's about to hit the fan."

Goodwin whispered back, "He must've read the article."

Sitting on the edge of their seats, they waited for the bomb to drop.

Lieutenant Foster took a sip of water, popped an antacid pill, and cleared his throat. He opened his mouth to speak when his phone rang. Foster picked up and said, "Good morning, Chief. Yes, I've read it. I just called them into my office. Okay, I'll put you on speaker."

"Good morning, Detectives. Have you read the latest article by Jeff Stone?"

"Yes, Chief, we have," replied Rose.

"Looks like Stone's getting on our case again. I just got off the phone with Mayor Hardy, and he's not a happy camper. He's concerned that our lack of progress in catching the Golf Club Killer is negatively affecting the city's economy. Tourists are staying away in droves. Hotels, restaurants, entertainment venues, and shopping malls are suffering severely. Have you made any progress in the case since we last talked?"

"Sorry, Chief, we haven't," Mike said.

"That's not what I wanted to hear. Maybe it's time we went in a different direction. Stone's suggestion to bring Patrick O'Connor out of retirement might be worth considering,"

"I've been in touch with Patrick O'Connor. I sat down with him and picked his brain. He said we're dealing with a smart individual who knows police procedure. He suggested that the killer could be an active member of the MNPD. We think it might even be someone fired for police brutality or another serious offense," McMahon said.

"Have you looked into any of these possibilities?"

"Yes, Chief, we have. We recently interviewed an officer fired for police brutality, but his alibi checked out, and he's no longer a suspect," Rose said.

"Chief," Mike suggested, "perhaps we should also look into retired MNPD personnel. Someone like Patrick O'Connor himself. In his case, his wife was killed by a spaced-out drug addict a few years ago. During our conversation, O'Conner told me he was extremely depressed and angry about his wife's murder. Maybe he decided to take the law into his own hands with a little vigilante justice."

"Good idea, Detective. However, I've known O'Connor since he first joined the MNPD. I find it hard to believe a distinguished and legendary detective such as Patrick is the Golf Club Killer. Perhaps I should give him a call. Maybe he would be willing to come out of retirement and help you and Detective Sergeant Goodwin. In the meantime, keep digging. Lieutenant Foster will keep me updated. Good day."

Foster gave Rose and Mike an icy glare. "Just because the chief was civil and didn't yell and scream doesn't mean I won't. Whether you know it or not, our asses are on the line. If you don't start making progress soon, I may have to consider replacing you two. Now get to work. Go through the list of cops who retired in the past several years and see if any red flags turn up."

CHAPTER 15

After spending the afternoon and evening researching cops who had retired in the past five years, no red flags surfaced. Rose yawned and checked her watch—9:18 p.m. She smiled and said, "Time goes by when you're having fun. It's almost my bedtime. Let's get out of here and start fresh in the morning."

McMahon picked up two bottles of whiskey at a liquor store and a chicken dinner from a KFC outlet on his way home. Sitting at the kitchen table, he dug in as he sipped from a glass half-filled with whiskey, two ice cubes, and a squirt of water. His mind kept flashing back to the Golf Club Killer crime scenes. By the time he had finished eating, thinking about the case was driving him crazy. He fixed another drink, went into the living room, flopped down on his recliner, and turned on the TV. The James Bond film *Casino Royale* was playing on the movie channel. Fifteen minutes later, McMahon was sound asleep. Shortly after midnight, he snorted and woke up. Mike turned the TV off and headed to his bedroom. He tossed and turned for one hour, but sleep wouldn't come. McMahon got out of bed and went into the kitchen. He downed two straight shots of whiskey and went back to bed. Almost instantly, he was out for the count.

As he was about to enter his car, sensing someone was behind him, McMahon turned just in time to see the raised golf club. Before it struck his head, he was jarred awake by the ringing of the telephone. He sat up quickly and fumbled for the switch on his bedside lamp. Turning on the light, McMahon glanced at the digital clock—2:17 a.m. He had a splitting headache, and when he reached for the receiver, he almost dropped it on the floor.

"Hello."

"Sorry to wake you, Mike. It's Dave Franklin. There's been a terrible accident."

"What...what kind of accident?"

"The bus...the bus the band was traveling on got T-boned by a freight train. I don't have all the details, but there are several deaths and survivors with injuries. As we speak, those who survived are on their way to Nashville General. That's all I know. Bill and I are heading there now."

"Where did it happen?"

"I'm not sure. Somewhere between Memphis and Nashville. They were on their way home from a concert in Memphis."

"Suzanne...do you know if Suzanne survived?" Mike asked, a lump in his throat, his heart beating like a drum.

"Sorry, Mike, I don't know. We'll find out when we get to the hospital."

"Okay, Dave, I'm on my way. I'll meet you and Bill there."

McMahon turned off the siren as the car squealed to a stop at the emergency entrance. He jumped out, dashed through the door and up to the reception counter.

The receptionist looked up from the magazine she was reading and said, "Can I help you, sir?"

Speaking rapidly, Mike said, "Yes. I'm looking for Suzanne Taylor. She was in an accident. Do you know where she is?"

"Do you know what kind of an accident, sir?"

"Yes. It was a bus that got hit by a train."

"I'm sorry, I don't have any names yet. The survivors recently arrived by air ambulance and were taken directly to critical care on the third floor."

"Do you know how many people survived?"

"No, sir, I don't. When you get off the elevator, walk straight ahead. The nursing station should have that information."

"Okay, thanks."

Just as the elevator door opened, Bill Ormond and Dave Franklin, the Frozen North partners, burst through the emergency entrance door. They were out of breath and had panic written on their faces.

Dave yelled, "Hold the elevator, Mike."

"Where are you going?" Bill asked.

"To the third floor. The survivors are there."

As they entered the elevator, Dave asked, "Were you able to find out who survived the crash?"

"No. The receptionist didn't know their names."

At the nursing station, Mike introduced himself to the nurse in charge and gave the reason they were there.

"Was one of the survivors a woman?" Mike asked, praying Suzanne was still alive.

"As far as I know, there were only three men."

Mike's chest tightened, and his stomach flipped. That was not the answer he wanted to hear.

"Are you positive there wasn't a woman amongst the survivors?"

"Yes, sir. I'm positive."

McMahon felt the blood drain from his face, and his body went numb.

"Can you tell us anything about their condition?" Bill asked.

"Sorry, sir, I don't have that information. Once the doctors have examined the survivors, you will get an update at that time. I suggest you take a seat in the waiting room down the hall. In the meantime, should you require a beverage or a snack, the cafeteria is on the lower level, and vending machines are on the first floor in the emergency waiting room area."

Seeing the distress on Mike's face, Dave said, "Maybe Suzanne and other survivors are at another hospital. Perhaps we should check with the Vanderbilt Medical Center."

"Good idea, Dave," Bill said. "I'll ask the nurse for Vanderbilt's number, and I'll give them a call."

Mike, in a daze, stood staring out the window into the darkness.

Ormond left and came back five minutes later.

"Sorry, guys, the person I spoke with at Vanderbilt said no accident victims from a bus wreck are at their hospital."

"That's too bad. I was praying there would be more survivors," Franklin said.

McMahon didn't seem to be listening. Bill and Dave were surprised when he turned around from gazing out the window and said, "The only other place left to check is the Davidson County Morgue."

"Before we do that, let's wait for an update on the three men. I want to find out their condition and who they are," Ormond said.

"You two can wait here while I go to the morgue. I've got to find out if Suzanne is there," Mike said. "I'll call you later, Dave."

"Okay," Franklin said as Mike ran toward the elevator.

CHAPTER 16

At the mortuary, Mike flashed his badge at the security guard and proceeded to the autopsy room. He was surprised to see Dr. Tony Capino at his desk, reading a file. Glancing up, he smiled when he saw Mike. "Detective McMahon, what brings you out at this ungodly hour?"

"I was going to ask you the same question, Tony."

"I was burning the midnight oil when several bodies came in from a tragic accident between a bus and a freight train."

"That's why I'm here. Suzanne was on that bus."

"Oh, no. Sorry to hear that, Mike."

"Is Suzanne's body here?"

"No. All the bodies were men. She could be with the survivors taken to Nashville General. You should go there."

"I just came from there. Suzanne wasn't with the survivors."

"That's odd. A state trooper said everyone on that bus was removed and either brought here or airlifted to Nashville General. Maybe Suzanne wasn't on the bus."

"That was her tour bus. It doesn't make any sense. She had to be on the bus."

"Have you tried calling her?"

"In all the confusion, I didn't even think of that."

As Mike reached for his cell phone, that's when he remembered in his haste to leave his condo; he left it on the night table.

"Shit! I left it at home."

"Here, call her on my phone," Capino said, handing Mike the receiver.

McMahon sat down and dialed Suzanne's cell number. No answer. After the fifth ring, he left a message stating the time of his call. He asked her to call him in a half-hour at the condo.

"Thanks, Tony. See you."

"Take care, Mike. I pray that Suzanne is all right."

McMahon was in the ensuite bathroom. He had just swallowed two extra-strength headache pills and was splashing water on his face when he heard the phone ring. Mike rushed into the bedroom and picked up. When he saw Suzanne's name on the screen, he breathed a huge sigh of relief.

"Hi, babe, thank God you're all right."

"Why wouldn't I be all right?"

"I'll tell you in a minute. Where are you?"

"I'm still in Memphis. I was asleep and didn't get to my phone in time. I listened to your message and figured you might be home by now."

"I just walked in the door. Why are you still in Memphis?"

"Before the show, I was autographing CDs and meeting fans. An old girlfriend from home surprised me. Nicole Tuttle and her husband Gary live in Memphis, and when she saw I was in town, they came to my concert. In our conversation, I told her I was coming home for a two-week break. She invited me to stay with her for a few days to reminisce and catch up. I accepted her invitation. I hope you don't mind? I was planning on calling you in the morning."

"I don't mind at all. I'm overjoyed. I'm so glad you're still in Memphis."

"Mike, why are you acting so strange?"

"As I said, there's something I need to tell you. Are you sitting down?"

"No, I'm standing. Why do you ask? You're starting to scare me, Mike."

"Please sit down. Are you sitting?"

"Yes."

"There's been a terrible accident."

"Oh, my God. What kind of accident?"

"Your tour bus was hit by a train."

McMahon went on to tell her everything he knew about the tragedy. Before he could finish, Suzanne was crying softly and gulping for air.

Mike let her cry for a few minutes before asking, "Suzanne, are you all right? Are you able to speak?"

In a weak whisper, she said, "No, Mike, I'll never be all right. I'll take a bus home first thing in the morning."

"Give me the address, and I'll leave now and come pick you up."

"That's crazy, Mike. The round trip will take about seven hours. Get some sleep, and I'll see you tomorrow. Don't worry about picking me up; I'll take a cab home."

"No way you're taking a bus. I'm coming to get you, and that's final. What's the address?"

Luckily, Suzanne had typed the address into her phone. She read it to Mike, and he wrote it down.

"Try to get a few hours rest. I'll see you in about three hours."

He hung up before Suzanne could protest.

Just as McMahon was about to leave, the phone rang. Checking the screen, it read Rose Goodwin.

"Hey, Rose. What's up?"

"Mike, I hope I didn't wake you. I couldn't sleep and was watching TV when a news flash came on the screen. Do you know about the terrible accident?"

"Yes, Rose, I do. I found out a few hours ago. Dave Franklin from Frozen North called me."

"Was Suzanne one of the survivors?"

"She wasn't on the bus. She decided to stay in Memphis for a few days with an old girlfriend she met at her concert."

"Thank God!"

Mike went on to tell Rose about his conversation with Suzanne.

"Sorry, I've gotta go. See you later."

"Don't worry about work. I'll inform Lieutenant Foster of the situation."

"Okay. Goodbye."

"Goodbye, Mike. Give Suzanne a big hug for me."

As Mike got into the car, he checked his watch—6:21. He entered the address Suzanne had given him into the GPS, fired up the engine, and squealed out of the parking garage. When McMahon hit the on-ramp to I-40, he flipped on the siren and floored the gas pedal.

Less than three hours later, he was pulling into the laneway of a sprawling ranch bungalow on the outskirts of Memphis. Suzanne was sitting on the front porch with two suitcases by her side. Mike jumped out of the car, rushed to her side, and gave her a long hug and a kiss.

"How are you, my dear?"

"I'm not too good. I couldn't sleep. I can't get the accident out of my head."

"Maybe you can catch a few winks on the drive home."

"I doubt it."

"What about your friend? Does she know what happened?"

"No. Nicole and Gary were both sleeping when we talked. I didn't want to wake them, so I wrote a note explaining what happened and left it on the kitchen table."

On the way back to Nashville, Mike didn't use the siren. Suzanne tilted her seat back and closed her eyes. Within five minutes, she was fast asleep.

Just as they entered the condo, Mike's cell phone rang. It was Dave Franklin.

"Hi, Dave."

"Hey, Mike. I talked to Dr. Pringle, and he said all the survivors are going to make it. Their injuries are all minor, nothing life-threatening."

"Did the doctor tell you who survived the crash?"

"Yes, he did. Jesse Potter, sound engineer, Marven Jones, and Brandon Barber, the fiddle player, all survived the crash. Marven Jones has a broken arm and some scrapes and bruises, nothing serious. The good news is Suzanne wasn't on the bus. Jones said she stayed in Memphis to visit a friend."

"That's good news about the survivors. After I left you, I found out Suzanne stayed in Memphis, so I drove there and picked her up. We just walked through the door."

"How is she?"

"As I'm sure you can imagine, she was devastated when I broke the news to her. Suzanne is having a hard time coming to grips with what happened."

"Give Suzanne our love and tell her Bill and I are relieved she's safe. Please have her call me when she's feeling up to it."

"Okay. Goodbye, Dave."

"Goodbye, Mike."

CHAPTER 17

McMahon decided to take some of his vacation time to keep an eye on Suzanne. He didn't want her to be alone. During the first week, they attended the funerals of Mark Bush, producer and bus driver, Doug Grant, lead guitar, Buddy King, bass guitar, Trey Thompson, steel guitar, Ken Curtis, drummer, and roadies Billy Walker and Nick Pulaski. By the time the funerals were over, Suzanne was a complete wreck. The members of the band and road crew had become her family. She became depressed, lost her appetite, and had a hard time sleeping. When Suzanne did manage to fall asleep for a few hours, nightmares about the accident caused her to wake up in a panic. After a few days of badgering, Suzanne finally took Mike's advice and began seeing a shrink that he had recommended. Several sessions later, her depression began to lift, her energy came back, and she started to look and sound like her old self again. Suzanne ate regular meals, the color came back to her face, and most nights was able to sleep without nightmares about the accident. Mike was pleased with the progress she was making.

After spending two weeks with Suzanne, McMahon went back to work. His first morning on the job, Lieutenant Foster called Mike and Rose into his office.

"Welcome back, Detective. How is Suzanne?"

"Much better, thanks."

"I'm glad to hear that. Please pass on my regards and best wishes."

"I will, Lieutenant."

Foster picked up his mug, took a sip of coffee, cleared his throat, and said, "Getting back to the Golf Club Killer case, it looks like he's stopped killing, at least for the time being. Do you have anything new to report, Detective Sergeant?"

"Sorry, Lieutenant, I don't. I think the killer is biding his time waiting for things to cool down before he strikes again," Rose said.

"I agree," Mike said. "I'm sure we haven't heard the last of him."

"You could be right. In the meantime, I've got a new assignment for you. Over the past few months, five men from the gay community have gone missing. So far, none of them have turned up. It's like they vanished from the face of the earth. The chief and I suspect we could be dealing with another serial killer. That's why he's taken the case away from the West Precinct and thrown it in my lap."

Lieutenant Foster handed Rose five sheets of paper.

"A picture and information about each missing person are on these printouts. They should help get you started. Keep me updated. Good luck."

As they left Lieutenant Foster's office, Mike said, "Why don't we get the hell out of here? Let's go to Starbucks for a caffeine fix. We can read the profiles and plan our strategy over a coffee."

"Sounds good to me."

Rose bit into her muffin, took a sip of coffee, then pulled out the first sheet from a file folder. After studying the picture and reading the information, she passed it across to Mike. They followed the same procedure for all five documents.

"According to every report, each man went missing from a gay bar. Is that a coincidence or what?" Mike said.

"I don't believe in coincidences," Rose said.

"Neither do I."

"Let's assume we're dealing with a serial killer stalking his victims in gay bars. He could be a straight person, who, for whatever reason, hates gays, or perhaps he's gay himself. If he's gay, he'll blend in with the crowd, and no one will suspect what he's up to," Goodwin said.

"If he is gay, that will make him harder for us to find."

"You're right. Let's hope the bars have security cameras. Maybe we'll get lucky and spot one or more of the missing persons leaving with the killer."

"Where do you want to start?" Mike asked.

"Let's start with the Krystal Club and then go to the Rainbow Bar & Grill. They're within a block of each other on Charles Street."

Checking his watch, Mike said, "We could have a problem."

"What kind of a problem?"

"It's ten-thirty. Most gay bars don't open until four or five."

"Let's try, anyway. We can knock on the door. If no one comes, we can go back later."

"All right. It's worth a try."

CHAPTER 18

At the Krystal Club, finding the door locked, clenching his hand into a fist, Mike rapped on the door. When no one came, he pounded harder. Just as they were about to leave, the door opened. A six-six, broad-shouldered, muscular man with a shaved head said, "Sorry, we don't open till four."

They produced their badges, and Rose said, "I'm Detective Sergeant Goodwin, and this is my partner Detective McMahon. We need to come in and ask you a few questions."

"Questions? Questions about what?"

"We'll tell you when we're inside," Mike said.

The man stepped aside and allowed the detectives to enter.

"Follow me," he said.

He went behind the bar, and McMahon and Goodwin sat on stools facing him.

"You look familiar," Mike said.

"Grant Wilson," he said, extending his hand. "You may have seen me on the football field. I played left tackle for the Titans for five years."

"That's why you look familiar. I've seen you interviewed on TV a few times and went to several of your games." Mike said.

"How did you get into this business?" Rose asked.

"In the first game of my sixth season, I got my right knee mangled in a pile-up. The next year I tried to make a comeback, but it didn't work out. That injury forced me into early retirement. A gay friend of mine was half-owner of this bar. His partner wished to retire, so he asked me if I wanted to buy him out. I knew it was a profitable business, so I decided to go for it. It gives me something to do and keeps me from brooding about my brief football career."

"Is your business partner also your life partner? Mike asked.

Wilson laughed. "No, he's just a friend. I'm as straight as an arrow. Believe it or not, most of our staff are not gay."

Mike's face flushed. Embarrassed, he said, "Sorry, but I had to ask."

"No problem, Detective. I've answered that same question at least a hundred times since I became a partner. Customers hit on me all the time, assuming I'm gay."

"I can understand that," Rose said. "You're a handsome man."

Changing the subject, Mike said, "Getting back to the reason for our visit. In the past few months, five men have gone missing—two from your bar."

Goodwin pulled out the missing person reports and handed them to Wilson. "Do you recognize either of these men?"

Wilson read the information then studied the pictures for a moment.

"Ross Raymond was a regular, and the other guy, Cameron Butler, came in occasionally. I didn't know their last names until now. I only knew them as Ross and Cam. I was wondering why I haven't seen them lately. Do you suspect foul play?"

"That's what we're trying to determine," McMahon said.

"Friends and relatives came forward and provided the MNPD with the information you see on these missing person reports," Rose said. "We believe the dates Raymond and Butler went missing are accurate."

"I see video cameras throughout your fine establishment," Mike said. "Do you keep a record on file of each day you're open?"

"Yes and no. We still use videotape. Each tape is kept for forty-eight hours and then reused. Sorry, we wouldn't have anything from the dates on these reports. I suppose it's time we updated our security system."

"That's too bad," Rose said.

"The last time Raymond and Butler were here, did you notice if either of them left with someone you hadn't seen before?" Mike asked.

"Not that I can recall." Wilson paused momentarily then said, "Come to think of it, around the date Reynolds went missing, he came in a little after nine. He sat at the bar and ordered a beer. Ross was excited. He told me he had met a new friend online on a dating site. While Reynolds waited for his friend to join him, his cell phone pinged. After reading the message, Ross typed a response and said his plans had changed. He paid for his drink and left. That was the last time I saw him."

"Do you have any idea where he was going?" Rose asked.

"No, Detective, but I think his new friend provided the address in the text message."

"That's great!" McMahon said. "Now, all we have to do is find Ross Reynolds's cell phone."

Goodwin asked, "What about Butler? Do you remember the last time you saw him?"

"Sorry, Detective, I don't. As I said, Butler wasn't a regular customer."

"Okay. Thanks for your time, Grant," Rose said, handing him her card. "Please call if you think of anything that might help our investigation."

"I will, Detective. It was a pleasure meeting you both. Good luck with your case."

They shook hands, and Wilson accompanied Mike and Rose to the door. As the detectives walked up the street, Goodwin said, "If the guy who sent the text killed Reynolds, I'm sure he would've destroyed the cell phone."

"Serial killers are weird. Sometimes they keep a personal item of a victim as a souvenir. A lot of them have left calling cards. Denis Rader, known as the BTK Killer, wrote letters and poems taunting the police, which ultimately led to his capture. Jack the Ripper mutilated bodies, taunted police with letters and kept body parts. The Zodiac Killer sent cryptic messages to the police, and the Night

Stalker drew pentagons with his victim's lipstick. I could go on and on," Mike said.

"That's not necessary, McMahon. I get the picture, enough with the gory details. I'm curious, how do you know so much about serial killers?"

"Ever since the Guitar String Strangler case, I've made it a point to educate myself on what past killers have done. I think it could help get inside their heads."

"I don't know how anyone can get inside the heads of those psychos. Psycho or not, it appears that our killer is intelligent. He finds his victims online and not in bars. That way, he doesn't expose himself to security cameras or people who can identify him."

"You're right. The Online Killer isn't making it easy. This case could be another tough one to solve."

"The Online Killer? Is that what you're calling him?"

"Yeah. I thought I'd give the killer a name before Jeff Stone did. Do you have a better name?"

"No, I don't. Since the killer finds his victims online, the name makes sense. So, Online Killer it is."

CHAPTER 19

Arriving at the Skylark Lounge, McMahon tried the door with no luck. The sign in the window indicated the opening time was 4:00 p.m. He knocked. No one came, so he pounded harder. No response.

Checking her watch, Rose said, "We have over an hour to kill. Since we haven't had lunch, let's go grab a sandwich."

"Good idea."

Shortly after four, they entered the Skylark Lounge and went straight to the bar. The place was empty. The bartender, a fit-looking man in his early thirties with short, straw-colored hair, sea-blue eyes, and a friendly smile, greeted them.

"Howdy folks, what can I get you today?"

"A little information," Mike said, presenting his badge. "I'm Detective McMahon, and this is my partner, Detective Sergeant Goodwin."

"Pleased to meet you. I'm Andrew Bloom, but everyone calls me Andy. What kind of info are you looking for?"

Rose pulled out two missing person reports and slid them toward Andy. "Do you recognize either of these two men?"

Bloom took a few minutes to study the pictures and read the information, then replied, "Yeah, I do. Roy Williams and Brandon Brown are both regular customers, but I haven't seen them for a while."

"Do you remember the last time you saw either of them?" Mike asked.

"I'm not sure. It could've been around the dates shown on these missing person reports."

"Please tell me that your security system keeps records longer than a few days," Goodwin said.

"Yes, it does. We have a state-of-the-art wireless camera system. It's not cheap, but it gives us about a year of storage capacity."

"Can you bring up the dates shown on these reports?" Mike asked.

"Yes, Detective, that won't be a problem." Bloom waved at a waitress. "Sally, can you cover the bar for a few minutes?"

"Sure, Andy," the young woman said.

"Please follow me, Detectives."

Bloom led them into a small room where a computer and monitor sat on a metal desk. The monitor's image changed every ten seconds, switching from one camera to the next on a rotating basis. Andy sat down in front of the keyboard, went into the cloud storage site, and typed in the date Roy Williams went missing. Scrolling through the video, he stopped when Williams appeared on the screen.

"Here it is," Bloom said. He continued to scroll through the video and stopped it when Williams pulled out his cell phone. After reading the message, Williams smiled and typed a reply. He finished his beer, threw a twenty-dollar bill on the counter, and left the bar. The timestamp showed that Roy Williams departed at 9:17 p.m.

A similar scenario played out on the night Brandon Brown went missing. Instead of a text message, Brown received a phone call. When the conversation ended, he settled his tab and headed out the door. The time on the monitor read 9:46 p.m.

"Thanks, Andy, we appreciate your help. Is it possible to get a copy of those videos?" Rose asked.

"No problem, Detective."

Five minutes later, Bloom handed Goodwin a flash drive.

"Here's my card. If you think of anything else, please call," Rose said.

"I will. Good luck, Detectives."

They shook Andy's hand, said goodbye, and left the bar.

As Mike started the car, Rose said, "It looks as if the unsub is playing it safe. He must use something enticing to lure his victims to him. Once they fall for his ruse, it's goodbye, Charlie."

"You're right. The killer never shows up in any of the bars. He must find his victims online and develops a rapport with them. When the timing is right, he arranges to meet in a gay bar, as he did with Roy Williams and Brandon Brown. At the last minute, the unsub sends a text or calls with some excuse why he can't make it. He suggests another meeting place without cameras or witnesses. I think the perp lures each unsuspecting man to his home or some secluded place, where he murders them."

"What you're saying sounds feasible. Now, all we have to do is figure out how to catch the son of a bitch."

"Easier said than done," McMahon said.

Five minutes later, Mike parked near the Rainbow Bar & Grill on Broadway Avenue. They got out and went inside. A short, balding, overweight man in his mid-forties was standing behind the bar, polishing a glass.

Showing her badge, Rose said, "I'm Detective Sergeant Goodwin, and this is my partner Detective McMahon. And you are?"

"My name is Gordon Granderson. How can I help you, Detectives?"

Granderson gave a crooked-toothed smile and offered a limp, fish-like handshake.

"We're working on a missing person case. Do you recognize this man?" Rose said, handing Granderson the missing person report for Charles James Brockman.

He studied the sheet, then said, "Yeah, I know Charlie. I was wondering why I haven't seen him lately."

"Would your security system have a video of the date shown on the missing person report?" Rose asked.

"I'm sure we do. Would you like to see it?"

"Yes, please," Goodwin said.

The Rainbow Bar & Grill had a similar security system to the one at the Skylark Lounge. The video showed Brockman sitting at the bar, engaged in a conversation with another man. At 10:06 p.m., he received a phone call. He spoke for a few minutes, paid his tab, and hurried toward the door.

Before the detectives left, Granderson made a copy of the video and gave it to McMahon.

"Thank you for your help, Gordon," Mike said, handing Granderson his card. "If you think of anything else, please call."

"I will, Detective."

They shook Granderson's hand, said goodbye, and left the bar.

CHAPTER 20

The next morning, after showing Lieutenant Foster the security videos and filling him in on the previous day's visits to the three gay bars, he sat back and pondered for a minute before speaking.

Leaning forward, he said, "It sounds like you've got a good idea of how the unsub operates. The perp stays away from cameras and witnesses. Do you have any ideas on how to collar the unsub?"

"We're going to set a trap for the Online Killer. I told Rose about my idea last night, and she agrees it might work."

"Online Killer? I guess that name makes sense. What kind of trap?" Foster asked, looking confused.

"I'll go undercover online and pose as a gay man to see if the perp takes the bait."

"That's a great idea," Foster said, grinning from ear to ear.

Feeling uneasy with Foster's delight in his idea, Mike quickly said, "I'm as far from gay as you can get. I hope I can pull it off."

"Did you ever act in a school play?" Foster asked.

"Actually, I did. I played Brutus in our high school play of *Julius Caesar*."

"Well, there you go. Playing a gay man is acting. Same as what you did in high school. Et tu, Brute," Foster said, laughing.

All this time, Rose sat silently, an amused smirk on her face.

"That was a long time ago, Lieutenant. I'm sure I'll be a little rusty."

"Nonsense. You'll do fine. Just be yourself. Many gay men don't have feminine traits and mannerisms that most people associate with being gay. Numerous men and women who play professional sports are gay, but you'd never know it to look at them."

"Okay, I'm willing to give it a shot if it'll help collar the killer."

"We'll set you up with a false ID and a new address. I have a friend who owes me a favor. He has a vacant furnished apartment close to downtown. I'll ask him if we can rent it for a few months. I'm sure he'll go along with our plan. Once we set you up on several gay dating sites, I'm sure that you'll attract plenty of contacts with your good looks. Hopefully, our perp will be one of them. We'll have a makeup artist create a new look for you. You won't even recognize yourself."

When they were back at their desks, Rose chuckled. "I know a gay patrol officer who is looking for a serious relationship. Should I have him give you a call, Brutus?"

"Hilarious, Goodwin. Couldn't resist a smart-aleck remark, could you?"

"Sorry, Brutus. I just couldn't."

CHAPTER 21

A week later, Mike moved into Lieutenant Foster's friend's apartment. Early that evening, he phoned Suzanne and caught her before she went on stage in Pittsburgh with her new band. McMahon told her about his assignment as an undercover gay man. She was curious to see what he looked like and insisted on Mike sending her a picture. Reluctantly, he took a selfie and sent it to her. When she received the photo, Suzanne laughed and said, "Wow! I almost didn't recognize you. Now, don't go cheating on me with some good looking gay guy."

Mike chuckled. "You never know, it might be tempting, especially if he's charming and rich."

McMahon became John Robert Woodman with a credit card, social security number, and a Tennessee driver's license. He received a cell phone registered under his new name. A picture showing Mike with short blond hair and dark horned-rim glasses and a fictitious bio appeared on three popular gay dating sites. The line was in the water. Now all they had to do was sit back and wait for the fish to bite.

Three days went by without any response. On day four, Mike received an email from a man named Martin Tuckman. Tuckman had included a recent photograph and a bio that said he was an architect at a local Nashville firm. After a few emails went back and forth, the two men decided to meet at the Skylark Lounge that evening at nine. They exchanged cell numbers should something come up at the last minute and one of them couldn't make the meeting.

An hour before heading to the Skylark Lounge, Mike slipped on a wireless recorder that looked like a wristwatch. Rose would record and listen to McMahon's and Tuckman's conversation from the car. Mike wore an earbud that allowed him to hear any comments or instructions from Rose. After a brief test, they were ready to go.

McMahon strolled through the door at five to nine and spotted Tuckman sitting at the bar sipping on a beer and chatting with the bartender.

"Good evening, Martin," Mike said as he sat down on the stool next to him.

"Oh, hi, John," Tuckman said, extending his hand. "I'm pleased to meet you in person."

After shaking hands, Mike asked, "Have you been here long?"

"About ten minutes. Can I buy you a drink?"

"That would be great."

"What are you having?" the bartender asked.

"A Bud Light in a bottle, please."

When Mike's beer arrived, Tuckman said, "Why don't we move to a table at the back where we can talk without all the noise?"

"Sounds good to me."

Tuckman paid for the drinks, and Mike followed him to a table for two located against the back wall.

"This is much better," Tuckman said. "At least we can hear ourselves think."

"I agree."

An hour and a half later, after two more drinks, they had run out of conversation. Tuckman checked his watch and said, "Sorry, John, I have to go. I'm late for another meeting."

"Don't worry about the tab. I've got it," McMahon said.

"Thanks, John, I've enjoyed our time together. You're a nice man. However, I don't think you and I would be a good fit. Best of luck. I hope you find true love."

Before Mike could say another word, Tuckman turned and headed for the door.

As McMahon got into the car, Rose smiled and said, "Sorry, you didn't find true love, Mr. Woodman."

"Couldn't resist, could you, Goodwin?"

"I like this new assignment. I haven't had this much fun since I can't remember when."

"I'm glad you're amused, Goodwin, but I'm not. Pretending to be gay is driving me crazy. I'll be happy when we catch the bastard, and things return to normal."

CHAPTER 22

Rose dropped Mike off at his car. Before going to his new home, Lieutenant Foster's friend's apartment, he headed to his condo to pick up a few things. As Mike waited for the elevator in the parking garage, a familiar voice yell, "Hold the elevator, please." McMahon turned and watched as Patrick O'Connor rushed toward him, a suitcase in tow. "Thanks," he said, a little out of breath.

"No problem, Pat."

O'Connor did a double-take. "I almost didn't recognize you, Mike. What's with the new look?"

McMahon laughed. "This is my undercover disguise. We're working another serial killer case, and I'm pretending to be gay."

Mike filled O'Connor in on the details.

"Are you and Sergeant Goodwin still assigned to the Golf Club Killer case?"

"Yes, we are. I can't get that damn case out of my head. I think about it every day. It's driving me crazy trying to figure out why he suddenly stopped killing."

"So, he hasn't murdered anyone while I've been away?"

"No. The Golf Club Killer hasn't been active for over a month. He's either lying low or hasn't found anyone worth eliminating. Perhaps he left town or took some time off. Maybe he went on vacation. Speaking of vacations, where did you go?"

"I took a trip to Paris with Joe Carson, my former MNPD partner. It was the trip that Cindy and I had planned before her untimely death. While we were there, we rented a car and toured most of Europe."

"I trust you had a good time."

"It was okay, but it would've been much better if Cindy had been with me. Joe and I had a few laughs because most people assumed we were a gay couple."

"Yeah, I can see where two men traveling together would give that impression," McMahon said as the elevator arrived. They rode in silence until the twenty-second floor.

When the door opened, Mike said, "See you later, Pat."

"Yeah, see you, Mike. Good luck with your cases."

Mike headed to his temporary home after picking up a few personal grooming items and his electric shaver. Before going to bed, he downed a few straight shots of whiskey and was sound asleep by twelve-thirty.

At eight the next morning, McMahon and Goodwin were drinking coffee and making small talk in the squad room. Mike was about to mention his unexpected encounter with Patrick O'Connor when a booming voice caused him to wince.

"Hey, Rico, I believe I see a fruit fly. What do you think? Is that a fruit fly?"

"You're right, Jack. I see it, too. It is a fruit fly."

Mike turned to see Jack Bowman and Rico Costa, two narcotics detectives, approaching. Bowman stood about six-six and weighted in around two hundred and fifty pounds. His gray hair was an old-school crew cut, and his long, slim face had a beaklike nose. Jack Bowman was arrogant and condescending—not Mike's favorite person. They never got along from the day McMahon became Goodwin's new partner. A few months before Mike got the job, Bowman had put in for a transfer to homicide, thinking he had the inside track. He was visibly upset when Mike ended up as Goodwin's new partner. Bowman openly showed his dislike for McMahon and Goodwin as well. During the Guitar String Strangler case, Bowman and Costa had chastized Mike and Rose for their inability to catch the killer. The confrontation almost resulted in fisticuffs between the two men.

Rico Costa was smaller and shorter than Bowman. In his early thirties, Costa was approximately eight years younger than his mentor. He had olive skin, dark, slicked-back hair, brown eyes, and a neatly trimmed black mustache. Over the past two years, Costa had become a miniature Jack Bowman.

Annoyed, Mike asked, "What do you idiots want?"

"Who are you calling idiots, fruit fly?" Bowman shot back.

"You and your little clone, that's who."

"Better watch your mouth, McMahon," Bowman taunted.

Jumping to his feet, Mike barked, "Or what, asshole?"

"Or you'll be picking your teeth up off of the floor."

Rose sprang into action and squeezed between the two men. "Hold on, fellas, let's cool down."

Bowman reached over Goodwin's shoulder and shoved McMahon. Mike moved around Rose and pushed back.

By this time, a crowd had gathered, expecting to see fists flying at any moment. Hearing the commotion, Lieutenant Foster rushed out of his office and demanded, "What the hell's going on here?"

"Just a little misunderstanding," Bowman said. "We're leaving, Lieutenant. Come on, Rico, we've got work to do. See you later, fruit fly."

As Bowman and Costa turned to go, Lieutenant Foster gruffly said, "Goodwin, McMahon, into my office. Now!"

Just as they were seated, Foster's phone rang. He viewed the screen, picked up the receiver, and sweetly said, "Sorry, honey, I can't talk now. I'll call you back later. Okay, then, I'll see you tonight."

After hanging up, the lieutenant took a sip of water and asked, "Would either of you care to tell me what that was all about?"

Mike and Rose both started to speak at the same time.

"Hold it. Ladies first."

"Detective McMahon and I were sitting at our desks minding our own business when Detectives Bowman and Costa walked up. They started harassing Detective McMahon about his undercover disguise. Bowman and Costa called him a fruit fly, and Detective McMahon took exception to their comments. Mike stood up and confronted Jack Bowman head-on. A heated verbal exchange took place. I got between the two men and told them to cool it. That's when you came charging in."

Foster's serious look dissipated, and he began to laugh. "Is that what I did, come charging in?"

"Yes, sir," Rose said. "You did."

Foster smiled and began to laugh once more. He glanced at McMahon and said, "Do you confirm Detective Sergeant Goodwin's version of what took place?"

"Yes, sir, I do."

"Well, then, it appears as if your undercover disguise is working. You do look like a fruit fly. Just kidding, Detective, just kidding. How about giving me an update on what happened last night?"

"I'll be right back, sir," Goodwin said. She went out to her desk. When she returned, Rose handed Foster a flash drive of Mike's meeting with Martin Tuckman.

After skimming through the conversation, Lieutenant Foster ejected the storage device and handed it back to Rose.

"I'm sure you both agree that Tuckman is not the unsub we're looking for."

"Yes, sir. We agree, Lieutenant," Mike said.

"Okay, then, keep at it. Sooner or later, I'm sure the real unsub will contact you."

"Before we go, Lieutenant, I dropped by my condo last night to pick up a few things, and I ran into Patrick O'Connor. He told me he just returned from a month's vacation in Paris and other places in Europe. Since we haven't had any murders by the Golf Club Killer in over a month, it might be a coincidence, but I still think O'Connor should still be considered a suspect."

"As you said, Detective, it's probably just a coincidence. Unless you have proof, I suggest you tread lightly suggesting that Patrick O'Connor had anything to do with those murders. The last time you brought up the subject, I told you I'd known O'Connor for a long time. I'm confident he's not our man. Your job, for now, is to solve the case of the missing gay men. Did I make myself clear?"

"Yes, sir. Crystal clear."

Back at his desk, Mike checked his email. There was a new message with a bio and a picture from a forty-five-year-old named James (Jim) David Matthews, a financial advisor. From his photograph, Matthews looked ruggedly handsome with a full head of brown hair. After exchanging a few more emails, a meeting was scheduled for nine the following evening at the Skylark Lounge.

CHAPTER 23

The next evening, Mike entered the Skylark Lounge at 9:12 p.m. wearing his wrist recorder and earbud. McMahon recognized Matthews from the picture he had sent. He was sitting at the bar, sipping from a bottle of beer. Since there wasn't an empty seat at the bar, Mike tapped Matthews on the shoulder and said, "Sorry, Jim, I'm a little late."

Turning his head, Matthews smiled and said, "No problem, John, glad you could make it."

The two men shook hands.

"Why don't we find a quiet table where we can carry on a conversation without having to shout," Mike suggested.

"Good idea."

Matthews paid for his drink and followed McMahon to the same table he and Tuckman had occupied the night of their meeting. After ordering and receiving his beer, Mike clinked bottles with Matthews and said, "Here's to a pleasant evening. Cheers."

"Cheers."

After two hours spent getting to know each other, Mike glanced at his watch and said, "It's past my bedtime. I've got a busy day tomorrow. It's been a pleasure meeting you, Jim. I'm sorry, but I don't think we're right for each other. Good luck. I hope you find true love."

"I appreciate your honesty, John. It was nice meeting you as well."

They shook hands, and Mike left. When he reached the car, Rose smiled and said, "Not too original, are you, Mr. Woodman? You used the same parting line that Tuckman used on you."

Mike laughed. "Couldn't think of anything better to say. I guess I'll have to work on it."

Three days after Mike's meeting with Tuckman, Lieutenant Foster didn't look happy when he asked Mike and Rose to join him in his office. After Goodwin and McMahon were seated, Foster said, "I just received another missing person report. I'm glad you're sitting down. You'll probably find this hard to believe; Martin Tuckman is now the sixth missing person."

Shock registered on both detective's faces.

"I wonder what happened?" Rose asked.

"Damn!" Mike said. "It's my fault. When Tuckman left me that night, he went to meet someone else. It didn't dawn on me that it could be our unsub. If I had been thinking straight, I should've followed him."

"Don't go beating yourself up," Rose said. "I was listening to your conversation, and I should have caught it, too."

"It's no one's fault. I listened to the recording, and I didn't catch it either," Lieutenant Foster said.

"It looks like our unsub used the same MO on Tuckman as he did with the other victims," Mike said. "He sets up an appointment to meet, then cancels at the last minute, luring the unsuspecting victim someplace without cameras or witnesses."

"The only way we're going to catch this monster is if he contacts you, Detective. Until he does, we have to be patient and hope no one else goes missing. By the way, how did things go at your last meeting?" Foster asked.

"Matthews was waiting at the bar when I got there. Since he showed up, that rules him out as our unsub," Mike said.

"Okay, keep at it. Sooner or later, our luck is bound to change."

McMahon and Goodwin were drinking coffee and making small talk at their desks when Mike's new cell phone pinged, indicating he had received a message. Checking the screen, McMahon was surprised to see a picture of a smiling, pleasant-looking older man with thinning gray hair, friendly blue eyes, and a neatly trimmed snow-white mustache and goatee.

"Hey, Rose, I just got a hit from an older dude named Bruce Morton, who goes by the name 'Silver Bear.' The bio says he's a self-employed landscaper. It states he's sixty-one, physically fit, likes to travel, is open to new adventures, and is looking for guys who have a kinky side. He says he would like to meet me in person so we can get to know each other."

Goodwin laughed. "You fit the bill perfectly, McMahon. I'm sure you have a kinky side and are looking for new adventures. It sounds like you and 'Silver Bear' are a match made in heaven. He could be the true love you've been searching for."

"You're a real comedian, Goodwin," Mike said as he began to answer the email. After texting back and forth, McMahon agreed to meet Morton at the bar in the Skylark Lounge that evening at nine.

CHAPTER 24

Mike arrived at the Skylark Lounge at 8:58 p.m., found a seat at the bar, ordered a beer, and waited. Fifteen minutes went by without any sign of Bruce Morton. At nine-thirty, his cell phone rang.

"Hello."

"Hey, John, it's Bruce. Sorry, I've got a problem. My van wouldn't start. I think the alternator's shot. If I give you my address, would you be willing to come here? I live on thirty acres on the edge of town. It'll take about a half-hour. We can spend a quiet evening getting to know each other over a few drinks and some soft music. How does that sound?"

"Sounds great! Text me your address, and I'll program it into my GPS."

"Okay."

McMahon paid for his beer and headed for the door. At the car, he got into the passenger side and asked, "Did you get the gist of my phone conversation with Morton?"

"Yes, I did," Rose said, excited. "I think we just found our unsub."

"I agree, Morton could be our man. How do you want to handle this?"

"Give me Morton's address, and I'll program it into the GPS. Since your car is just down the street, I'll follow you. If I lose you, the GPS will get me there."

"Do you think we should call for backup?"

"Not at this time. The two of us should be able to handle it."

"Okay. Do you think I should take a gun with me?"

"Yes, but don't take your Glock. It'll be too bulky. Use the pistol in your ankle holster instead."

"Good idea."

It took thirty-five minutes from the time McMahon started his car until he arrived at Morton's property. As Mike turned into the laneway, he noticed a sign that read Morton Landscaping, Inc. A few hundred yards later, he arrived at a modern ranch-style red brick bungalow with a double attached garage. McMahon parked in the circular driveway near the front entrance. Feeling a little apprehensive, Mike took a few deep breaths before getting out of the car, then slowly walked up to the door, rang the bell, and waited.

In less than thirty seconds, the door opened, and a smiling Bruce Morton extended his hand and said, "John, I'm so glad you could make it. Come on in."

After shaking hands, Mike said, "It's good to meet you in person, Bruce."

"Likewise, John. Did you have any trouble finding the place?"

"My GPS brought me right to your door."

"Good. Let's go into the living room. What can I get you to drink?"

"A bottle of beer would be great."

"Would you like a glass?"

"No, thanks."

"I'll be right back."

Mike took a seat on an expensive-looking beige leather couch and surveyed the professionally decorated room.

Once McMahon had turned into the driveway, Rose parked her car on the shoulder of the main road. She got out and silently crept toward the home using the abundance of trees as cover. Peering through the living room window, Goodwin saw McMahon sitting on the couch. He appeared to be apprehensive as he bent over to make sure his ankle holster was still there. Rose ducked down just as Morton entered the room, carrying a bottle of beer in each hand.

"I hope Bud Light is okay?" Morton said, handing Mike a bottle.

"Bud Light is my favorite brand."

Morton smiled and said, "There you go, we've already got something in common. Cheers."

"Cheers," Mike said.

After clinking bottles, Morton asked, "What type of music do you prefer?"

"I like most music, but tonight I'm in the mood for some blues."

"Okay, blues, it is."

Morton went over to a stand that contained a few hundred albums. He pulled out a disc and inserted it into the player. A few seconds later, the Muddy Waters song "I Can't Be Satisfied" played softly in the background.

"I love Muddy Waters," Mike said.

"He's one of my all-time favorites," Morton said as he came back to the sofa and sat down next to Mike. "Your bio says you're a self-employed painter. Do you do commercial or residential?"

"I do both. If the job is more than I can handle alone, I have a retired friend who helps me. What about you, Bruce, do you work alone?"

"No, John, I have three experienced landscapers who do all the grunt work. At my age, I'm content to quote on jobs and supervise the work my men do. Sometimes I help out on rush jobs. Actually, I've been thinking of retiring soon. By the way, would you be interested in giving me a quote on painting my bedroom?"

"I'd be happy to," Mike said, wondering what was going on.

"Would you like to take a look at it?"

"Now?"

"If you don't mind?"

"I'd be glad to."

"Okay. Come with me."

Mike followed Morton down the hall to a large master bedroom with a fireplace across from a king-size bed. The room contained a spacious walk-in closet and a five-piece ensuite bathroom. There was a window on each side of a sliding door that led to an oversized cedar deck.

"Your bedroom looks fine to me," Mike said. "Why do you think it needs painting?"

"The blue is too dark. I want to brighten it up. I think something more neutral would work better. What do you think about pink?"

"Pink?"

"I'm pulling your leg, John. I want something a little more neutral. What about beige?"

"Beige is a good choice. To completely cover the dark blue, you'll need at least two coats, maybe even three."

"How much will it cost?"

"How does five hundred sound, including paint and taxes?"

"Sounds good to me. When can you start?"

"Unfortunately, I'm swamped. I'm booked solid for the next three weeks. Is that a problem?"

"Not at all. Call me with a date when you're free."

"Will do."

Morton grinned. "While we're here, would you like to try out the bed? It's comfortable."

Mike let out a nervous laugh. "I don't think so. I make it a point not to go to bed on the first date. I guess I'm a little old-fashioned."

"I'm kidding. I feel the same way. Why don't we go back to the living room and continue getting to know each other?"

"That's fine with me," Mike said, relieved.

McMahon returned to the couch while Morton went into the kitchen. Within a few minutes, he came back with a bowl of pretzels and two more Bud Lights.

After thirty minutes of conversation, the Muddy Waters CD ended. Mike glanced at his watch and said, "It's getting late. I probably should be going."

"Stay for a bit. It's not that late. Do you like new country music?"

"Yeah, most of it."

"I just bought a CD by a new artist. She's got an amazing voice. Let me play you a few songs."

"Okay."

Mike was surprised to hear a familiar tune. It was Suzanne singing one of her recent hits, "The Power Of My Love."

When the song ended, Morton asked, "What do you think? Has she got a great voice, or what?"

"Who is she?" Mike asked, pretending not to know.

"Her name is Suzanne Taylor. She's a beautiful woman. I predict she's going to become a superstar."

"I agree; she does have a captivating voice. Come to think of it, I recall seeing a video on CMT with her and a guy named Marven Jones singing a duet together. For the life of me, I can't remember the name of the song."

"It's called 'Don't Throw Our Love Away.'"

"Oh yeah, now I remember," Mike said.

Catching McMahon entirely off guard, Morton said, "I read somewhere she's engaged to an MNPD homicide detective."

Mike paused for a few seconds. *Does he know who I am?* "Oh, I didn't know that. I'd say that detective is one lucky guy."

"I remember seeing the detective doing a TV interview during the Guitar String Strangler case. If I recall correctly, his name is Detective Mike McMahon. For some reason, you remind me of him."

Shit! Did Morton recognize me? "They say everyone has a double. Maybe this McMahon guy is my double," Mike said, his stomach beginning to churn.

"Could be," Morton said, checking his watch. "It's getting late, and I've got a busy day tomorrow. I usually don't work on Saturday, but I promised a customer we'd finish his job tomorrow. I've enjoyed meeting you, John. Sorry, but I don't think you and I are a good fit."

Not knowing what else to say, Mike asked, "Do you still want me to paint your bedroom?"

"No, that's all right. I think it's best if we don't see each other again."

"No problem, Bruce. Goodnight."

"Goodnight, John."

The two men shook hands, and Mike left.

When he reached the main road, he spotted Rose in the unmarked police car. McMahon made a u-turn, parked behind her, got out, and slid onto the passenger seat.

"What do you think, did he make me?" Mike asked.

"It's hard to tell, but I think Morton was starting to get suspicious. He probably didn't recognize your physical appearance, but he might have recognized your voice. That's why he made an excuse to get you to leave."

"Shit! Do you think so? I should've tried to disguise my voice, too. Now, what do we do?"

"I don't know. Since it's Friday night, let's sleep on it over the weekend. We can start fresh on Monday morning."

CHAPTER 25

After McMahon had started his car and disappeared, Morton went into the kitchen and returned to the living room with a fresh beer. That's when his mind shifted into high gear. *Something doesn't feel right. Are the cops on to me? Are my suspicions that John Woodman is Detective Mike McMahon correct, or am I becoming paranoid?*

Morton sat up until the wee hours of the morning drinking and reviewing his evening with John Woodman. At four, he finished his drink and stumbled into the bedroom. As soon as his head hit the pillow, Morton was snoring loudly. He awoke at seven with a piercing headache and a gigantic hangover, but with the definite conviction that John Woodman was indeed Detective Mike McMahon.

On Monday morning, as Mike sat down at his desk, Rose took one look at him and laughed.

"Going on a trip?"

"On a trip? What are you talking about?"

"Are you going on a trip? I see your bags are packed."

Finally, McMahon caught on. "You're a barrel of laughs, Goodwin."

"You look like death warmed over. Did you get any sleep on the weekend?"

"Not a hell of a lot. Last night, before going to bed, I drank a half bottle of whiskey, but it didn't help. I ended up with very little sleep and a massive hangover. I couldn't get Morton out of my mind. The more I think about it, the more I believe he made me. My gut tells me he's our guy, but now we might never catch the bastard."

"Don't be so negative. If Morton is our perp, we'll find a way to collar him."

"If we could obtain a search warrant, I'd like to take a team of cops and go over his property with a fine-tooth comb. But we don't have probable cause. No judge in his right mind would issue a warrant on my gut feeling."

"You're right about that, but maybe there's another way," Rose said.

"What are you thinking?"

"If you spend your nights in gay bars, you might get lucky and spot the killer's next victim. You can watch for someone who receives a text message or receives a phone call and leaves shortly afterward. You and I can follow that person, and hopefully, he'll lead us to Morton or whoever the perp is."

"I sure as hell don't want to spend all my nights in gay bars. That could take forever. I've got a better idea."

"Okay. I'm all ears."

"When I read the missing person reports, they showed that all the men disappeared on a Friday or Saturday night. It would appear as if Morton works from Monday through Friday at landscaping and kills his victims on the weekend. If that's the case, it would be easier if we staked out his place on those nights and watched for a lone male driver entering his laneway," Mike said.

"That's a much better plan."

"Let's start this Friday."

"Okay," Rose said.

"Before I forget, I'd like to check something." McMahon went into his computer and brought up the DMV website and typed in the name Bruce Morton. Under the name Bruce Daniel Morton, two vehicles came up in the registry. One was a three-year-old white Chevrolet panel van, and the other a recent-model white Ford Escape. "Just as I thought. That bastard has two vehicles. Morton lied about his van breaking down. He must have used the same ruse on his other victims as he did on me."

Just then, Lieutenant Foster appeared and said, "The chief's been bugging me. I need to give him an update on the missing person case. Could you step into my office for a minute, please?"

"Okay, Lieutenant, we'll be right there," Rose said.

Before the detectives sat down, Foster asked, "Are you making any progress?"

"Yes, sir. I think we have a suspect, Lieutenant," McMahon said.

"That's good news. Do you have a name for me?"

"His name is Bruce Daniel Morton. He's a landscaper who lives on thirty acres just outside the city off Interstate 65 North."

Mike went on to tell Foster about Friday night's meeting and conversation with Morton. He also mentioned their plan to stakeout Morton's property on Friday and Saturday nights.

"Based on what you just told me, Detective, I think this Morton guy could be our suspect. It sounds like he recognized your voice, having seen you on TV during one of your past interviews. Let's hope your surveillance plan works. Too bad we don't have probable cause for a search warrant. If he is our killer, Morton has more than enough acreage to hide the bodies and maybe even the vehicles of his victims."

"He sure does," Goodwin agreed.

"I'd better call the chief. I hope your plan works. Keep me updated."

"Will do, Lieutenant," Rose said.

"What about my undercover assignment? Should I discontinue it?" McMahon asked.

"Let's hold off for now just in case you've made a mistake, and Morton isn't the unsub."

When they returned to the squad room, Mike said, "I've got an idea. First thing tomorrow morning, why don't we go to Morton's place and search the grounds? Maybe we'll find something that ties him to the missing men."

"If we do find any evidence, you know we can't use it since it'll be an illegal search."

"Yeah, I know, but I need to satisfy my curiosity."

"Oh, all right, but it'll probably be a waste of time."

"Humor me, Goodwin. Are you coming or not?"

"Yeah, I'm coming. What's your rush?"

"As I said, I'm curious. I've got to find out if Morton's our man. If he is, we'll find a way to nail that son of a bitch."

CHAPTER 26

Early the following morning, dressed in jeans, casual tops, and sneakers, McMahon and Goodwin headed to Morton's place. As they approached the laneway, a white panel van with Morton Landscaping Inc. printed on the side turned on to the road a hundred yards in front of them and headed in the opposite direction.

"That was close," Mike said. "I hope he didn't spot us."

"I'm sure he didn't. We were too far away. You sound like you're getting paranoid."

"No, I'm not. I'm just pissed that Morton may have made me."

"Should we hide the car and walk-in?" Goodwin asked.

"No, let's drive; it'll be quicker."

"Okay," Rose said, not sounding too sure of Mike's decision.

As they entered the laneway, under the Morton Landscaping Inc. sign, Mike got a chuckle out of another posting he had missed the night of his visit with Morton. In bold letters, it read:

WARNING

NO TRESPASSING

VIOLATORS WILL BE SHOT

SURVIVORS WILL BE SHOT AGAIN

"Did you see that sign, Rose?"

"How could I miss it?"

McMahon laughed. "Maybe that's what Morton will use as his defense. He'll say the men he killed were trespassing."

"Yeah, maybe. With our luck, Morton will probably get off."

They drove by Morton's home, past a sizeable glass-enclosed greenhouse, and a white aluminum-sided storage building. A hundred yards down the road, McMahon pulled into a secluded opening in the woods.

"Okay, partner, let's do a little exploring," McMahon said. He got out and removed a long-handled spade from the trunk.

"There's a lot of ground to cover. Do you think we should split up?" Rose asked.

"No. Let's stick together. I don't want you to get lost in the woods. Besides, we only have one shovel."

Rose shot back. "I'll have you know I was a girl guide when I was young. I've had lots of experience in the woods."

"I bet you have."

"What's that supposed to mean?"

"Nothing. I'm just kidding."

"Okay, Mr. Kidder, where do you want to start?"

"Let's follow the road and see where it leads."

After walking for five minutes, they came across a vast clearing that contained a variety of newly planted small trees and shrubs. A yellow backhoe sat next to an elevated stainless steel fuel tank.

"It looks like this is where Morton grows greenery for his business," Rose said.

"Yeah, it does, and that backhoe over there would sure come in handy for digging graves and covering up bodies."

"If Morton is our killer, what did he do with the bodies?" Goodwin asked.

"If I were him, I'd bury the remains and then plant trees and shrubs on top of them. This field would be the ideal place."

"I don't think your shovel is the best tool for digging up human remains under all these shrubs and trees. They'd be way too deep, and it would take forever. Do you know how to operate a backhoe?"

"No, and I don't think I want to learn. I've got a better idea," Mike said.

"Okay, let's hear it."

"When we go back to the station, I'll call Sergeant Barry Reeson of the Canine Unit. We worked together when I was a patrol officer. I know his dog, Hunter, has been trained to find buried bodies."

"Good idea, but do you think Reeson will agree to an illegal search?"

"I don't know, but it can't hurt to ask."

"Since we won't be doing any digging today," McMahon said, Let's go back and check out the storage building and greenhouse."

"I like that idea. It's better than digging up bodies," Rose said as they headed back to the car.

Mike had no sooner parked the car when Goodwin jumped out and hurried to the door, "Damn! It's padlocked," she grumbled.

Pulling a pick out of his pocket, McMahon said, "Step aside, partner, let an expert go to work."

In less than thirty seconds, Mike had the lock picked. Rose found the light switch and flipped it on.

"Looks like Morton uses this building to store his landscaping equipment and gardening tools," Goodwin said.

The building contained two riding mowers, a golf cart, shovels, rakes, hedge clippers, and other landscaping and lawn maintenance equipment. Nothing appeared to be out of place until they spotted a large freezer, a double stainless steel sink, and a tap with a garden hose rolled around a metal wall holder. An oversized butcher's block stood next to the sink. A bucket of cleaning chemicals, an electric saw, a hatchet, and an assortment of different sized knives sat on top of the blood-stained butcher's block.

"Holy shit," Mike said. "Morton's not just a landscaper. He's a butcher, too. I dare you to open the freezer?"

Without hesitating, Goodwin opened the freezer. "Yuck," she said, turning away in disgust.

Bewildered by Goodwin's reaction, Mike stepped up to the freezer and looked inside. He saw frozen animal parts that Mike guessed was the deer's carcass whose head hung on the wall above the butcher's block.

McMahon smiled and tried not to laugh as Goodwin bent over the laundry tub and rinsed her mouth out with water from cupped hands. "Is this why you're so upset? From the way you reacted, I thought you had seen a chopped-up human body."

"I don't know what I expected to see, but that poor animal wasn't at the top of my list."

Mike pulled out his cell phone and snapped photos of the freezer, its contents, the sink, and the butcher's block displaying Morton's tools. When he had finished, McMahon slipped the phone back into his belt holder and said, "So far, the only thing Morton's guilty of is hunting out of season. But I still think Morton is our killer. Let's get the hell out of here before he comes back and catches us on his property. I don't relish the thought of being shot for trespassing."

The words had no sooner left McMahon's mouth as the distinct sound of tires crunching on gravel broke the silence.

"Shit," Mike said, "Someone's coming."

"It must be Morton. Who else could it be?"

"I don't know. Let's go take a look."

Out of sight behind a cedar hedge, they watched Morton's panel van approach. The garage opened, and the vehicle disappeared inside.

"Once the door closes, let's hightail it out of here. By the time Morton gets out of his van and into the house, we'll be long gone," McMahon said.

They ran to the car and took off. As Mike turned on to the main road, Rose said, "That was a close call. I hope he didn't see us."

"Morton might have heard the car, but I doubt he saw us."

"Even if he did see the car, there's no way he'd know who we were," Goodwin said.

"I've been thinking. I bet Morton uses the butcher's block and all those tools to chops up the bodies of his victims. I'm guessing he buries the parts somewhere on his property. Serial killers are a weird breed. Ted Bundy took Polaroid pictures of his victims, Ivan Milat kept his victims' camping supplies, Jerome Brudos killed women and kept their shoes. Who knows what Morton is doing? Maybe he keeps their fingers or heads."

"That's gross, Mike. Let's not talk about it anymore."

Changing the subject, McMahon said, "To get to Morton's place, his victims have to drive there. When he kills them, what does he do with their vehicles?"

"That's a good question. Morton's got plenty of land. Maybe he digs holes with his backhoe and buries them."

"That sounds logical. Maybe Morton is greedy and sells the vehicles to a scrapyard."

"How would he be able to do that? Wouldn't he have to show that he was the owner?"

"Normally, yes, he would," Mike said. "But Morton probably knows a shady scrapyard owner who will look the other way if he can buy the cars for a song."

"If we can prove Morton has sold his victim's vehicles, that could be the evidence we need to get a judge to issue a search warrant for his property."

"I still want to speak to Sergeant Reeson about bringing his dog out to Morton's place to sniff for human remains," McMahon said.

"Are we going to tell Lieutenant Foster what we've been up to?" Rose asked.

"I don't know. If we don't tell the lieutenant and he finds out later, we'll be in deep shit."

CHAPTER 27

When they arrived at the station, Rose headed to the ladies' room while Mike called Sergeant Reeson. As he hung up the phone, Goodwin returned, looking relieved and refreshed.

"I'm ready, let's go face the music," she said.

As they walked through the door, the boss looked up from a pile of paperwork and did a double-take. "I didn't know it was casual Friday. What's going on?"

"We took a little side trip this morning, Lieutenant," Mike said.

"Side trip? Where?"

"We went to Morton's place," Mike said.

"Why in hell did you do that?"

He explained what they had found on the property and showed Foster the pictures he had taken in the storage building.

Just as McMahon finished, Foster scowled and barked, "What were you thinking? Those pictures don't prove squat. Since your search was illegal, even if you found dead bodies on Morton's property, the evidence wouldn't be admissible in a court of law. You know that, don't you?"

"Yes, sir, we do," McMahon said. "We suspect Morton doesn't just use the butcher's block and all those tools to chop up wildlife. I strongly believe the remains of the missing men are buried somewhere on his property."

"And what do you believe, Sergeant?"

"To be honest, I don't know what to believe."

"Suspecting Morton is our killer, and proving it, legally, is another matter," Foster snapped.

"That's what we intend to do," Mike said, showing his annoyance.

"And how do you plan on doing that?" Foster barked back, his face crimson, and the vein on his forehead was beginning to pulse.

Noticing McMahon's blood pressure starting to rise, Rose jumped in before Mike said something he would regret. "We'll continue to stake out Morton's property and catch him before he kills his next victim. We plan to check out local scrapyards to see if Morton has sold any of his victims' vehicles."

Foster laughed. "Good luck with those two long shots," he said sarcastically.

McMahon glanced at Goodwin, who gave him a look that said, "bite your tongue." Mike turned back to Foster, cleared his throat, and calmly said, "If Morton is a serial killer, he's bound to try again. We'll be waiting when he lures his next victim out to his property."

"For your sake, I hope your plan works. I don't think it would be wise for me to inform Chief Cummings of what you two have been doing with your time. I have a feeling he wouldn't be too pleased."

Foster reached for his bottle of water as the detectives stood to leave and quickly swallowed an antacid tablet.

On their way back to the squad room, Mike was visibly upset.

"That went over like a fly in your soup. The boss wasn't too pleased about us trespassing on Morton's property," McMahon said.

"Yeah, I'd say he was slightly pissed."

"Slightly pissed? That's an understatement. And thanks for your support, partner. What's with: 'To be honest, I don't know what to believe.'"

"I'm sorry, Mike, but that's how I feel. I'm not sure Morton's our killer."

"He's our killer all right, and somehow we'll prove it. Let's get the hell out of here and go have a coffee at Starbucks."

Goodwin waited as Mike went to his desk and retrieved a cell phone from the middle drawer. He pulled out a phone book and thumbed through the yellow pages, jotted down a number, then gave the sticky note and phone to Rose.

"What's going on?"

"I've got an idea. When we get to Starbucks, I want you to call Morton Landscaping."

"Why do you want me to call Morton?"

"I'll fill you in when we get there."

McMahon placed a coffee in front of Rose and sat down. She took a sip and said, "Well, don't keep me in suspense. What's this bright idea of yours all about?"

"I want you to call Morton and pretend that you're a potential customer looking for a quote on a landscaping job."

"Why can't you call him?"

"Because he might recognize my voice."

"And why do I need a quote on landscaping?"

"Because we need to find out where Morton will be working tomorrow. We'll hide off the main road with Sergeant Reeson and his dog, Hunter. I called Reeson while you were in the ladies' room, and he agreed to help. Once Morton takes off, we'll go to the field with the shrubs and trees and have Hunter sniff for buried bodies."

"And you want me to use a burner phone, so Morton won't know who's calling."

"That's right. You can tell Morton you and your husband just moved into a new home and would like a quote to have it landscaped. If he asks, give him a phony name and a fake address."

"Okay, here goes."

Goodwin picked up the phone and dialed the number. After three rings, a voice said, "Morton Landscaping."

"Is this Mr. Morton?"

"Yes, this is Bruce Morton. How may I help you?"

"My husband and I recently moved into a new house and want to get a quote on having it landscaped."

"That's great! I'm sorry, but I'll be away until next Tuesday. I have to attend a funeral in Knoxville on Monday. If you give me your phone number, I'll be happy to call you when I return, and we can set up an appointment."

Having obtained the information they required, Goodwin hung up.

"So, what did he say?" Mike asked.

"Morton said he had to go to Knoxville to attend a funeral. He said he'd be back on Tuesday and would call when he returned. That's when I hung up."

"Good. It looks like we're on for tomorrow."

Mike pulled out his cell phone and dialed Sergeant Reeson. After a brief conversation, they agreed to meet at Starbucks on Church Street at five the next morning.

CHAPTER 28

Sergeant Barry Reeson, six-foot-one, had the build of a running back. After paying for his coffee, he noticed McMahon waving and casually walked over to their table. Mike introduced Reeson to Rose.

After shaking hands, Reeson asked, "What's the plan?"

"If you have room, can we go in your vehicle?" Mike asked.

"No problem. My van has plenty of space."

"Great, we'll leave our car here until we get back," Rose said.

Reason pulled the van off the main road, and they waited. At 7:10 a.m., Morton drove out of his driveway and turned right.

Five minutes later, they parked in the field with the newly planted trees and shrubs. Mike and Rose each grabbed a long-handled spade. They waited while Reeson opened the cargo door, unlatched the cage, and a grateful Hunter jumped out. The German Shephard sniffed the ground for a few seconds, made a circle, lifted his leg, and relieved the pressure.

When the dog had finished watering a pine tree, Reeson said sternly, "Hunter, come sit."

Immediately, Hunter stopped his sniffing, returned, and sat by his master's side.

"What a beautiful dog," Rose said. "How old is he?"

"Hunter recently turned five," Reeson replied.

"It's hard to believe your dog can sniff out buried human remains," Mike said.

"Hunter is smart, and he has one of the best noses in the business. He's a cadaver dog, trained to search for cadavers and human remains. Believe it or not, a cadaver dog can detect human remains through concrete, buried underground, or at the bottom of a body of water."

"That's amazing," Goodwin said.

"Where would you like to start?" Reeson asked.

"I think we should start here in this field," Mike said.

Sergeant Reeson looked down at his dog, who was still sitting by his side, and said, "Hunter, find bodies."

The dog jumped up, and with his nose to the ground, he began to sniff among the trees and shrubs. It didn't take long before Hunter stopped at the base of a small spruce tree, barked, and started to claw at the dirt.

"Good boy, Hunter. It looks like he found something," Reeson said.

Mike and Rose picked up their shovels and began to dig. Ten minutes later, with sweat pouring down their faces, they removed the tree. After searching for a few more minutes, they spotted two human hands severed at the wrist and two feet chopped off above the ankle.

"Oh, my God, that's disgusting," Rose said. "You were right, partner. Morton is our killer."

Hunter continued his work, and two exhausting hours later, they discovered several more body parts, including the head of Martin Tuckman.

"Gross," Goodwin said when she saw the severed head. "That Morton is one sadistic bastard."

"You've got that right," McMahon said as he proceeded to take pictures of the hands, feet, head, and several other body parts. When he had finished, they reburied the remains and replanted the trees and shrubs, leaving the field similar to how they had found it.

"Since our search was illegal, how do you plan to catch Morton?" Reeson asked.

"That's a good question," Rose said.

"We'll find a way," Mike said. "I've got a few ideas on how to collar Morton legally. It might take a little time, but we'll get the son of a bitch."

After dropping Mike and Rose off at their car, Reeson wished them luck, said goodbye, and he and Hunter drove away.

Before starting the car, McMahon turned to Goodwin and said, "Now that we know Morton is our killer, we've got to develop a plan to prove it legally. Do you have any suggestions?"

"The two things we talked about previously might work. We can visit the scrapyards in the area. Maybe Morton tried to sell his victims' vehicles. We can stake out his property on Friday and Saturday nights and watch for anyone entering his driveway."

"Since today's Saturday and Morton's out of town, I don't think he'll be killing anyone tonight. Let's grab a quick lunch, and we can visit a few scrapyards this afternoon," Mike suggested.

"Okay. My stomach's starting to growl. Where do you want to go?"

"How about The Longhorn on Murfeesboro?"

"Sounds good to me."

While waiting for his meal to arrive, Mike used his cell phone to Google area scrapyards. He jotted the names and addresses down in his notebook, looked up, and said, "There are only three in Nashville."

"I don't know why, but I thought there'd be a lot more."

"Me, too."

CHAPTER 29

When they arrived at Cumberland River Scrap Processors, Mike parked the car in front of a small wooden building with white, peeling paint. A faded sign above the door said OFFICE.

As they entered the building, a middle-aged man with pale skin and greasy, black hair sat behind an antique oak desk. He glanced up from the *Playboy* magazine he pretended to be reading and gave a gap-toothed smile. He put the magazine down, picked up a cigarette from an ashtray, took a deep drag, and slowly released smoke into the already stale-smelling room.

Flashing their badges, Rose said, "I'm Detective Sergeant Goodwin, and this is my partner, Detective McMahon."

"Good afternoon, Detectives. How can I help you?" he said in a raspy smoker's voice.

"Are you the owner of this scrapyard? Goodwin asked.

"Yes, I am."

"And what is your name, sir?" Mike asked.

"My name is Bill Stoutt. What's this about?"

"We need to ask you a few questions, Mr. Stoutt," Goodwin said.

"Questions? About what?" Stoutt asked, a concerned look on his face.

Rose pulled out her cell phone, brought up Morton's picture, and showed it to Stoutt. "Have you ever seen this man?"

He stared at the picture for a few long seconds, took another drag on his cigarette, inhaled, and blew the smoke straight at Rose. Goodwin waved the cloud from her face and glared at Stoutt.

"Sorry, Detective, I wasn't thinking."

Visibly upset, Rose repeated, "Have you seen this man? Think hard, and don't give us any bullshit."

Finally, Stout said, "He does look familiar."

"Did he try to sell you a vehicle?" Mike asked in a demanding tone.

"About two or three weeks ago, he came in driving a recent-model blue Cadillac SUV."

"Did he give you a name?" asked Goodwin.

"I believe he said his name was Martin. No, I think it was Morton. Can't remember his first name."

"Does Bruce Morton ring a bell? Mike asked.

"Yeah, that's the name—Bruce Morton."

"Was the car registered in his name?" Rose asked.

"I think it was."

"Was it or wasn't it?" McMahon snapped.

Stoutt paused and scratched his head. "Morton said he won the car in a poker game."

"And you believed him?" Goodwin said.

"I had no reason to doubt him."

"Did he provide you with proof of ownership?" Mike asked.

"Yes, he did. The back of the title form showed him as the new owner."

"Do you recall the name of the original owner?" asked Mike.

"Sorry, Detective, I don't."

"Weren't you a little suspicious as to why Morton wanted to sell what appeared to be a valuable vehicle for scrap?" Goodwin asked.

"I was, but when I asked him why he didn't go to a used car dealer or try to sell the car privately, he said he wanted a quick sale. Morton said he just wanted to recoup enough to pay off the five thousand owing to him from the gambling debt."

"Surely you knew the car was worth at least ten times that amount," Mike said.

"Of course I did, but why look a gift horse in the mouth? I knew I could sell the car for a lot more than I paid Morton."

"Is that what you did?" Rose asked.

"Yes. I have an arrangement with a used car dealer. The next day, he came by, gave me a check for twenty grand, and left a happy camper. He probably sold it for a hefty profit and laughed all the way to the bank."

"What's the name and location of the car lot?" McMahon asked.

"It's called Smitty's Auto Sales on Murfreesboro Road. I can't remember the exact number."

"That's okay," Mike said. "We'll find it. Who is the owner?"

"His name is Bernie Smith."

"Give me a minute," Rose said. She went out to the car and returned with a folder containing the missing person reports. "Here it is. That car belonged to Martin Tuckman."

"I see you have security cameras on your premises," Mike said. "Do you think you can find a video from the day Morton came in with the car?"

"That shouldn't be a problem, Detective. I think he came in a few weeks ago. Let me check and see what I can find."

It didn't take long for Stoutt to find the video from the day Morton had visited him. He waved the detectives into a small room. The screen showed Morton driving through the gate and getting out of Tuckman's Cadillac. The footage showed him entering the office and the ensuing deal-making conversation with Bill Stoutt. As soon as Morton received the cash, he made a phone call, and fifteen minutes later, he got into a taxicab and left.

Mike smiled. "Bingo! We got the bastard."

"Can you make a copy of this video for us, Mr. Stoutt?" Rose asked.

"I sure can. Am I in any trouble for buying the car and reselling it, Detective?"

"I wouldn't worry, Mr. Stoutt. We've got bigger fish to fry," Goodwin said.

Stoutt breathed an audible sigh of relief and pulled out a flash drive.

Five minutes later, with the evidence in his pocket and a smile on his face, Mike started the car and headed for Murfreesboro Road.

The lot at Smitty's Auto Sales was jam-packed with at least a hundred vehicles of all makes, shapes, and sizes.

As the detectives walked through the door, a short, beefy, bald man in his mid-fifties, smoking a cigar, greeted them warmly.

"Howdy, folks. I'm Bernie Smith. How can I help you?"

Smith looked like a typical old-school car salesman in his red and white checkered sports coat, dark blue dress pants, a lime-green dress shirt, and a red silk tie.

Presenting his badge, Mike said, "I'm Detective McMahon, and this is my partner, Detective Sergeant Goodwin. We're looking for a car."

"Great!" Smith said, dollar signs flashing in his eyes. "You've come to the right place."

"I hope so," Goodwin said. "We're looking for a recent-model Cadillac SUV."

"You're in luck. I just purchased one recently. It's on the lot. Would you like to see it?"

"We sure would," Mike said.

Smith led them to the front row facing the street and stopped at Tuckman's Cadillac SUV.

"I hope you like blue."

"I love blue. It's my favorite color," Rose said.

"It's a honey of a car, and I can offer you a sweet deal. Would you like to take it for a test drive?"

"That won't be necessary," Rose said.

"Which one of you will be buying it?"

"Neither of us," Mike said.

Confused, Smith said, "I thought you said you were looking for a recent-model Cadillac SUV?"

"We are," Rose said. "We'll have an MNPD tow truck pick it up within the hour."

"Wait a minute! What the hell's going on here?" Smith demanded.

"You purchased this car from Cumberland River Scrap Processors, didn't you?" Rose said.

"Yes, I did. Legal and above-board."

"Sorry, but the car is evidence in a murder investigation," McMahon said.

"You've got to be kidding me. Is the MNPD going to reimburse me the twenty grand I paid for it?"

"That's not our problem," Goodwin said. "Maybe you should talk to Bill Stoutt about that."

"I'll phone that crooked bastard right now," Smith scowled. He turned and rushed back to his office.

While Rose made a few calls, Mike walked across the street for coffee. When he returned, they waited in the car, drinking their java and making small talk. In less than an hour, the MNPD tow truck arrived and hooked up the Cadillac.

As McMahon drove away, he said, "Since this is Saturday, why don't we put everything on hold until Monday. The forensics people should have the car processed by then. Once Foster sees the video, I'm sure he'll agree we have enough evidence to obtain a search warrant for Morton's property."

"Good idea. Morton's out of town until Tuesday, so we can't arrest him until then. We can both use a day off to recharge our batteries."

"You've got that right. I think I'll sleep all day tomorrow."

CHAPTER 30

Monday morning, Mike felt rested and raring to go. When he arrived at his desk, he uploaded the video from the flash drive onto his computer.

"Good morning," Rose said as she sat down next to him. "Did you get your batteries charged?"

"Yeah, I did. I slept most of the day yesterday. How about you?"

"I slept in and didn't think about work all day. I picked up Jill after lunch, and we went to a movie. Before driving her home, we stopped for pizza. It was the best day I've had in a long time."

"It sounds as if you and Jill had a fun day."

"We did. It was nice to spend some time with my daughter for a change."

Shortly after eight, as he and Goodwin entered Foster's office, McMahon handed him the flash drive and explained what it contained. Mike also mentioned that Tuckman's vehicle was in the garage being processed by forensics.

After watching the video, Foster leaned back and smiled. "Good work, Detectives. This evidence should get us the warrants to search Morton's property and arrest him for first-degree murder. I'll contact the Canine Unit and have a team ready to roll as soon as a judge signs the paperwork."

"No rush, Lieutenant," Goodwin said. "We found out Morton is out of town and won't be back until tomorrow."

"And how do you know that?"

Rose told Foster the story about how she had called Morton, pretending to be a potential customer.

"So, Morton's in Knoxville attending a funeral?"

"That's what he said," Goodwin confirmed.

"Okay. First thing tomorrow morning, I want you two to stake out Morton's property. When he shows up, call me, and I'll send a team with the warrants."

"Will do, Lieutenant," Goodwin said.

"By the way, Lieutenant, can I quit the undercover assignment now and get back to normal?" Mike asked.

"Yes. Close the gay dating sites and go back to living in your condo." Foster laughed. "And get rid of that blond hair. It doesn't suit you."

"Gladly, Lieutenant."

"In the meantime, you might want to go to the garage and check to see how forensics are making out," Foster said.

As they stepped out of the elevator, Mike spotted the Cadillac in a parking space facing the end wall.

"It looks as if forensics have finished their work," McMahon said.

"Either that or they haven't started yet," Rose replied.

"Let's check with George," Mike said.

George Mason, the garage manager, was in his office with his feet up on his desk, talking on the telephone. As the detectives approached, he quickly removed his feet from the desk and ended his conversation. Mason gave an embarrassed smile and said, "Good timing, Detectives. I was just about to bring the forensics report up to you when my wife called."

"Oh, were you now? You're sure you were going to deliver it today?" Goodwin said sarcastically.

"Yes…yes, I was," Mason stammered.

He handed the report to Rose.

Goodwin burst out laughing. "Had you going there, didn't I, Georgie?"

"Rose, you rascal, you got me again."

McMahon was trying hard to keep a straight face. He knew that Rose was pulling Mason's chain.

Goodwin and Mason, who was one year away from retirement, had been friends for many years, and they enjoyed bantering with one another.

Back in the squad room, Rose opened the report, and with Mike hovering over her shoulder, they each began to read.

When they had finished, Rose said, "Just as I suspected, forensics found two sets of prints in the vehicle. The unidentified set would be Tuckman's. The other prints came up in the registry under the name Bruce Daniel Morton."

"I recently checked and found out that Morton got arrested for driving under the influence five years ago. That's why his mug shots and prints are in the system," Mike said.

CHAPTER 31

Tuesday morning at five-forty, McMahon hid the car off the main road near Morton's laneway entrance. They had a clear view that allowed them to see any vehicles entering and leaving the property.

"I'm sure we're here early enough," Mike said. "I don't think Morton will get home until late morning or early afternoon."

"You're probably right. In the meantime, all we can do is sit and wait," Rose said, pouring coffee from a large thermos into a mug.

"I'm glad we each brought a thermos of coffee and sandwiches. We could be here for a long time, so I'm going to take a catnap," Mike said, tilting back his seat.

"Hey, McMahon, how come you get to sleep, and I've got to stay awake?"

Mike laughed. "Because I thought of it first. Goodnight, Goodwin."

"If you snore, you'll be getting a poke in the ribs."

Two hours later, Rose elbowed McMahon in the ribs.

Mike's eyes flew open. "Ouch," he said. "Was I snoring?"

"Yes, you were. You've had your snooze, and now it's my turn to catch a few Zs."

Goodwin woke up just before noon. She stretched and yawned.

"That felt good. Any sign of Morton?"

"No," Mike replied. "All quiet on the Western Front."

"I've got to stretch and move around before rigor mortis sets in," Rose said, opening the door.

"Good idea. I think I'll do the same."

Just as they returned to the car, Morton's panel van zoomed past and turned into the laneway.

"That's odd," Mike said, "you'd think he would've taken his car to the funeral in Knoxville."

"You're right. It doesn't make any sense. Unless Morton came home earlier than expected."

"What do you want to do? Should we go in and arrest him now?" McMahon asked.

"No. Foster told us to call when Morton returned. He said he'll send a team with the warrants. We'd better do as he asked; otherwise, he'll get pissed off."

Foster answered on the second ring.

"Morton's back," Rose said.

"Good. I've got the warrants. The team should be there within the hour. Make sure Morton doesn't leave the property."

"Copy that," Goodwin said.

An hour later, a black SUV and Sergeant Reeson's Canine Unit van drove past the detectives and turned into Morton's driveway. Mike started the engine and followed.

All three vehicles stopped in front of the house. Four officers got out of the SUV. The driver, Sergeant Brock Davies, saw McMahon and Goodwin approaching and held up his hand.

"Here are your warrants, Detectives."

"Thanks, Sergeant," Goodwin said, taking the papers.

"How do you wish to proceed?" Davies asked.

"Send two of your men to guard the back door," Rose said. "I'd like you and the officer with the battering ram to accompany Detective McMahon and me to the front door." Turning to Sergeant Reeson, she said, "Sergeant, you and Hunter go with the officers to the back of the house. If Morton tries to run, he won't get far with Hunter on his heels."

When everyone was ready, McMahon said, "All right, let's do this."

Rose rang the doorbell. Several seconds later, the door opened. Goodwin was expecting to see Bruce Morton. Instead, a middle-aged man she had never seen before stood in the doorway, looking bewildered.

The detectives introduced themselves and presented their badges.

"Who are you?" Goodwin asked.

"I'm Harvey Broadbent."

"Show me some identification, please," Rose said.

Broadbent pulled out his wallet and showed her his driver's license and two credit cards.

Satisfied, Goodwin asked, "Where is Bruce Morton?"

"I don't know for sure. Bruce said he might go up to Canada for a few weeks."

"Shit! Where in Canada?" Mike asked.

"I don't know. Bruce didn't say."

"How come you're in Morton's house?" Rose asked.

"I work for Bruce. I'm house-sitting and running the business while he's on vacation."

Holding up the paperwork, Goodwin said, "We have a warrant to search the property, all the buildings, and vehicles. And a warrant for the arrest of Bruce Daniel Morton on six counts of first-degree murder."

Broadbent's jaw dropped. "Holy shit! No wonder Morton took off in such a hurry."

CHAPTER 32

Before his telephone rang, Lieutenant Foster was in a good mood.

"Lieutenant Foster." He listened briefly, then barked, "I can't believe it. Morton took off and is in the wind. How the hell did that happen?"

"As I said before, the night I met Morton, I suspect he made me," Mike said. "He figured we were on to him, and so he decided to get out of Dodge."

"Damn! It's too late to watch the airport, bus terminal, and the train station. Do you have any idea what Morton is driving?"

"Yeah. Morton owns a late-model Ford Escape."

"Do you have the description and plate number?"

"It's in my notebook."

"Give me the details, and I'll put out a nation-wide BOLO."

After receiving the information, Foster slammed the receiver down without saying goodbye. He pounded his fist on the desk, accidentally knocking his coffee mug to the floor, sending coffee and shards of glass in all directions.

"Shit, shit, shit," he bellowed.

When she heard glass shattering and Foster cursing, Nancy Allman came charging through the door.

"What happened, Lieutenant?"

"I just spilled my coffee. Bring some paper towels, a broom, and a dustpan, please."

"I'm glad you made that call," Goodwin said. "How did Foster take the news?"

"He was pissed."

"If Foster is pissed, wait until he tells the chief. That's when the shit will hit the fan."

"This might be a good time to take a leave of absence or go on a long vacation," Mike said.

"That sounds like one hell of a good idea, partner. I think I'll catch a plane to Timbuktu."

"Can I come? I've never been to Mali."

After a tension-relieving laugh, Rose asked, "Where do you think Morton's going?"

"I don't have a clue. Morton is smart. I bet he's already put stolen plates on his vehicle and is long gone. He probably travels by night and hides by day in a cheap motel off the beaten path."

"That's what I would do if I were Morton. It looks like he made his escape in his Escape," Rose said, grinning from ear to ear.

"Made his escape in his Escape. Good one, Goodwin."

"Good one, Goodwin. That's a good one, too, McMahon."

Mike chuckled. "You'll have to tell that one to the boss. I'd be curious to see his reaction."

"Somehow, I don't think he'll see the humor in it. Better keep that joke between you and me, McMahon."

Good idea, Goodwin."

Both detectives let out a half-hearted laugh, hoping to ease the tension, but it didn't work.

Chief Cummings was like a provoked hornet when he received the update from Lieutenant Foster. "What steps are you taking to collar Morton?" he snapped.

"I've just sent out a nation-wide BOLO with Morton's picture and vehicle details. I'm not holding my breath that we'll find him any time soon. Morton's no dummy. He's had a few day's head-start and could be anywhere by now."

"Did your detectives drop the ball on this one?"

"I don't think so, Chief. Goodwin and McMahon had no way of knowing Morton suspected they were on to him."

"Well, let's hope your BOLO works. Has the search team found any evidence yet?"

"They're just getting started. I'll keep you updated as soon as I know anything."

"Okay. You do that, Lieutenant. Goodbye."

"Goodbye, Chief."

Hunter did an excellent job. He sniffed out chopped-up body parts in the field with the recently planted trees and shrubs, including the severed heads of all six victims.

At the back of the property, the searchers dug up five vehicles buried in a gravel pit.

Looking at the unearthed cars, McMahon noticed it immediately.

"Hey, Goodwin, What's missing?" Mike asked.

"What's missing? I don't have a clue what you mean."

"If you look closely at the vehicles, they all have license plates except for one."

"You're right. That's odd."

"Not really. I'm sure the missing plates are on Morton's Ford Escape. He was thinking ahead. All we have to do is check to see which of the victims drove that Honda Accord. Once we get the plate number, we can have Lieutenant Foster reissue the BOLO."

The MNPD now had the evidence they needed to convict Bruce Daniel Morton on six counts of first-degree murder. The only problem, Morton was in the wind, and no one had any idea where to start looking.

CHAPTER 33

In preparation for the day of his departure, a few weeks earlier, Morton had obtained a false ID under the name James Donald Edwards. He purchased a gray wig that looked like real hair and got rid of his glasses, replacing them with contact lenses that made his eyes appear blue instead of brown.

All the funds from Morton's Nashville bank accounts now sat in an offshore account in the Cayman Islands. The balance on the statement of James Donald Edwards totaled over two million dollars.

At eleven the night Morton hit the road, he removed his emergency fund of one hundred thousand dollars from a safe at a rented storage unit and stuffed the cash into his briefcase.

Not wanting to attract the attention of state troopers, Morton stuck to the speed limit. It took twelve and a half hours to cover the seven hundred miles from Nashville to Tampa Bay.

At 11:20 a.m., Morton checked into the Days Inn on North 50th Street using his false ID. The accommodation was clean, comfortable, had a swimming pool, and was reasonably priced. The daily rate included breakfast and WiFi.

After a quick lunch at a nearby diner, Morton spent the afternoon by the pool, drinking beer and napping on a chaise lounge. He was relaxed and enjoying himself until he watched the six o'clock news. That's when he saw his picture come on the screen.

The male news anchor said, "This man, Bruce Daniel Morton, is wanted by the Metropolitan Nashville Police Department. He is a murder suspect and is considered to be armed and dangerous. The police believe Morton is driving a newer white Ford Escape with either of the two Tennessee license plate numbers now on your screen. If you see this man, do not approach him directly. Please call this toll free number immediately." The number flashed on the screen. "In other news—"

Morton turned off the TV and sat in stunned silence momentarily.

"Shit," he said out loud. "The cops must've found the buried cars and figured out what happened to the missing plates from the Honda Accord. It's time for a new plan."

Morton took a drive as soon as the sun had set and found a dimly lit side street lined with cars. He pulled over and checked to make sure no one was around. Not seeing anyone, he quickly removed the plates from his vehicle and replaced them with Florida plates from a white Honda Civic.

When he arrived back at the Days Inn, Morton tossed the Tennessee plates into a dumpster. To help ease the tension, he poured himself a generous drink of Scotch on the rocks. Feeling better, he turned on the TV and watched the last half of *The Silence of the Lambs*.

Detectives Goodwin and McMahon had mixed emotions. They were happy the search had turned up overwhelming proof implicating Morton as the killer of the six missing men. However, they blamed themselves for his escape. The evidence meant nothing unless Morton could be collared and brought back to stand trial.

The day of the search had been long. McMahon was exhausted, and every bone in his body ached. It was eight-fifteen when he opened the door to his condo. Mike was looking forward to a few stiff drinks and a good night's sleep.

After pouring himself a whiskey on the rocks, McMahon was about to head to his recliner and watch TV when something on the kitchen table caught his attention. A diamond ring sat on top of a folded piece of paper.

"What the hell?" he said aloud.

Mike placed his glass on the table and pulled up a chair. He unfolded the paper and began to read.

Dear Mike:

I'm taking the easy way out by leaving you this Dear John letter.

For the past several months, our lives have taken us in different directions. Because of my career, we seldom see each other anymore. I need some time and space to think about the future.

I've decided to return your ring until I can sort things out. In the meantime, please don't attempt to contact me.

Suzanne

Mike sat dumbfounded, staring at the note, his heart pounding and his mind racing like a runaway train. He reread the letter once more, picked up his drink, and downed it in one gulp.

What the hell's going on? Am I so wrapped up in my work that I missed the signs? Has Suzanne fallen out of love with me and in love with someone else? A member of her band? She didn't even sign the note with the word love.

Mike checked and found all of Suzanne's clothes, shoes, and personal grooming items were gone. He went back to the kitchen, poured a double shot of whiskey, walked into the living room, and slumped into his recliner. He awoke at two-thirty, went back into the kitchen, and finished off the bottle of Crown Royal before crashing on his bed fully clothed.

McMahon took a long, hot shower the following morning, hoping it would help his hangover and ease the migraine headache jabbing in his head. By the time he entered the squad room, it was nine-fifteen. He sat down and placed the black coffee on his desk. Mike turned to Rose, working on a crossword puzzle, in a world of her own, and said, "Good morning, Goodwin."

Without looking up, Rose said, "Good afternoon, Detective. You decided to come to work, did you?"

"I don't need your sarcasm today, Goodwin."

Surprised by McMahon's response, Rose glanced up and said, "What's with the bad mood? By the way, you look like death warmed over, McMahon, and you reek of alcohol. What the hell's going on?"

"It's a long story, and I'd rather not get into it now if you don't mind."

"I'm not letting you off the hook that easy. Tell me what's going on, or I'll bug you all day until you do."

"Oh, all right. To put it bluntly, Suzanne broke off our engagement. When I got home last night, I found a note and her ring on the kitchen table. She took all her things and moved out. It shocked the shit out of me, so I had a few too many trying to drown my sorrows."

"Oh, Mike, I'm so sorry. That's not what I was expecting to hear."

"That's not what I was expecting either. I just wanted to unwind from our long day with a drink or two and watch some TV. Now that you know, I would appreciate it if we don't talk about it anymore. And please keep it to yourself."

Before Goodwin could reply, Nancy Allman appeared and said, "The boss wants to see you two in his office immediately."

"Here," Rose said, pulling out a mint from her pocket. "suck on this. It will help freshen your breath."

When they were seated, Lieutenant Foster glanced at McMahon. "Have a rough night, Detective?"

"Yes, sir. I didn't get much sleep."

"Getting back to business, it looks like the search of Morton's property turned up the evidence we need to nail that monster. So far, we haven't had any leads from the BOLO I issued. It's like Morton disappeared off the face of the earth. He could be anywhere by now. Maybe even out of the country."

"Let's hope not," Goodwin said.

Just as Mike was about to say something, Foster's phone rang.

"Lieutenant Foster." He listened for a few moments, then said, "That's excellent news. The detectives assigned to the case are with me in my office. Let me put you on speakerphone. It's Chief Hanson from the Tampa PD. Okay, go ahead, Chief."

"Good morning, Detectives. We collared your suspect yesterday."

"That's great news," Goodwin said.

"How did you happen to find him, Chief?" Mike asked.

"Mostly by luck. Two officers on routine patrol spotted a white Ford Escape parked at a local Days Inn. The vehicle had Florida plates, but the officers decided to call it in. It turns out the plates were stolen the day before from a Honda Civic. After searching in an onsite dumpster, the officers discovered two Tennessee plates that matched the ones in your BOLO. They checked the VIN. The registration showed the name, Bruce Daniel Morton. After checking with the front desk, they obtained the occupant's room number. A few minutes later, the suspect was in custody. Morton had changed his appearance, and he had several pieces of fake ID under the name James Donald Edwards."

"So how do you wish to handle this, Chief?" Foster asked.

"We'll keep Morton in a holding cell until you can arrange to send someone to pick him up."

"Okay, Chief. I'll send Goodwin and McMahon. They'll leave later today and will pick Morton up first thing in the morning."

"Have them call me in the morning, and I'll arrange to have Detective Randy Mullens pick them up at their hotel."

After writing the phone number down, Foster said, "Thanks, Chief. Goodbye."

Foster buzzed Nancy Allman and explained what he required. Ten minutes later, she called back.

"Go home, freshen up, pack an overnight bag, and head to the airport. Your tickets will be waiting for you at the American Airlines check-in counter. Your plane leaves at four-forty."

The short flight was uneventful. Goodwin and McMahon spent the night at the Hyatt House near the Tampa International Airport.

At eight the next morning, as previously arranged, Mike called Chief Hanson. Thirty minutes later, Detective Randy Mullens picked Rose and Mike up at the front entrance and drove them to the District One Patrol Division, where Bruce Morton was waiting in a holding cell. Goodwin presented the warrant for Morton's arrest and signed the form releasing him into their custody. Detective Mullens then drove the detectives and Morton to the airport for their 11:00 a.m. flight.

When they arrived back at the station house, Morton was booked and processed, after which he was placed in a holding cell.

As Mike and Rose walked into his office, Lieutenant Foster smiled and said, "Welcome back, Detectives. I trust everything went well."

"As smooth as icing on a cake," Rose said.

"Good. What did Morton say when you arrested him?"

Mike laughed. "Like most criminals, after we Mirandized him, he said he was innocent and wouldn't speak without his lawyer present."

"Are you going to interview him today?"

"Yes, we are," Goodwin said. "Morton called his lawyer, and he should be here within the next thirty minutes."

"I'm curious. Who did Morton hire?"

"My ex-husband."

CHAPTER 34

Paul Goodwin was allowed a private meeting with his client before a guard escorted them to the interview room where Mike and Rose sat waiting.

The guard handcuffed Morton's right hand to the table and left the room. Seated next to his client, Paul Goodwin made eye contact with the two detectives and said in a pleasant tone, "Good afternoon, Detectives."

"Good afternoon, Paul," Rose said.

"Good day, counselor," Mike said.

"Before we get started, I want to make one thing clear. You do not speak directly to my client. All your questions go through me. Is that understood?"

"Yes," Rose said.

Mike nodded and said, "To prevent any misunderstandings, we would like to record this interview. Do we have your permission to do that?"

"Yes, you do," Paul Goodwin said.

Mike turned on the video recorder, gave the location, date, time, and the names of those present.

Rose glared directly at her ex-husband and said, "Your client, Bruce Daniel Morton, has been charged with six counts of first-degree murder. How does he plead?"

"Not guilty." Paul Goodwin said.

"During our investigation, we found a car of one of the missing men. It was sold to a scrap dealer by your client," McMahon said.

Mike placed a flash drive into the laptop computer, hit "play," and turned it around so that Morton and his lawyer could view the screen.

"As you can see," Rose said, "this security video shows your client driving through the entrance and getting out of Martin Tuckman's vehicle. Inside the office, you will see your client negotiating the sale of the car with the owner, Bill Stoutt, of Cumberland River Scrap Processors."

When the video had finished playing, Paul Goodwin turned to his client and whispered into his ear. Morton whispered back.

"My client says he bought the car from Mr. Tuckman legally before he went missing."

"If that's true," McMahon said, "we'd like to see your client's receipt and proof of payment."

Once again, Paul Goodwin and Morton whispered back and forth. Finally, the solicitor said, "My client says he lost the receipt and paid cash for the vehicle."

"That's a cock and bull story if I ever heard one," Rose said, showing her annoyance. "Your client told the scrapyard owner, Bill Stoutt, he won the car in a poker game."

"Stoutt lied," Morton shouted, his face flushing with anger.

"Shut your mouth," Paul Goodwin barked. "I told you before. I'll do the talking."

"Sorry," Morton said sheepishly.

Rose opened a folder, pulled out several colored photos, and placed them on the table.

"As you can see, these two pictures show body parts and the severed heads of the six missing men. This one shows the unearthed cars of five of the missing men, and this picture is a photo of a blood-stained butcher's block. The blood on the block was tested and found to be both animal and human. We took these pictures after presenting a search warrant to the employee house-sitting your client's property."

"With all this overwhelming evidence, does your client wish to change his plea?" Mike asked.

Without consulting his client, Paul Goodwin said, "No, he does not, Detective. Mr. Morton is being framed. This interview is over. We'll see you in court."

The next afternoon at 2:00 p.m., Paul Goodwin, ADA Clair Coleman, Mike, and Rose sat in the courtroom, awaiting the arrival of Bruce Morton and Judge Thomas Wells. At five minutes after two, Morton entered the room cuffed and shackled. He wore an orange jumpsuit and was accompanied by a sheriff's deputy. Two minutes later, the bailiff said, "All rise—the honorable Judge Thomas Wells presiding." As the judge sat down, the bailiff said, "Please be seated."

Judge Wells cleared his throat, took a sip of water, then said, "This arraignment hearing is now in session. Would the accused please stand?" Paul Goodwin and Bruce Morton stood and faced the judge. The judge continued. "Bruce Daniel Morton, you are charged with six counts of first-degree murder. How do you plead?"

"Not guilty, Your Honor," Paul Goodwin and Bruce Morton said in unison.

The defense and prosecution were each given fifteen minutes to state their cases regarding bail.

When they had finished, the judge said, "I have carefully studied the information presented by the defense and the prosecution. I have decided to grant a bond of $100,000 on each charge of first-degree murder. Before his release, the accused will surrender his passport and be fitted with an ankle monitor to ensure he does not take any unexpected trips."

"But Your Honor," Clair Coleman protested, "the accused is a flight risk, having already fled before his arrest in Florida. I strongly suggest he be held in custody without bail."

"Enough, Ms. Coleman. I have made my decision, and it's final."

"But—"

"I said enough. A preliminary hearing will be held one week from today in this same courtroom at 2:00 p.m. At that time, the prosecution and defense will have the opportunity to argue their cases.

Once the evidence is presented, I will decide if this case will proceed to trial or be dismissed."

CHAPTER 35

By the time Mike arrived home that evening, he was mentally exhausted. He was looking forward to a drink or two and stretching out in front of the TV. As he walked through the door, he heard a female voice coming from the living room. Suzanne was talking on the phone. As soon as Mike walked in, she said, "I've gotta go. I'll see you later, Joyce."

"Suzanne, what a pleasant surprise. I didn't expect to see you here."

"Hi, Mike, I hope you don't mind; I kept my key. We need to talk."

"I thought your letter said it all. What's on your mind?"

"First of all, I'd like to apologize for leaving you a note instead of speaking to you in person. I took the easy way out, and it's bothered me ever since. I'm so sorry for doing that."

"Your letter caught me entirely off guard. It was like being stabbed in the heart. I thought we were still good. What happened? What did I miss?"

"I thought we were still good, too. The problem is we've been living separate lives. My career takes me away, and we very rarely see each other anymore. When I come home for a few days, I'm usually so exhausted and mentally drained that all I want to do is sleep. And most of the time, your job has you stressed out. I've noticed that you try to relieve your anxiety by drinking more than you used to. And our love life has gone down the drain."

"I'll cut back on my drinking and start working out regularly. It's an excellent way to relieve stress, and I need to lose a few pounds.

You're right. Our love life has gone down the drain. It's turned as cold as snow."

"Working out and cutting back on your drinking sounds like a good start."

"I promise I'll work on it. Getting back to you, ever since the bus crash, you haven't been the same. Is that still bothering you?"

"I'd be lying if I said it wasn't. The people who died in that crash were my family. I still have nightmares about it. Why was I spared? I should've been on that bus."

"You can't beat yourself up about that. Feeling guilty won't help you get on with your life. The good Lord spared you for a reason. Are you still seeing your shrink, Suzanne?"

"The odd time when I'm home, but traveling the way I do doesn't help."

"Maybe you need to take a break and stay home for a while and get things sorted out. You'll need professional help to do that."

"I can't right now. I've still got two more tours booked. I can't let the band and the label down."

"Screw the band and screw the label. Your health is more important. What happens if you have a nervous breakdown?"

"Oh, Mike, I don't even want to think about it."

"Suzanne, you've got to think about it before it's too late. You can't put your head in the sand like an ostrich, hoping it'll go away."

"I know…I know, but I can't right now."

"Is there someone else? Is that why you broke off our engagement?"

The expression on Suzanne's face showed that she wasn't expecting that question. "No, Mike, there's no one else in my life. To be honest with you, a band member tried to hit on me recently, but I told him to bug off. I wasn't interested."

"I want you to know that I still love you very much, Suzanne. Do you still love me?"

"I'm not sure if I can love anyone right now. I don't even know if I love myself."

"Take my advice, Suzanne. You'll need professional help to get you through this."

"I promise, after my last tour, I'll take time off and get my head straightened out."

"Suzanne, you're not listening to me. You need to take time off right now before it's too late."

"Sorry, Mike, I can't. I have to go. " She held out her hand. "Here's your key."

"Keep it. You may need it again."

"No, Mike, I don't think I will."

Reluctantly, he took the key.

"Where are you staying?"

"I'm staying with Joyce and Bill Ormond. I've moved into their basement apartment."

McMahon opened his mouth to say something, but it was too late. Suzanne had walked out the door.

"Shit!" Mike bellowed to the empty room.

He was about to pour himself a drink when a little voice in his head said, *Stop, McMahon, what the hell are you doing?* He went into his bedroom, changed into his tracksuit, and headed down to the gym.

When he returned, the stress had left his body, but his mind was still moving at warp speed. He knew he wouldn't be able to sleep, so he went into the bedroom and picked up his guitar. The lyrics and melody to a song began to take shape in his head. As he started to play and sing, Mike occasionally stopped to jot words down on a legal pad. Thirty minutes later, he reread the lyrics.

AS COLD AS SNOW

By Mike McMahon

Every time we try to talk, you seem so far away
It hurts me when I know you block out every word I say
You and I are heading down a road of no return
I pray each day it's not too late to fix the bridges burned

Chorus:
Every time we try to talk, we don't communicate
I only know I still love you and hope it's not too late
You and I once touched the sky not so long ago
The passion that we felt back then has turned AS COLD AS SNOW

Every time I kiss your lips, your feelings have gone
You pretend I'm someone else. I feel I don't belong
And when I look into your eyes, I try to believe
I'd like to think that I am wrong and you still love me
Repeat Chorus
Tag:
The passion that we felt back then has turned AS COLD AS SNOW

CHAPTER 36

At Bruce Daniel Morton's preliminary hearing, Judge Thomas Wells ruled that the prosecutor's evidence far outweighed the "my client was framed" argument used by the defense. "The trial will begin in three months," Judge Wells said before leaving the courtroom.

The next morning in the squad room, Mike spotted an article in the *Nashville Star Daily* by his "favorite reporter" that read as follows:

SUSPECTED SERIAL KILLER ARRESTED

By Investigative Reporter: Jeff Stone

Over the last few months, six men from the local gay community have gone missing. Detective Sergeant Rose Goodwin and Detective Mike McMahon are working on the case. During their investigation, the detectives obtained video evidence that a suspect had sold the car of one of the missing men to a local scrap dealer. An arrest warrant and a search warrant for the buildings and property of Bruce Daniel Morton, a local landscaper, were issued. Somehow, before the police obtained the warrants, the suspect figured out what was about to happen and took off.

The MNPD presented the search warrant to an employee house sitter and began combing the buildings and thirty-acre property, looking for evidence. The police found the mutilated remains of all six missing men and five buried vehicles.

Immediately the MNPD put out a nationwide BOLO for Morton's arrest. A few days after his escape, Bruce Daniel Morton was found hiding at a Days Inn in Tampa Bay, Florida. The suspect was arrested and returned to Nashville. Believe it or not, at his arraignment, Morton was granted bail and is currently awaiting trial.

When contacted, Morton's lawyer, Paul Goodwin, the former husband of Detective Sergeant Rose Goodwin, said that his client was framed and planned to prove it in court.

Thank you, Detective Sergeant Goodwin and Detective McMahon, for a job well done. You have made the streets of our beautiful city safer.

As Rose sat down at her desk, Mike said, "Hey, partner, I can't believe what I just read. Jeff Stone thanked us for collaring Bruce Morton."

McMahon passed the newspaper to Goodwin.

After reading the article, Rose said, "Enjoy it while you can, Mike, he may not be so nice if we don't collar the Golf Club Killer soon."

"We may not have to worry about that. The GCK hasn't killed anyone recently. Maybe he's left town."

"So that's what you're calling him now. The GCK. I think the GCK is laying low until he finds another victim."

Mike was about to speak when Lieutenant Foster appeared, his face flushed, the vein on his forehead working overtime.

"I need to see you now. In my office, please." When everyone was seated, Foster continued. "I just received a call from one of our officers. The Golf Club Killer has struck again."

"Who was his victim this time?" Rose asked.

"Take a wild guess," Foster said.

"It's someone you both know well."

"Don't keep us in suspense," Goodwin said. "Who is it?"

"It's Bruce Morton."

"You've got to be kidding. Bruce Morton?" Mike said.

"I can't say that I'm sorry," Goodwin said.

McMahon laughed.

"What's so funny?" Foster asked.

"I find it ironic that one serial killer murdered another serial killer."

"Come to think of it, it is ironic," Foster said with a slight grin. "The Golf Club Killer broke into Morton's house and did his thing. Morton was found by his employee, Harvey Broadbent, around eight this morning. When Morton failed to answer the door, he used his key and found Morton lying on his bed with the killer's usual calling cards. When a patrol car arrived, the officers noticed that the killer broke through the back deck's sliding door. The CSU team is on their way. You two had better get your asses over there right now."

By the time the detectives arrived at the crime scene, the front and back entrances were sealed off and guarded by patrol officers. They logged in and headed straight to Morton's bedroom. As Goodwin and McMahon walked through the door, ME Tony Capino and his team were just beginning their work.

"Good morning, Detectives," Capino said. "How are you this fine morning?"

"As good as can be expected under the circumstances," McMahon said. "At least we didn't have to get up in the middle of the night this time."

Capino laughed. "Sometimes, killers are so considerate, aren't they?"

As per the Golf Club Killer's MO, Bruce Morton's body lay on the bed face up, a golf club in his right hand and a red golf ball in his mouth. Dried blood from Morton's caved-in skull saturated his pillow.

"Any clues so far, Tony?" McMahon asked.

"Same old, same old, Mike. Nothing."

"Why am I not surprised," Goodwin said.

Mike snapped several pictures with his cell phone, then turned to Rose and said, "If the GCK keeps this up, our murder book will be as thick as Webster's dictionary."

"You're right. The way things are going, we may end up with two or three books before we solve this case," Goodwin said.

Three hours later, they were back in Lieutenant Foster's office. After completing their update, the boss wasn't happy.

"Damn," Foster said. "You'd think by now we'd catch a break and find a clue or two. I can't believe this guy."

"Yeah, he's something else," Mike said. "I still believe we're dealing with someone with experience in law enforcement."

Foster frowned. "It certainly looks that way. Keep at it, Detectives. Sooner or later, you're bound to catch a break. For now, I'll do my best to keep the chief and mayor off your backs."

The next morning at ten, Mike and Rose attended Bruce Morton's autopsy. On their way back to the squad room, Mike picked up the *Nashville Star Daily*. After sitting down at his desk, he saw a new article by Jeff Sone.

SERIAL KILLER MURDERS ALLEGED SERIAL KILLER

By Jeff Stone, Investigative Reporter

Hold on to your hat, folks. In a weird turn of events, the alleged serial killer of six men from Nashville's Gay Community, Bruce Daniel Morton, was murdered yesterday by the Golf Club Killer.

The article went on to explain that Morton was out on bail. It said he was in his home wearing an ankle monitor to keep track of his whereabouts. The story went into detail about Morton's murder.

When McMahon finished reading, he handed the paper to Rose.

"Here, read Jeff Stone's article about Morton's murder. I still can't figure out where he gets all his information."

After putting the paper down, Rose said, "That Stone doesn't miss a beat. I couldn't describe things any better, and you and I were at the crime scene."

"I hate to say it, but that arrogant bastard is a damn good reporter," Mike admitted.

Four days after Bruce Morton's murder, another victim was found near a wooded walking trail in Percy Walter Park. The GCK had struck again.

"Have you identified the body yet?" Rose asked ME Tony Capino.

"Yes. Tyron Parker is the name on his ID."

"Tyron Parker, Tyron Parker," Goodwin repeated. "Why does that name sound familiar?"

"I know who Parker is," McMahon said. "He's the maniac who went on a killing rampage a few years ago in the Opry Mills Mall food court. Parker gunned down several people and wounded a few others. One of those who died was Cindy O'Connor, Patrick O'Connor's wife."

"Wasn't Parker convicted and sent to prison?" Rose asked.

"No. During Parker's trial, the testimony of a psychiatrist who interviewed Parker said he wasn't responsible for the murders due to his drug-induced state. After deliberating a few hours, the jury agreed with the defense, and Parker was found not guilty. Instead of going to prison, where he belonged, he ended up in a country club mental health facility for treatment."

"It looks like Parker was released back into society recently, and the GCK was waiting for him," Goodwin said.

"Usually, people with Parker's problems get released to a halfway house to help them integrate back into society."

Mike pulled out his cell phone and Googled halfway houses in Nashville. Thirty names came up. The closest one to Percy Walter Park was called Hickory Terrace on Old Hickory Boulevard.

"Parker was probably staying at a halfway house called Hickory Terrace. It's within walking distance of this park," Mike said.

"You're probably right. Somehow the GCK found out where Parker was staying, watched for him to leave the building, and followed him into the park."

"I remember Pat O'Connor said during our conversation that Parker was due to be released soon. With his connections, I'm sure he found out where Parker was staying. I still think that O'Connor could be the GCK."

"O'Connor definitely had a motive to want Parker dead," Rose said.

"Now, all we have to do is to connect the dots and prove Patrick O'Connor is the GCK."

"Easier said than done," Goodwin said, turning back to Capino. "Do you know who found the body, Tony?"

"It was a woman out walking her dog early this morning. She called 911 from a phone booth."

"Did she give her name?" asked Goodwin.

"No. The caller said she wanted to remain anonymous."

"How long has Parker been dead?" McMahon asked.

"Judging from the temperature and condition of the body, the victim has been dead for about sixteen hours." Capino glanced at his watch. "I'd say the TOD was between seven and eight last evening. The cause of death was blunt force trauma to the head. Same as all the others. I'll be doing the autopsy at ten tomorrow morning if you care to stop by. I'll send you pictures and a report within a few days."

"Okay. Thanks, Tony, we'll see you in the morning." Mike said.

On their way back to the station, they stopped at Hickory Terrace halfway house. After the administrator confirmed Parker's registration, Goodwin informed him of Parker's murder.

CHAPTER 37

On his way home that evening, Mike stopped by Patrick O'Connor's unit. He rang the bell and waited. No answer. McMahon rang the bell again. He was about to give up when the door opened.

"Hi, Mike. Sorry, I took so long. I'm still not used to walking with these damn crutches."

Mike's jaw dropped. It took a moment to get over the shock.

Finally, he said, "What...what happened to your foot?"

"I went out jogging a week ago, tripped in a pothole, and twisted my ankle. I thought I had just sprained it, but X-rays showed that I have a calcaneus fracture of the heel bone."

"What the hell does that mean?"

"It means I've got a broken heel."

"How did you get to the hospital?"

"Another jogger saw me fall and came over to see if I needed help. Since I couldn't walk without excruciating pain, he went and got his car and drove me to Nashville General."

"How long will you have to wear that boot?"

"It's called a removable fracture boot. The emergency room doctor said I'd have to wear it for about six to eight weeks. The boot is removable so I can work on ankle and foot motion during the healing process. When it comes off for good, I still may need physical therapy after that."

"That's not good news."

"It'll drive me crazy not being able to exercise and jog for a few months. And I won't be golfing or bowling for a while."

"Yeah, that would drive me crazy, too."

"Forgive my bad manners. Come in, Mike. Would you care for a beer?"

"No thanks, Pat, I'm good. I won't take up much of your time. I wanted to stop by to tell you before you read it in the paper or see it on TV that Tyron Parker is dead. He was murdered last evening by the Golf Club Killer."

"No, shit! I can't say that I'm sorry. Where did it happen?"

"In Percy Walter Park. Just around the corner from the halfway house where Parker was staying."

"I heard Parker was going to be released soon, but I wasn't expecting this."

Gazing down at O'Connor's boot, Mike chuckled. "Damn. It looks like I'll have to take you off my suspect list, at least for now, Pat."

O'Connor laughed. "I hope so, Mike. Knowing that I'm no longer on your list will help me sleep soundly tonight."

McMahon smiled, extended his hand, and said, "Take care, Pat. I wish you a speedy recovery."

"Thanks, Mike." O'Connor grinned. "By the way, congratulations on solving the missing gay men case. It's nice to see you without your disguise. You look much better."

McMahon laughed. "I feel better, too. Goodnight."

"Take care, Mike."

When McMahon opened the door to his unit, he decided to unwind with a drink. He poured a double whiskey on the rocks and went to the living room, slumping down in his recliner. Taking a sip from his glass, he picked up the phone and dialed.

After three rings, he heard, "Hey, partner, what's up?"

"I just eliminated my number one suspect in the GCK case."

"Your number one suspect? I didn't know you even had a suspect. Do you mean Patrick O'Connor?"

"Yeah. I thought for sure O'Connor was our killer."

Mike went on to tell Rose about his visit with O'Connor. When he had finished, Goodwin said, "I agree he had a motive when it came to Tyron Parker, but not for the other victims. It's improbable he could've killed Parker with that boot on his foot using crutches to walk."

"You're right. It looks as if we're back to square one. But I still think the GCK has something to do with law enforcement."

"Should we go back to the drawing board and review fired, suspended, and retired cops again? Maybe we missed something," Rose said.

"Honestly, I don't know what we should do. Why don't we sleep on it and talk about it in the morning."

"Okay. Goodnight, partner."

"Goodnight, Goodwin, sleep tight."

When McMahon arrived in the squad room at eight the following morning, Rose was at her desk drinking coffee and reviewing files.

"You been here long?" Mike asked.

"I came in at seven."

"What are you doing?"

"I'm going back over the information on the cops we checked before."

"So, did you find anything new?"

"Not so far. But I found three retired cops we missed."

"Who are they?"

"Patrick O'Connor's former partner, Joe Carson. The other two are Fred Thomas and Steve Larkin, former narcotics detectives."

"Have you had a chance to check their records?"

"Yes. All three men have spotless records. Not one single misdemeanor."

"That doesn't sound too promising. I don't think any of those cops would have a reason to become a vigilante."

"You could be right, but you never know."

"It's a delicate situation. We'll have to tread lightly," Mike said. "Do you think we should inform the boss of what we're up to?"

"Not at this time. I don't think Lieutenant Foster would approve. By the way, how are you making out?"

"Making out?"

"How are you coping since your breakup with Suzanne?"

"Okay, I guess. So far, I haven't thought about it much," Mike lied.

"Good. If you need to talk—"

"I know, I know, you'll be there for me. Let's go see the boss and give him an update on yesterday," McMahon said.

"Give me a minute to finish my coffee and put the file away."

When the two detectives arrived at his door, Lieutenant Foster was on the phone. He waved them in and continued his conversation.

"Yes, Chief. My detectives have just arrived. I'll call you back with an update later. Goodbye." He glared at Mike and Rose. "The chief isn't happy the Golf Club Killer is back in business. He's concerned the city will go into panic mode, and the mayor and media will be hounding him relentlessly until the killer is collared. Are you making any progress?"

"Yesterday's crime scene looked the same as all the others. No clues and no witnesses," Goodwin said.

"Who was the latest victim?"

"He's Tyron Parker," Mike said. "Parker killed and wounded several people about three years ago at the Opry Mills Mall."

"Isn't he the druggie who murdered Patrick O'Connor's wife?"

"Yes, Lieutenant, he is. At his trial, Parker was found not guilty due to his drug-induced state during his killing spree. He was sent to a rehab facility and recently released to a halfway house near the crime scene," Mike said.

"What about a motive? Who would want Parker dead?"

"The only person I can think of would be Patrick O'Connor," Mike said. "But it wasn't him."

McMahon went on to tell the story of his meeting with O'Connor the previous evening.

"Keep at it. In the meantime, I don't know what the hell I'm going to tell the chief."

"I'm sure you'll think of something," Mike said.

CHAPTER 38

The meeting took place at a Starbucks location on Murfreesboro Pike at three that afternoon.

Patrick O'Connor's former partner, Joe Carson, was the first through the door, followed by Fred Thomas and Steve Larkin. Goodwin stood up and waved them over to the table. Rose, who knew the three retired detectives personally, introduced them to McMahon. After shaking hands, Mike took orders, and five minutes later, he returned with a tray filled with coffee and doughnuts.

"Thank you for coming, gentlemen," Rose said with a smile. "As I mentioned on the phone, Detective McMahon and I could sure use your expertise in helping us solve the Golf Club Killer case."

"We'd love to help in any way we can," Joe Carson said.

"What's on your mind, Detective Sergeant?" Larkin asked.

"You all know someone has been taking the law into his own hands, vigilante-style. Several of his victims have been prominent people, who, for some reason, the killer decided to eliminate. The killer's MO is the same. He uses a golf club to bludgeon each person and leaves the club in their hand and a red golf ball in their mouth as his calling card. The only thing he doesn't leave is a clue of any kind. No prints or DNA have been found at any of the crime scenes. Detective McMahon and I believe we could be dealing with someone who knows what we look for at a crime scene. Mike and I suspect we're dealing with a cop or even a forensic expert. If our killer is a cop, he could be an active cop, a disgruntled fired cop, or even a retired cop who is tired of criminals slipping through cracks in the justice system."

Fred Thomas laughed. "Based on what you're saying, Sergeant Goodwin, the three of us fall into your suspect category."

Rose smiled. "You're right. Would any of you like to confess and make our job easier?"

"I don't think so," Joe Carson grinned. "We want you to earn your paychecks just like we had to when we were active cops."

"Since you fall into our suspect category," Mike said, "we wouldn't be doing our job if we didn't ask each one of you where you were between seven and nine last evening?"

The three retired detectives all laughed.

"Glad to see you're doing your job, Detective," Larkin said. "As former cops, we wouldn't expect anything less."

"I was home with a migraine headache. Normally, on Wednesday evening, I'd be at the bowling alley with my team," Carson said.

"Was there anyone at home that can confirm you were there?" asked Goodwin.

"I live alone. My wife passed away last year. Would my dog, Sparky, qualify?"

"Sorry about your wife," Rose said.

"You have my condolences," Mike said.

"And, no, Sparky doesn't qualify as a witness unless he can speak." Rose laughed.

"Oh, he can speak all right," Carson chuckled, "but unfortunately, he can't speak English. He's got a language all his own."

"As for Steve and I, we were bowling at Music City Lanes," Fred Thomas said. "We're on the same team as Joe and Pat. You can check with the owner, Terry Baker. He will confirm we were there from seven until around ten. Also, I'm sure their security video will show we were bowling with two subs. Patrick O'Connor broke his heel recently and is recuperating at home, and Joe just told you he was home with a migraine."

"Now that you're off our suspect list, we would appreciate your thoughts on the Golf Club Killer case. Do you think Detective McMahon and I are on the right track?"

"Based on what you said about not finding a single clue at any of the crime scenes, I'd agree the killer knows what he's doing. You're on the right track. Stick with it. Your theory is sound," Joe Carson said.

"I agree," Steve Larkin said.

"So do I," Fred Thomas chimed in.

"Do you have any suggestions?" Mike asked.

"Based on my experience as a homicide detective," Carson said, "keep at it. Go back over every crime scene photo to see if you might have missed a small detail. When I worked with Patrick O'Connor, the one thing that helped us solve some tough cases was his photographic memory. Persistence pays off. Even the smartest criminal will eventually make a mistake. That's when you'll nail him."

"I agree with Joe," Larkin said. "Stay positive. Sooner or later, you'll collar the bastard."

"I hope it's sooner than later," Goodwin said. "In the meantime, more people could die."

Fred Thomas said, "You have no way of controlling that. Keep at it. Eventually, you'll catch him. Good luck."

On their way back to the squad room Mike and Rose took a detour, stopping at Music City Lanes. Terry Baker and the security video confirmed that Steve Larkin and Fred Thomas were bowling the night of Tyron Parker's murder, eliminating them as suspects.

CHAPTER 39

McMahon had just finished his third whiskey and was about to retire for the night when his cell phone rang. He checked his watch—11:12 p.m. The name on the screen showed Dave Franklin.

"Hi, Dave. What's up?"

"Hey, Mike. I hope I didn't wake you."

"No problem, Dave, I'm still up."

"Even though you and Suzanne broke up, I thought you'd like to know. Suzanne and her new band recently returned to the concert tour. I just received a call from our road manager, Doug Mercer. He told me Suzanne collapsed backstage at the end of her concert in Chicago. She's unconscious, and an ambulance is taking her to the hospital. Mercer said he would call back when he had more information."

"Shit! I warned Suzanne that something like this might happen if she didn't slow down and take more time off. No matter the hour, call me back as soon as you get an update."

"I will, Mike. I'll phone you as soon as I hear back from Mercer. It shouldn't take long. Doug said he'd call again from the hospital."

"Thanks, Dave. I'd appreciate it."

After hanging up, Mike decided that sleep was out of the question. He went back into the kitchen, poured another stiff drink, and headed for his recliner.

McMahon's mind went into overdrive. The signs were all there. Suzanne was a time bomb waiting to explode. He should have insisted that she stop touring and seek professional help. Mike prayed it was just exhaustion and that Suzanne wasn't taking drugs to relieve the stress in her life.

Without waiting for Franklin to call back, Mike went into his bedroom, pulled out a carry-on suitcase from the walk-in closet, and began to pack. Just as he finished packing, his phone rang.

"Hey, Dave."

"Hey, Mike. I just received a call from Doug. He, the band, and the crew are at Northwestern Memorial. Suzanne is in ICU, and as far as he knows, she is still unconscious. Bill and I are taking an early morning flight."

"Would you mind if I join you?"

"Not at all, Mike. Bill and I would be pleased if you did."

"What time is your flight leaving?"

Franklin went on to give McMahon the details. As soon as they hung up, Mike called American Airlines and made a reservation. Next, he called Rose, and after four rings, a sleepy voice answered.

"Hey, partner. Sorry to bother you so late. I just received a call from Dave Franklin from Frozen North." He explained what had happened, said he was going to Chicago for a few days, maybe longer, and asked her to inform Lieutenant Foster.

"Sorry to hear the bad news, Mike. I'll update Foster in the morning. In the meantime, take care, and give Suzanne my love and best wishes for a speedy recovery. Keep me posted, okay?"

"I will. Thanks, Rose. I'll see you soon. Goodbye."

"Goodbye, Mike."

McMahon arrived at the airport at 6:00 a.m., one hour before departure. He picked up his boarding pass at the American Airlines counter and stopped for a coffee at Starbucks. Looking around, he spotted Bill Ormond and Dave Franklin sitting at a table drinking coffee and munching on bagels.

"Good morning, gentlemen," Mike said, sitting down next to Franklin.

"Good morning, Mike," they both said.

"Have you heard any more news about Suzanne's condition?"

"Doug called around four with some good news. Suzanne regained consciousness in ICU and is now in a private room. The doctor won't allow any visitors. He said she was exhausted and needed to sleep for several hours."

"That's good news, Dave. Do they know why she collapsed?"

"Not yet. Doug said the doctor was running some tests, but he hadn't heard anything before he called."

"By the time we get to the hospital, the results should be back," Mike said.

"I hope so," Bill said. "I'm sure Suzanne will come through with flying colors."

"I'm sure she will," Dave agreed.

"I pray you're both right," Mike said.

Just then, an announcement came over the loudspeaker that their flight was ready for boarding.

An hour and fifty minutes after takeoff, the Boeing 737 touched down smoothly at O'Hare International. After deplaning, the three men piled into a taxi, and twenty-five minutes later, the cab pulled up to Northwestern's emergency entrance. Dave Franklin insisted on paying the seventy-five dollar fare, tipping the driver twenty-five dollars.

Pulling their carry-ons behind them, they stopped at the reception desk.

"Last night, Suzanne Taylor was brought here by ambulance and taken to ICU. We were informed she is now in a private room. Do you know where that might be?" Mike asked the receptionist.

"Let me check on my computer, sir." A moment later, she said, "Ms. Taylor is on the seventh floor in room 724." She pointed. "The elevators are over there on the right."

"Thank you," McMahon said.

Dave Franklin introduced himself to the nurse at the nursing station on the seventh floor and inquired about Suzanne's status.

"Ms. Taylor is sedated and sleeping peacefully at the moment. There's a waiting room down the hall on your right. You will find several of her friends there. It could be another hour or two before she is awake. At that time, only two visitors will be allowed in her room at once. Doctor's orders."

When they reached the waiting room, six band members, two roadies, Doug Mercer and Marven Jones, were sprawled out on chairs and couches, looking tired and worried.

As soon as he saw the three men, Mercer got out of his chair and rushed toward them.

After shaking each man's hand, he said, "I'm sure glad to see y'all."

Spotting Mike, Marven Jones walked over and shook his hand.

"Mike, it's good to see you again."

It's nice to see you too, Marven. I just wish it was under better circumstances."

"So do I, Mike, so do I."

After Mercer introduced McMahon to the band and road crew, Mike asked, "How is Suzanne doing?"

Before Mercer could respond, a tall, slim man in his mid-fifties with short, gray hair and sleepy brown eyes, wearing a navy business suit, entered the room.

"Gentlemen," he said in a deep baritone voice, "I'm Doctor Carlton. I've been attending to Ms. Taylor, and I'm here to give you an update on her condition. Shortly after she arrived in ICU, Ms. Taylor regained consciousness. We performed several tests. The good news is that the toxicology test came back negative. The bad news is that we have determined that Ms. Taylor has a severe case of dehydration."

"Dehydration?" Mike repeated.

"Ms. Taylor is on intervenous and resting comfortably. Once rehydrated, she is going to need a week or two of complete rest before resuming normal activities."

"How long will Suzanne be hospitalized? Dave Franklin asked.

"Hopefully, she will be well enough to be released in a few days. Ms. Taylor is awake and in good spirits. You can now visit her briefly. Two at a time, please."

"If the rest of you don't mind, Detective McMahon and I will go in first. I suggest we limit each visit to ten minutes in order not to tire Suzanne out too much," Bill Ormond said.

Everyone agreed.

As Ormond and McMahon entered the room, Suzanne's face lit up like a light bulb, and tears of joy filled her eyes.

"Mike, Bill, what a pleasant surprise. I'm so happy to see you both."

CHAPTER 40

Three days later, Mike went back to work, while Suzanne rested in her apartment under Joyce Ormond's care.

As McMahon entered the squad room, Rose smiled and said, "Welcome back, partner. How did it go?"

"So far, so good. Suzanne will require a lot of time to recuperate. She was severely dehydrated. She's back home, and Joyce Ormond, like a mother hen, is keeping a watchful eye on her."

"That's good news. How are things between you and Suzanne?"

"Fine, I think. Suzanne was surprised to see me but said she was glad that I came."

"Do you have any idea how long it will take for her to recover?"

"I don't have a clue. Once Suzanne gets hydrated and feels better, I believe she'll need some therapy. I suspect she's suffering from a bad case of depression, maybe even PTSD."

"Sorry to hear that. Do you have any idea why?"

"She has a hard time sleeping. Suzanne continues to have nightmares about the bus accident. She feels guilty that members of her music family died, and she is still alive. Suzanne told me she was supposed to be on that bus. And I suspect her close call with death when she was abducted by the Guitar String Strangler still haunts her."

"I can't even imagine what that poor woman is going through."

"Neither can I, but I'm going to be there for her no matter what."

"Lieutenant Foster said he wanted to meet with us as soon as you returned."

"I guess now is as good a time as any," McMahon said. "I'm sure the boss will want an update on the case. I think we should tell him about our meeting with the three retired detectives."

When they arrived at his office, Foster was on the phone. He waved them in and said, "Sorry, my dear, I've got to go. See you tonight." After hanging up, he said, "Welcome back, Detective. How is Suzanne doing?"

"She's home and feeling much better." Mike went on to give Foster a brief update.

"When you see her, please say hello and pass on my sincere wishes for a speedy recovery."

"Thank you. Luitenant, I will."

"Getting back to business, where do things stand on the Golf Club Killer case?"

Rose glanced at Mike, and he nodded.

"Before Detective McMahon left for Chicago, we interviewed three retired cops. With their years of experience, we wanted to pick their brains on who they thought the unsub might be. All of them agreed with our theory that the killer has a connection to law enforcement," Goodwin said.

"I'm curious, who are they?"

"The retired cops are Patrick O'Connor's former partner, Joe Carson, Fred Thomas, and Steve Larkin, former narcotics detectives."

"Did you check to see where they were the night of Parker's murder?"

"Yes, sir," Goodwin said. "Larkin and Thomas were at Music City Lanes from around seven until ten. They bowl on the same team in a men's ten pin league. The manager and security video confirmed their alibi. Joe Carson said he didn't bowl that night because of a migraine headache. Since he lives alone, no one could confirm his alibi."

"I'm confident Joe Carson isn't our unsub. Do you have any other suspects at this time?"

"Sorry, Lieutenant, we don't," McMahon said.

"That's not what I wanted to hear, Detective. I know I'm starting to sound like a broken record, but I suggest you go over every victim file in your murder book with a fine-tooth comb. Maybe you missed something. I know we're all frustrated by the lack of progress. The chief and mayor have been on my back, looking for something positive to tell the media hounds. And Jeff Stone is driving me crazy. He calls every day, wanting to know what we're doing to catch the Golf Club Killer. No wonder my stomach ulcer is on a rampage." Foster paused, put an antacid pill in his mouth, and gulped it down with water. He cleared his throat and continued, "Jack Bowman has recently been transferred from narcotics to our homicide unit. I'm seriously considering adding him to help you with the case if I don't see results soon. That's it for now."

As they left Foster's office, Mike said, "If I have to work with Bowman, I'm sure it wouldn't take long before we'd be at one another's throats."

Rose laughed. "Let's hope that doesn't happen. If we have to work with Bowman, I might just decide to apply for a transfer."

"I might just do the same."

Goodwin and McMahon spent the rest of the morning going through the murder book files, searching for any clues they might have missed. After taking a lunch break for soup and a sandwich, they returned without finding anything new.

Closing the murder book, Rose said, "None of the victims except for councilor Mitch McConnell and Anthony Garanti had any connections. Everything still points to a vigilante who decided to take the law into his own hands for unknown reasons."

"God, this case is getting so fucking frustrating," Mike said. "Let's get the hell out of here and call it a day."

"Good idea."

CHAPTER 41

McMahon parked his car in the driveway, picked up the bouquet of red roses off the passenger seat, slid out, and walked up to the front door. He rang the bell, and a moment later, Joyce Ormond greeted him with a welcoming smile.

"Detective McMahon, it's nice to see you again."

"Hi, Joyce, how are you? Mike, please call me Mike."

"I'm fine, Mike. Are you here to see Suzanne?"

"Yes, Joyce, if she's up to it."

"Please come in. I'll go tell Suzanne you're here."

"If you don't mind, I'd like to surprise her if I can?"

"No problem. The stairs on your left lead down to Suzanne's apartment. I'm sure those roses will cheer her up."

"I hope so. Thanks, Joyce."

Suzanne was sitting on the sofa, a glass of red wine in her hand, watching a movie on TV.

"Mike, what are you doing here?"

"Hello to you, too, Suzanne. I came to see you," he said, handing her the flowers. "Is that a problem?"

"Sorry for snapping at you. It's just I didn't expect to see you so soon. Thanks for the roses, Mike, they're lovely. You didn't need to bring me flowers."

Suzanne got up, went into the kitchen, found a vase, filled it with water, and placed the roses inside. When she came back into the living room, Mike was sitting on the couch. She put the flowers on the coffee table and sat down next to him.

"Would you like a glass of wine or a beer?"

"No, thanks. I'm trying to cut back on my drinking."

"How's that going?"

"I'm making progress," Mike lied.

"That's good to hear."

"How are you feeling, Suzanne?"

"Much better, thank you. Physically I feel much stronger."

"You look much better than the last time I saw you in Chicago. You've lost weight you couldn't afford to lose. You need to pack on a few pounds."

"That shouldn't be a problem. Joyce is keeping me hydrated and well-fed."

"How have you been sleeping?"

"Not great. Most nights, the same old nightmares keep coming back."

"Have you made any arrangements to see your psychiatrist?"

"Yes. I have an appointment tomorrow at three. Dr. Hamilton wants to assess my current condition and work out a schedule to treat me."

"That sounds good. Before you know it, you'll be back to your old self again."

"I pray you're right."

"Have you told your brother what happened in Chicago?"

"No. I didn't want to worry Steve. He has enough on his plate with the business and his family."

Just then, Joyce appeared in the doorway.

"Sorry to interrupt. Bill will be home soon. We'd love to have you stay for supper, Mike. I hope you're a meat and potatoes guy. We're having roast beef, mashed potatoes with gravy, and Ceasar salad."

"Thanks, Joyce. I would be delighted to stay for supper."

It was ten minutes to eleven by the time Mike arrived home. Before retiring for the night, he poured a drink and headed to the living room. He sank into his recliner, picked up the remote, and clicked on the TV. It was time for the eleven o'clock news.

McMahon was thinking about his evening with Suzanne and the Ormonds when his cell phone rang. It was dispatch.

He turned the TV off and said, "Detective McMahon."

"Hi, Detective. It's Sergeant Harding. I know I'm beginning to sound like a broken record, but the Golf Club Killer has struck again. A man was found in a parking lot behind an office building on Second Avenue. The first officers on the scene identified him as lawyer Paul Goodwin."

"Shit! He's my partner's ex-husband. Is he dead?"

"I'm not sure. As far as I know, Goodwin was still alive when the ambulance arrived."

"Do you know where they took him?"

"The officer I spoke with said he's at Vanderbilt."

"Do you have any idea who found Goodwin?"

"Yes. It was a homeless man. He ran to the front of the building and flagged down a police cruiser. When the officers checked, they found the victim unconscious and still breathing."

"Do you have any idea what happened to the homeless man?"

"After taking the man's statement, the officers brought him here. They figured you would want to talk to him. He's waiting in interview room two."

"Okay. Have you contacted my partner yet?"

"I was just about to call her."

"Don't bother. I'll do it. Keep the homeless guy comfortable and feed him, if necessary. It could be a while before I get there. Once I call Sergeant Goodwin, we'll probably head to the hospital first."

"One other thing, Detective, the attacker left a golf club at the scene. The officers brought it in and left it on your desk. I'm sure you'll want to have forensics check it for fingerprints."

"Okay, Sergeant, thanks."

After hanging up, Mike sat there, stunned. His mind was trying to figure out why the GCK would attack Paul Goodwin.

Finally, he picked up the phone. It took four rings before Rose answered.

"Hey, Mike. What's up?"

"Did I wake you?"

"No. I was just getting ready to go to bed. I stayed up later than usual, reading a good book."

"Rose. I just received a call from dispatch. I've got something to tell you."

After he broke the news as delicately as he could, there was a moment of silence. Suddenly, Goodwin broke down completely. He waited patiently until the loud sobs tapered off to a few sniffles before asking, "Are you all right, partner?"

"I think so, Mike," Rose whispered. Without warning, she screamed, "That fucking maniac. Why did he try to kill Paul?"

"I don't know. Slow down, and take a few deep breaths."

"I've got to get to the hospital. Where did they take Paul?"

"He's at Vanderbilt. Try to stay calm and drive safely. I'll meet you there."

Mike grabbed his jacket and headed for the door. A few minutes later, he was in his car, squealing out of the underground parking garage. When he hit the street, McMahon flipped on the siren and floored the accelerator pedal.

McMahon pulled into a parking spot near the emergency entrance, jumped out, and rushed through the door. He glanced around the waiting area, but there was no sign of Rose. McMahon introduced himself at the desk and showed his badge, then asked the receptionist, "Do you know if a man named Paul Goodwin was brought in by ambulance recently?"

"I'm sorry, sir, I don't have a name, but about two hours ago, paramedics took someone to ICU."

"How would I find out if it's Mr. Goodwin?"

"ICU is on the sixth floor of the Critical Care Tower. The nursing station should be able to help you."

"Thanks."

Out of breath, Rose came dashing through the door and hollered, "Mike."

As McMahon turned, she ran into his arms, and they hugged. When Rose released him, tears were streaming down her face.

"Thanks for coming, Mike. Do you know where Paul is?"

"The receptionist suggested I check with ICU. That's where I'm heading."

Goodwin pulled out a tissue and wiped her eyes. "Okay. Let's go."

They identified themselves at the nursing station, and Rose asked, "Do you know if Paul Goodwin is one of your patients?"

"I believe that was the name the doctor mentioned. Let me just confirm that for you." She checked on her computer and said, "Yes, that's his name."

"Do you have any information on his condition?" Rose asked.

"Not at the moment, I don't. All I can tell you is that Mr. Goodwin is in surgery. As soon as the operation is over, I'm sure our neurosurgeon, Dr. Swartz, will give you an update. Until then, please try to make yourself comfortable. The waiting room is at the end of the hallway."

When they entered the waiting room, it was empty. Rose walked over to the window and stared into the night. Mike went and stood beside her, put his arm around her shoulder, giving her a gentle squeeze.

"Don't worry, partner, I'm sure Paul is going to make a full recovery."

"I hope you're right, Mike. Jill will be devastated if she loses her father, and so will I. Believe it or not, we still have feelings for each other. Paul and I have been exploring the possibility of getting back together."

"That's good to hear. Is Jill at home with her nanny?"

"Yes. At this hour, Jill will be fast asleep." Tears returned to Goodwin's eyes. "I don't know how I'm going to break the news to her if Paul doesn't make it."

For a long moment, Mike couldn't think of anything to say. Finally, he said, "Paul's a fighter. He'll make it. Why don't you sit down? I'll go get you a coffee?"

It appeared as if Goodwin hadn't heard him.

"Rose?"

"Sorry, Mike. I was thinking about Jill. Coffee sounds good."

When McMahon returned, Rose was in a chair, a blank look on her face. He handed her the coffee and said, "It's hot. Careful you don't burn your lips."

"Thanks, Mike."

Two hours later, Rose jumped to her feet when a tall, slim, middle-aged man wearing light blue scrubs entered the room.

"Hello, I'm Dr. Swartz. Are you Mrs. Goodwin?"

"I'm Detective Sergeant Rose Goodwin, Paul Goodwin's ex-wife, and this is my partner Detective Mike McMahon."

After shaking hands, Dr. Swartz said, "Mr. Goodwin was unconscious when admitted. He has a TBI or, in layman's terms, what we call a traumatic brain injury. When we did a scan, it revealed a blood clot and that his brain had swelled. To relieve the pressure on his skull, I performed an operation called a craniotomy. I don't want to bore you with all the medical details. Mr. Goodwin came through the procedure but is not out of the woods. The next forty-eight to seventy-two hours will be a critical period. He is currently in a recovery room but is still unconscious. It might be best if you go home and try to get some rest. Leave your number at the nursing station, Mrs. Goodwin, and a nurse will call you when Mr. Goodwin is in a private room. Do you have any questions?"

"Can I go see him?"

"Sorry, I'm not allowing visitors at this time."

"What are the chances of Paul making a full recovery?"

"It's too early to tell. All we can do is hope for the best. A few prayers wouldn't hurt. Mr. Goodwin will have a nurse by his side twenty-four hours a day, monitoring his progress."

As soon as Dr. Swartz had left the room, Mike said, "Why don't you go home and get some rest? I've got to go to the station to interview the person who found Paul."

"If I go home, I won't be able to sleep. I'll be worried sick about Paul. It's better if I stay here."

"Are you sure?"

"I'm positive." Rose nodded. "That couch looks comfortable."

"Okay. I'll be back as soon as I can."

"When you finish the interview, you should go home and get some sleep."

"I don't think I'll be able to sleep either. I'll come back later."

CHAPTER 42

When McMahon entered the room, the putrid stench of body odor almost made him gag. An older man with an untamed white beard and shaggy gray hair sat devouring a ham and cheese sandwich.

Breathing through his mouth, Mike said, "I'm Detective McMahon. I'm sorry to have kept you waiting, sir."

"Not a problem, Detective. The officers who brought me here were kind to me. They got me this sandwich and a coffee."

"That's good. An officer told me your name is Hatter. Is that correct, sir?"

"Yeah, my name is Matt Hatter." He laughed. "All my friends on the street call me 'Mad.' You know, like in 'Mad Hatter' because they say I'm a little crazy sometimes."

"Nice to meet you, Mad," Mike said without offering to shake hands. He sat down opposite Hatter, pulled out his notebook, and continued. "I was informed you are the person who found the victim in the parking lot earlier this evening."

"Yeah, that's right."

"Can you tell me about it?"

"Well, I was lookin' for anythin' of value that I could sell, like refundable bottles. I usually check the dumpster in that lot every week. As I pushed my shoppin' cart round the corner, I see this man about to strike another man with a golf club, so I yell, stop."

"What happened next?"

"The attacker struck the guy on the back of the head, threw down the club, turned around, and ran past me like a scared rabbit."

"Did you manage to get a good look at the attacker?"

"Yes and no. The guy was about six feet tall, with an average build. A black hood covered his head, and a black ski mask covered his face."

"What about his pants and shoes?"

Hatter closed his eyes and paused for a moment as if trying to envision what he had seen. When his eyes opened, he said, "It all happened so fast. Everything was black except for his hands."

"So, the man was dressed in black, except for his hands," McMahon repeated as he scribbled in his notebook.

"Yeah. The guy's clothes were all black except for his hands.."

"Did he have white hands?"

Once more, Hatter paused for a moment. "I don't know for sure. I think he had on a pair of white gloves. The kind surgeons wear."

McMahon pulled out a pair of cream-colored latex gloves from his pocket and placed them on the table.

"Like these?"

"Yeah, just like those."

"After the attacker ran away, what did you do next?"

"I rushed over to the man on the ground to see if he was still alive. I put two fingers on his neck and found a faint pulse. Then I ran to the street, flagged down a cop car, and told the officers what had happened. They checked the guy and called an ambulance. The cops asked me a few questions, and after the ambulance came and went, they brought me here. Said a detective would need to interview me."

"Is there anything else you can think of?"

"Nah, Detective, that's about it."

"Do you have an address or phone number where I can reach you, Mr. Hatter?"

Hatter bent over and began to laugh until tears filled his eyes. Finally, he straightened up and said, "That's a good one, Detective. I don't have an address or a phone. I'm homeless."

"Sorry, Mr. Hatter, I knew that. I wasn't thinking."

"Call me Mad, Detective. I don't know who Mr. Hatter is."

"Okay, Mad. Do you have a place to stay tonight?"

Hatter chuckled. "Yeah. I'm stayin' at the Cardboard Box Hotel down by the Cumberland River. That's where my sleepin' bag is stashed."

McMahon was amused by Hatter's sense of humor and the mischievous twinkle in his blue eyes.

"How long have you been sleeping there?"

"Ever since my friends and I got kicked out of the park near the downtown library. Someone said a developer from Chicago was building a high-rise condo there for rich people."

"That's right. How did you feel about that?"

"I was pissed off. But I learned a long time ago you can't fight city hall. Those rich bastards always win because money talks. The little guy doesn't stand a chance."

"Do you mind if I ask you a personal question?"

"Go ahead, Detective, I got nothin' to hide."

"How did you end up on the street, Mad?"

"For years, I couldn't talk about it, but the passing of time has helped me come to grips with what happened."

"If you'd rather not, I understand."

"It's okay, Detective. No problem, I can talk about it now."

"Are you sure?"

"Yeah, I'm sure. Back in 1972, we lived in a small town just outside of Green Bay. My wife and ten-year-old son went Christmas shoppin' in the big city. A few hours after they left, the weather turned nasty. When Carol and Fred didn't return home by evenin', I got worried and called the cops. It took two days before a state trooper noticed a broken guard rail and spotted a car at the bottom of a ravine. When the cops came to my door and told me that my wife and son were dead, my whole world fell apart. I started drinkin' and gamblin'. It didn't take long before I lost my job, house, and the money I had saved. That's how I ended up on the street."

"I'm so sorry, Mad. I can't even imagine what you went through."

"Thanks, Detective. I'm okay now."

"How did you end up in Nashville?"

"I just had to get away from all those bad memories. Since I write country songs, I thought I'd try my luck in Music City. Besides, it's a hell of a lot warmer here than it is in Wisconsin."

"Have you had any luck pitching your songs?"

"All the places I've tried can see I'm homeless and tell me to get lost, or they'll call the cops. I haven't written a song since some idiot stole my guitar about a year ago."

"How would you like to spend the night in a place where you can take a hot shower, get some fresh clothing, sleep in a comfortable bed, and eat a hearty breakfast in the morning?"

"That would be nice, Detective, but I ain't got no money to stay at Ritz."

"It won't cost you a penny. Give me a minute to make a phone call."

McMahon stepped out of the room and returned wearing a smile.

"It's all set, Mad. I'll drop you off at Mission House on Broadway. Father Monaghan is expecting you."

CHAPTER 43

At 4:15 a.m., McMahon entered the waiting room and found Rose on the couch, fast asleep. Not wanting to wake her, he sat in a wingback chair, sipping a coffee he had picked up on the way. After finishing his drink, Mike closed his eyes and was out like a light. McMahon was dreaming about playing baseball as a kid back in Dearborn when he was jarred awake by someone shaking his shoulder.

Startled, Mike said, "What…what is it?"

"It's Paul," Rose said, tears rolling down her face. "He's taken a turn for the worse. A nurse just told me that he went into cardiac arrest, and they had to resuscitate him. He's hooked up to a ventilator and is in critical condition."

"Shit! When did that happen?"

"I don't know. I'm guessing about a half-hour ago. The nurse said Dr. Swartz would give me an update as soon as possible."

McMahon stood up, wrapped his arms around Rose, and whispered into her ear. "Try not to worry, partner. Paul's in good hands. He's a fighter."

"It doesn't sound good, Mike. I feel so helpless."

"I know, I know. All we can do is wait and pray for the best."

At that moment, Dr. Swartz entered the room, a grim look on his face.

"Mrs. Goodwin," he said, "as the nurse informed you, Mr. Goodwin suffered a cardiac arrest. We were able to resuscitate him, but he is in critical condition. At the moment, Mr. Goodwin is still unconscious and breathing with the help of a ventilator. There's nothing more I can do at this time. Dr. Swan, a heart specialist, is with Mr. Goodwin as we speak. Please go home and get some rest. We will contact you immediately if his condition should change."

"Thank you, Doctor, but I prefer to stay right here."

"Okay, Mrs. Goodwin. I'll check in with you later."

As soon as Dr. Swartz was gone, Rose turned to Mike and said, "There's no sense in you staying here. Go home and get some sleep."

Mike glanced at his watch. It was 5:05 a.m.

"Okay. I'll call you later."

When he arrived at his condo, the first thing McMahon did was take a long, hot shower. Feeling better, he changed into fresh clothing and brewed a pot of coffee. Mike fried three eggs, toasted two slices of bread, put on peanut butter and strawberry jam, then poured a mug full of hot, black coffee. As he ate his breakfast, he thought about the Golf Club Killer. Why did the GCK select Paul Goodwin? The only reason he could think of was that Goodwin had gotten a lot of slimeballs acquitted that should have been convicted and sent to prison. Another reason could be that Bruce Morton had hired Paul Goodwin to defend him.

Before walking out the door, Mike dialed his partner's cell phone.

"Hi, Mike," Rose said.

"I'm on my way to the station. Thought I'd give you a call to see how Paul is doing and how you're holding up."

"I don't know. No one has updated me since you left. I guess no news is good news. As far as me, I'm okay, I guess."

"Good. I'll be back later. I'd better talk to the boss and fill him in on what happened last night."

"Foster already knows. He called me a few minutes ago."

"Okay. Take care. I'll get back to you later."

McMahon was on his computer, typing up a report of his interview with Matt Hatter when Lieutenant Foster appeared.

"Please come to my office, Detective. We need to talk."

Mike picked up his coffee and followed Foster. Once they were seated, the lieutenant said, "I spoke with your partner earlier, and things don't sound too good. She told me that Paul is still alive but in critical condition. So far, he's the first victim who survived an attack by the Golf Club Killer."

"You're right. The intervention by the homeless man saved Goodwin's life. At least for now."

McMahon went on to tell the story of his interview with Matt Hatter.

"Regardless of what happens to Paul Goodwin, I insisted that your partner take some time off. I don't think her head will be in the game if she returns to the job."

"How long will Rose be off?"

"That will depend on what happens to her ex. I'm thinking at least a month, maybe longer."

"Not to worry, Lieutenant, I'm sure I can work the case alone."

"I'm sure you can, Detective, but in the meantime, I'm going to assign you an interim partner."

"Oh, and who might that be?"

"Detective Jack Bowman is now part of our Homicide Division. He'll be your partner starting tomorrow until Detective Sergeant Goodwin returns to active duty."

Mike cringed at the mention of Bowman's name.

"You've got to be kidding me, Lieutenant. I'm sure you know that Bowman and I don't get along. To put it bluntly, we hate each other's guts."

"For God's sake, Detective, you and Bowman are men, not little children. You'll have to learn to put your differences aside and work together as a team."

"Isn't there anyone else besides Bowman?"

Foster glared at McMahon, his face turning red. "Quit your whining, Detective. That's my decision, and it's final. Jack Bowman is your new interim partner. Be in my office at eight sharp tomorrow morning."

CHAPTER 44

After leaving Foster's office, McMahon went back to typing his interview with Hatter. With the image of Bowman's scowling face filling his head, Mike found it hard to concentrate.

Fifteen minutes later, the report completed, McMahon decided to get the hell out of the squad room. He didn't want to risk another run-in with Foster.

When he arrived back at the hospital, Rose was alone in the waiting room.

"Hi, partner," Mike said as he walked through the door.

"Oh, hi, Mike. Glad you made it back."

"How are things with Paul?"

"Dr. Swartz gave me an update about an hour ago. So far, Paul's condition has improved slightly. He's hanging in there."

"That sounds positive."

"I suppose so. But I did get some bad news. When Foster called, he said he's placing me on indefinite leave with pay. He insists I take some time off to deal with what's going on in my personal life."

"Yeah, that's what he told me. In the meantime, he's assigning me a new partner until you return. Guess who?"

"I have no idea."

"Would you believe it's Jack Bowman?"

"Jack Bowman? I thought he was still in narcotics."

"Not anymore, he's not. Starting tomorrow, he'll be working with us."

"Did you ask Foster if there was anyone else available?"

"I tried, but he got angry and said Bowman is my partner, and that's final."

"That sucks. Do you think you and Bowman can put your differences aside and work together?"

"That's the sixty-four-thousand-dollar question. We'll have to wait and see."

"Good luck. I think you're gonna need it."

The following morning, when McMahon walked into Foster's office, Jack Bowman was already there, a smug smile on his face. The two men nodded at one another without shaking hands.

Lieutenant Foster checked his watch and said, "Glad to see you're on time, Detective. Please take a seat." He cleared his throat and continued. "I know there's no love lost between the two of you, but it's time to put your differences aside. I need you to work together as a team, and I won't tolerate any nonsense. Do you understand me?"

"Yes, sir," Bowman said.

"Yes, Lieutenant," McMahon said.

"The first thing I want you to do is to bring Detective Bowman up to speed on the Golf Club Killer case."

"Yes, sir," Mike said.

"Are there any questions before you get started?"

Neither man spoke.

"Okay, then. Dismissed."

Back in the squad room, Mike sat down at his desk, and Bowman took Rose's chair. McMahon pulled out the murder book and tossed it in front of Bowman. "For starters, I'd like you to go through the book and get familiar with each homicide. Maybe you'll spot something we missed. Let me know if you have any questions. While you're doing that, I'll get us coffee. How do you take yours?"

"Black."

When McMahon returned, he placed the cup down in front of Bowman.

"Thanks for the coffee," Bowman said, as he continued to read the murder book.

"Looks like you've still got a long way to go in getting up to speed on the case. I've got an errand to run. I'll be back by eleven."

"Don't hurry back on my account, Detective."

Mike could hardly believe Bowman was civil. He must have taken Foster's warning to heart.

Forty minutes later, McMahon walked through the door at Mission House carrying a guitar case.

Spotting Mike, Father Monaghan said, "Good morning, Detective. Coming to entertain us, are you?"

"Good morning, Father. Don't I wish I were good enough to do that. I've brought a guitar for Matt Hatter, the homeless man I dropped off a few hours ago. Is he still sleeping?"

"Yes, he is. Would you like me to give the guitar to him when he wakes up?"

"That would be great, Father. I would appreciate it. Thanks."

"What do you want me to tell him?"

"Just say Detective McMahon is looking forward to hearing the songs he writes. Oh, and I almost forgot, give him this digital recorder as well. I'm sure he'll figure out how to use it."

"If he can't, I'll be glad to show Mr. Hatter how it works."

"Before I go, Father, would it be okay if Matt leaves the guitar and recorder with you for safekeeping? A while ago, someone stole his guitar, and I wouldn't want that to happen again."

"That won't be a problem, Detective. Leaving the guitar and recorder with me will give Mr. Hatter a good reason to visit us more often."

"I hope so. Thanks again, Father."

When Mike arrived back in the squad room shortly after eleven, Bowman wasn't at Rose's desk. He checked the break room and found him drinking coffee and chatting with Nancy Allman, Lieutenant Foster's administrative assistant.

Seeing McMahon, Bowman got to his feet and said, "Looks like the slave driver is back. It's been nice talking with you, Nancy."

"Likewise, Detective."

As they walked into the squad room, Bowman said, "While you were gone, the LT stopped by and helped me clean out the personal items from your partner's desk. He took the box and said he'd store it in his office closet for now."

Mike should have bit his tongue, but he didn't. He said, "The boss didn't waste any time moving an asshole into her spot."

"Hey, watch your mouth, you jerk. What's with the asshole comment?"

Remembering Foster's warning, Mike said, "Sorry, Jack, it's not your fault. I apologize."

Neither man realized Foster had been standing behind them.

"What did I say about putting your differences aside?"

"Sorry, Lieutenant," McMahon said. "It won't happen again."

"It better not. For your information, I just got off the phone with Chief Cummings. He wants to meet with us tomorrow morning at eight to discuss the case. Make sure you're on time."

After Foster had left, McMahon said, "Did you manage to get through the murder book?"

"Yeah, I did."

"What are your thoughts?"

"Everything points to a brilliant and meticulous killer. He seems to know a lot about crime scenes and how we operate."

"Rose and I agree. We suspect we could be dealing with someone who has law enforcement experience."

"I was thinking the same thing. Have you done any checking to see if the perp could be a cop?"

"We've checked retired cops, and cops disciplined for using excessive force, the whole gamut. At the moment, we're at a dead end."

"Did any calls come in from the composite drawing and video released at the press conference?" Bowman asked.

"Not even one call. That leads me to believe no one recognized the suspect because he was wearing a disguise."

"You could be right. Do you mind if I take the book home tonight? I'd like to go through it again."

"Be my guest. Just don't forget to bring it back in the morning. We might need it for our meeting with the chief. It's almost noon. Let's grab some food. "

Although his heart wasn't in it, Mike decided to treat Bowman to lunch at a nearby diner. By the time lunch was over, McMahon was glad to get back to the squad room. He was sick of hearing Bowman brag about all his drug busts.

They spent the afternoon reviewing and discussing all the cops Rose and Mike had interviewed as possible suspects. When five o'clock came, they decided to call it a day. Bowman picked up the murder book, said good night, and headed for the door.

After Bowman had left, McMahon sat at his desk, thinking about his new partner. Jack Bowman was still an arrogant asshole, but McMahon was determined to put up with him until Rose returned. Hopefully, his anger management sessions would start to pay off.

CHAPTER 45

When he walked into the waiting room, Rose was not there. Mike waited fifteen minutes before he decided to give her a call.

After two rings, Rose answered her cell phone.

"Hi, Mike, what's up?"

"I'm in the waiting room at the hospital. Where are you?"

"I went to see Jill and her nanny. I'm on my way back. We can catch up when I get there."

"Okay. I'll be here."

Twenty minutes later, her face showing the strain, Rose walked through the door carrying two cups of coffee. She handed one to Mike and said, "Thought we could use some java."

"Thanks, partner. I appreciate it. You look exhausted. How do you feel?"

"I feel like my body went through a wringer."

"Did you manage to get any sleep?"

"Not much."

"How did it go with Jill?"

"It was hard. I tried to break the news gently, but there was no easy way to do that. By the time I was ready to leave, Jill had cried herself out and had calmed down. It broke my heart to see my little girl in such pain. Maria will keep her occupied with games, books, and TV. I'm going back later and will spend the night there."

Mike went over to Rose and wrapped his arms around her. "I can't even imagine how devastated Jill must feel and how difficult it was for you to tell her about her father."

At that moment, McMahon's cell phone rang. He stepped away and pulled the phone out of his belt holder. It was Bowman.

"Hey, Jack, what's up?" Mike asked in a civil tone.

"I've been going through the murder book again, and I have a question about one of the cops you interviewed."

"Which one?"

"Patrick O'Connor. He has a motive after what happened to his wife. I think he could be our guy."

"We thought the same thing, but his alibis were solid. He's not a suspect at this time. Can we talk about it tomorrow? I'm at the hospital with Rose."

"Sure, Mike. Sorry to have bothered you. Tell Sergeant Goodwin my thoughts and prayers are with her and Paul. See you in the morning."

"Sounds like that was your new partner."

"Interim partner," Mike corrected. "I can't believe it. Bowman was polite and even said his thoughts and prayers are with you and Paul."

"That doesn't sound like Jack Bowman."

"He must've taken Foster's warning about putting our differences aside seriously."

"You could be right, but if I were you, I'd watch my back. I don't trust that man."

"Not to worry, partner. I won't let down my guard. I don't trust him either."

"I called my sister Marilyn this morning. She stopped by earlier and stayed for about an hour. It was nice to see her. Unfortunately, we don't get together too often anymore."

Mike was about to say something when Dr. Swartz entered the room, wearing a broad smile.

"Mrs. Goodwin, I've got some good news. Mr. Goodwin has regained consciousness and is off the respirator. He's still a bit confused, but his heart seems to be working fine." Swartz chuckled. "The first words he spoke were: 'Where the hell am I?'"

"That is good news."

"If you wish, I can take you to his room for a brief visit. We don't want to overwhelm Mr. Goodwin, so I suggest Detective McMahon stay here."

When Rose entered the room, Paul appeared to be sleeping.

Dr. Swartz said, "Nurse Lee, this is Mrs. Goodwin. I'm allowing her a brief visit. No more than ten minutes."

The nurse nodded, and Dr. Swartz left the room.

Tears filled Rose's eyes as she took Paul's hand in hers. A few seconds later, his eyes fluttered open, and he smiled.

"Hi, Rosie," Paul whispered.

"Hello, my dear," Rose said, kissing him on the forehead.

"Why am I here? What happened?"

"Do you remember anything?"

"No, I don't."

"You were attacked by the Golf Club Killer."

Paul let out a weak laugh. "Looks like he failed. I'm still alive. I must have a thick skull."

Rose smiled. "Lucky for you that you do."

"Does Jill know what happened and where I am?"

"Yes, she does. I told Jill a few hours ago. She'll be glad to hear you're on the road to recovery. I'm staying with her until you're back home."

"Thanks. You're a saint. When I get out of here, I'd like us to become a family again. I made a big mistake, and I'm so sorry."

"Let's not worry about that now."

Without another word, Paul's eyes closed, and he drifted off to sleep.

As soon as Rose returned to the waiting room, Mike asked, "How is Paul?"

"He recognized me and was able to talk for a few minutes. It breaks my heart to see Paul with his head bandaged, and all those tubes and monitors hooked up to his body. Hopefully, he'll improve with each passing day."

"I'm sure he will."

"There's nothing more we can do here. I'm exhausted. I think I'll go and spend some time with Jill before bedtime. The hospital will call if Paul's condition worsens. You should go home and get a good night's sleep. You'll need all the energy you can muster to deal with Bowman."

"You've got that right. Keep me updated if you hear anything new about Paul's condition."

"Will do. Take care."

"You, too."

CHAPTER 46

McMahon and Bowman were waiting in Foster's office when Chief Cummings arrived at eight the next morning. He sat down in Lieutenant Foster's vacated chair and placed a styrofoam coffee cup on the desk.

"Good morning, gentlemen."

"Good morning, Chief," they all said in unison.

Cummings looked directly at Foster, who was sitting next to Bowman, and said, "Thank you for allowing me the use of your office, Lieutenant."

"My pleasure, Chief."

"Welcome to homicide, Detective Bowman."

"Thank you, Chief. I'm glad to be here."

"By the way, Detective McMahon, how is Paul Goodwin making out?"

"We received some excellent news yesterday evening, Chief. Paul regained consciousness and appears to be on the road to recovery. The doctor is cautiously optimistic."

"Sergeant Goodwin must be relieved. Please pass on my regards and tell her I wish Paul a speedy recovery."

"I will, Chief."

"As you are aware, I'm here to discuss the Golf Club Killer case. Have you been brought up to date, Detective Bowman?"

"Yes, Chief, I have."

"What are your thoughts on the case?"

"Well, Chief, after reviewing the murder book thoroughly, I've concluded that we're dealing with a psychopath who could have a background in law enforcement. He appears to be highly organized and plans his attacks carefully. I suspect he stalks his victims beforehand to establish their routines and plans his attack making sure there are no security cameras or witnesses in the area."

"That sounds logical. Good work, Detective."

McMahon remained calm on the surface, but he was seething inside. Bowman was taking credit for coming up with the killer's profile. Mike could almost see the honey dripping off his lips as he verbally puckered up and kissed the chief's ass.

Lieutenant Foster, seeing what Bowman was doing, broke his silence.

"Detectives McMahon and Goodwin came to that same conclusion weeks ago."

Like a kid caught with his hand in the cookie jar, Bowman's face flushed, and he lowered his head.

Noticing Bowman's embarrassment, the chief said, "Well, it seems like you're all on the same page, then. Is there anything else?"

"Based on the statement I took from the person who witnessed the attack on Paul Goodwin, we now have a physical description of the unsub. Unfortunately, the attacker wore a ski mask," Mike said.

"How did the witness describe Goodwin's attacker?"

"He said the man was about six feet, average build, and looked to be physically fit, judging by how fast he ran away from the crime scene."

"Any idea how old the suspect might be?"

"Sorry, Chief, I have no idea."

Lieutenant Foster said, "Well, at least the physical description is more than we had a few days ago."

"Before I leave, I want to remind you that catching this maniac is your top priority. The longer this case goes unsolved, the more flak we're going to take from the mayor and the media. Put your thinking caps on and go back to the drawing board. Review every cop, active, suspended, and retired, to see if anything turns up. I'm counting on you to come up with a plan to collar the perp. Lieutenant, please keep me informed of any new developments."

"You got it, Chief."

When they returned to the squad room, Mike was about to call Bowman out for taking credit for the killer's profile. Instead, he bit his tongue and went to the break room. When he returned, Bowman asked, "Where's my coffee, dickhead?"

"Sorry, asshole, I'm not a fucking waiter. Get your own coffee." Mike snapped as he placed the cup on his desk.

Agitated, Bowman got up and left. A few minutes later, he came back with a coffee. He took a sip and said, "Let's call a truce. I know we don't like one another, but we've got to put our differences aside. Do you agree?"

"Yes, I agree."

"Good. I'd like to continue our conversation from last evening about Patrick O'Connor."

"What do you want to know?"

"How thoroughly did you and your partner investigate him?"

"Like you, I felt he had a motive because of what happened to his wife. His alibis checked out, and at the moment, he's on the back burner."

"Do you know where O'Connor was the night Tyron Parker, his wife's killer, was murdered?"

"O'Connor lives in my condo building. After I left the crime scene, I rang his bell. He came to the door on crutches with a support boot on his foot. He suffered a broken heel in a jogging accident. I don't think he was in any condition to be out killing anyone with a golf club."

"So, at this point in the investigation, we don't have any suspects?"

"It looks that way."

"I've never met Patrick O'Connor. Do you think you could arrange a meeting? I'd love to pick his brain."

"I've already done that. O'Connor agrees with our theory. If you want to meet him, why don't we go there now? Since he's not too mobile, I'm sure he'll be at home."

CHAPTER 47

McMahon rang the bell, and they waited. Thirty seconds later, he punched the button again. He placed his ear to the door—silence.

"Maybe he's not home," Bowman said.

Frustrated, Mike punched the button again several times.

"For Christ's sake, stop ringing my bell. Who is it?" O'Connor yelled.

"Patrick, it's Mike McMahon."

"Hold on, Mike, I'm coming."

Standing on crutches, a few minutes later, O'Connor opened the door.

"Sorry I took so long. I dozed off on the couch. To what do I owe the pleasure?"

"Pat, I'd like you to meet Detective Jack Bowman, my interim partner. He wanted to meet you and get your take on a few things. Can you spare a few minutes?"

"Sure. Come in. It's nice to meet you, Detective Bowman. Hope you don't mind if we don't shake hands."

"I understand," Bowman said. "It's a pleasure to meet you as well, Patrick."

"Interim partner?" Where's Detective Sergeant Goodwin?"

"She's on temporary leave because of what happened to her ex-husband, Paul Goodwin."

"I'm sorry, but I haven't heard. What happened to Goodwin?"

"He survived an attack by the Golf Club Killer and is in serious condition at Vanderbilt. It's been in the papers and on TV."

"Since I retired, I very seldom read the newspaper, nor do I watch TV news as much as I used to. These days all the news is terrible. I'm sick and tired of it. How is Detective Sergeant Goodwin holding up?"

"She's taking it hard. Rose is practically living at the hospital."

"Say hello and tell her that I wish Paul a speedy and complete recovery."

"I certainly will. Do you know Paul Goodwin well?"

"Not on a personal basis, but we did tangle in court several times when I was a homicide detective."

"I hear Goodwin's a damn good lawyer," Bowman said. "How did you fare against him?"

O'Connor ignored Bowman's question and said, "Go take a seat in the living room while I make a pot of coffee."

"Do you need any help?" McMahon asked.

"No, thanks, Mike, I'll manage. It'll beep when it's ready."

A few minutes later, O'Connor joined the two detectives and slowly eased himself down onto a wingback chair.

"Nice place you have here," Bowman said.

"Thanks, Jack. It's the same plan as Mike's condo."

"Since we've never met before, I'd like to say how sorry I am about what happened to your wife," Bowman said.

"Thank you, Jack, I appreciate that."

"How did you feel when you heard the Golf Club Killer murdered your wife's killer?" Bowman asked.

"Are you asking me if I was pleased when Detective McMahon stopped by to tell me what had happened?"

"Were you?"

"Yes and no. Part of me was glad that son of a bitch was dead, but I don't condone vigilante justice."

"I don't either," Bowman agreed. "However, sometimes that's the best way to get justice. God only knows our court system doesn't always work."

Mike was sitting silently listening to their conversation when the coffee maker beeped.

"I'll get it," Mike said.

As McMahon got up, O'Connor said, "There's cream in the fridge and sugar on the kitchen table, the mugs are in the cupboard above the stove, and there's a tray on the counter."

"Do you want cream or sugar, Pat? We drink our coffee black."

"I do, too. It must be a cop thing."

McMahon returned in a few minutes, looking like a waiter with three mugs on a silver serving tray.

"Thanks, Mike," O'Connor said.

Taking a sip, Bowman said, "That's excellent coffee, Patrick. It sure beats the hell out of the mud we drink at the station."

"I agree," Mike said. "What brand do you use?"

"It's Folgers dark roast. It's my favorite brand."

"Now that I've been assigned to work the Golf Club Killer case with Detective McMahon, I'd like to get your thoughts on what you think we're dealing with."

"I've already talked to Mike about that. Didn't he mention it to you?"

"Yes, he did. I was hoping you may have come up with something new since you spoke to Detective McMahon."

"Not really. I agree with Mike and his partner's thinking that the unsub is smart, well organized, and might have a law enforcement background. I believe they're on the right track. What are your thoughts, Detective?"

"Having read the murder book, I agree. Now, all we have to do is figure out who the hell he is and collar the psychopath."

"Good luck with that, Detective. I think you're gonna need it."

Mike could sense O'Connor was getting irritated with Bowman. He stood up and said, "Thanks for the coffee, Pat. We appreciate you seeing us. Come on, Jack, it's time for us to leave and let Patrick get on with his day."

"How long before your boot comes off?" Bowman asked.

"I'm not sure. It'll depend on how fast it heals. I hope you don't mind if I don't walk you to the door?"

"Not a problem, Pat. Thanks again for your time," McMahon said.

Both men remained silent in the elevator until the door opened, and they stepped out into the underground garage.

"So what did you think of the legendary Patrick O'Connor?" Mike asked.

"O'Connor's no fool. He didn't get his reputation by accident. Patrick O'Connor is smart and has a sharp mind."

"Actually, O'Connor has a photographic memory. That's one of the reasons he was able to solve so many homicides. He remembered every little detail at crime scenes."

"Was he really that good?"

"That's what they say."

"For some reason, he seemed hesitant to talk about the Golf Club Killer case. I wonder why?"

"As O'Connor said, he already gave me his thoughts on the case. Besides, he's retired. He probably wants to forget about murders and crime scenes."

"Maybe, but my gut tells me there's another reason."

"Do you think it's because he's the Golf Club Killer?"

"I don't know what to think. You said O'Connor's alibis checked out."

"At the time, they did, but there's one thing bugging me."

"Oh, what's that?"

"When I went to see him after Tyron Parker's murder, I could swear the boot was on his right foot. Tonight, if I remember correctly, it was on his left foot."

"Are you sure?"

"I wish I was. I probably would be if I had a photographic memory."

CHAPTER 48

On their way to the station, they stopped for lunch at Mike's favorite diner. This time Bowman offered to pick up the tab.
When they returned to the squad room, the first thing Mike did was to turn on his computer. He logged into Google and typed in three words. Several options appeared on the screen.
"What are you doing?" Bowman asked.
"I'm bringing up sites that sell ankle and leg supports."
"Are you thinking what I think you're thinking?"
"That O'Connor might be faking his injury?"
"Yeah. Do you?" Bowman asked.
"It's worth checking. At the moment, our suspect list is sitting at zero."
Mike went on Amazon and typed in ankle and leg supports. He scrolled through the various makes until he found what appeared to be the exact brand O'Connor was wearing.
"Bingo," Mike said. "I think I've found it."
Bowman leaned over McMahon's shoulder and said, "It sure looks similar. The specs show the boot is available in different sizes but nothing about the left or right foot."
"That must mean the boot fits either foot. It took a long time for O'Connor to answer the door. He said he had fallen asleep on the couch and didn't hear the bell at first."
"Yeah, that's what he said," Bowman agreed.
"I think O'Connor lied. He was probably scrambling to find and put on the boot. In his haste, he must've put it on the left foot by mistake. I'm almost certain it was on his right foot when I dropped

by to break the news of Tyron Parker's murder. If O'Connor is faking his injury, he could be the GCK."

"GCK?"

"Short for Golf Club Killer," Mike said.

"Oh. If O'Connor is the GCK, as you call him, how do we prove it? Our suspicions won't be enough to get a judge to sign a search warrant."

"You're right. Even if we did get a warrant, I don't think we'd find anything to prove O'Connor killed anyone. He's too smart to leave evidence lying around in his car or condo. We have to catch him in the act," Mike said.

"And how do we do that?"

"It won't be easy. We'll need to come up with a plan."

"A plan? How do we do that when we don't know who his next target will be?" Bowman asked.

"We'll need to set a trap."

"A trap? What do you have in mind?"

"I've been studying the victims the GCK has murdered. Councilman Mitch McConnel was rumored to have taken bribes. Developer Anthony Garanti displaced homeless people with his condo project; Steven Starr stole a song from a young songwriter, Samson Smoke allegedly sold drugs that killed people. Tyron Parker murdered innocent people in a mass shooting, including O'Connor's wife. His latest victim, lawyer Paul Goodwin, represented criminals and scumbags. Goodwin's latest client is Bruce Morton, the man we arrested for murdering six gay men. The one thing all these people had in common—they made headlines in the papers and on TV."

"I see what you're getting at. The GCK selects his victims from the news. What if we try to put ourselves in his shoes and pick the next victim the same way?" Bowman said.

"That's what I'm thinking."

"Okay. Say we pick a possible victim from the news. How do we know we've picked the right target?"

"We don't. That's the hard part. We watch the news and take an educated guess. Once we select a person we think the killer will target, we watch that person twenty-four-seven. And when the GCK strikes, we'll be there to collar him."

"That's one hell of a big job. How are we gonna to do that?"

"We each work a twelve-hour shift seven days a week."

"Your plan sucks. We won't even have time to scratch our asses."

"It shouldn't take long. If the GCK follows the same pattern he did with the first six victims, he'll strike within a week after the news breaks. If you can come up with a better idea, I'm all ears," McMahon said.

"I think we should bounce your plan off the boss. Once we find a possible victim, maybe Foster can spare a few officers to help us with surveillance."

"Let's not put the cart before the horse. I'd prefer to wait until we pick the possible victim before talking with Foster. Besides, I don't think he'll be keen on using uniforms to help us with all the recent budget cuts."

"Okay. But I still think your plan could take forever," Bowman grumbled.

Mike smiled, and his eyes lit up. "I've got a better plan. We can attach a GPS tracking device to O'Connor's car. One of those new cellular devices. When the car moves, we'll be alerted on our cell phones. That way, we can follow him to his next victim and nail him before anyone else dies."

"Now, you're talkin'. I like that plan."

Before leaving, they uploaded the app on their cell phones, and Mike picked up several tracking magnets from the supply room.

CHAPTER 49

After Bowman was gone, McMahon went into the DMV website and obtained Patrick O'Connor's vehicle information. He jotted down the make and plate number and headed for the door. After parking his car, McMahon checked, and no one else was in sight. He found O'Connor's vehicle and placed the tracking device under the passenger side front fender.

Mike had just pushed the button for the elevator when his cell phone rang. He checked the screen, half expecting to see Bowman's name, but instead, it was Rose.

"Hey, partner, what's up?"

In a panic-stricken voice, Rose said, "I'm on my way to the hospital. Dr. Swartz wants to see me as soon as possible."

"Do you know why?"

"When I asked, the nurse said she didn't know why. I'm guessing she did but wouldn't tell me because it must be serious."

"That doesn't sound good. I'm on my way. I'll be there soon."

Mike turned around and ran back to his car. He jumped in, started the engine, and squealed out of the parking garage. When he hit the street, he flipped on the siren.

Rose was sitting on the couch in the waiting room, staring at the floor when McMahon came through the door. He rushed over and sat down beside her. Taking her hand in his, Mike softly asked, "Did you speak with Dr. Swartz yet?"

She looked up with tear-filled eyes and shook her head. "No, not yet. Thanks for coming, Mike."

"Are you okay?

"Not knowing what's going on is killing me."

Just as McMahon released Rose's hand and placed his arm around her, Dr. Swartz came through the door. He ignored Mike and squatted down in front of Rose.

"I'm sorry to have to tell you this, Mrs. Goodwin, but Mr. Goodwin has had a setback. He's unconscious again and back on a ventilator. At this time, I doubt he would survive another operation. I don't wish to speculate as to what happened. We'll do another scan and see what shows up. I will update you as soon as I have more information. Please go home and try to rest."

"Going home won't help. I'll stay here and wait for your update, Doctor."

"As you wish, Mrs. Goodwin."

After Dr. Swartz had left, Mike convinced Rose to go to the cafeteria for something to eat. On the way, they informed the nursing station nurse where they would be and said to call Rose's cell number if Dr. Swartz arrived before they returned.

Rose sipped coffee and picked at her garden salad without speaking while Mike wolfed down a hot roast beef sandwich.

Finally, Goodwin broke the silence. "How are you and Jack Bowman getting along?"

Between mouthfuls, McMahon said, "So far, we've had a couple of dust-ups. Even though there's no love lost between us, we called a truce and agreed to put our differences aside and concentrate on the case. So far, it seems to be working."

Mike went on to tell Rose about Patrick O'Connor's support boot story and that he was now their one and only suspect. He also mentioned their plan to track O'Connor's movements hoping he would lead them to his next target.

"It looks like you and Bowman are making progress. I hope your plan works."

McMahon was half-way through his meal when Goodwin's cell phone chimed.

"Hello." Rose listened for a few seconds, then said, "I'm on my way."

"What's up?"

"Dr. Swartz is back and is looking for me."

"Okay. Let's go."

"Stay and finish your meal. Don't let good food go to waste."

"No way. I'm going with you," Mike said, pushing back his chair and getting to his feet.

Dr. Swartz was at the nursing station when they got off the elevator. Seeing the two detectives, he said, "I'll meet you in the waiting room shortly."

When Dr. Swartz walked through the door, he joined Rose on the couch.

"The scan showed more swelling has developed, pushing down on the brain stem. Swelling can damage the RAS or Reticular Activating System. The RAS is a part of the brain that's responsible for arousal and awareness. That's the reason Mr. Goodwin has slipped back into a coma. At the moment, there's nothing more I can do. He wouldn't survive another operation. We'll have to let nature take its course and pray for the best."

"What are Paul's chances, Doctor?" Rose asked.

"Based on similar cases, I'd say he has a fifty-fifty chance of a full or partial recovery."

As Rose's eyes filled with tears, she asked, "What does a partial recovery mean?"

"A partial recovery could leave Mr. Godwin with brain damage that may affect his speech and thought process."

"Oh, no," Rose whispered as she dabbed at her eyes with a tissue.

"I'm so sorry, Mrs. Goodwin. I wish I had better news. From what I've seen, Mr. Goodwin is a fighter. Please don't give up hope. He may just surprise us all and make a complete recovery. In the meantime, he is back in the same room under twenty-four-hour supervision. Go home and get some rest. We'll call you if Mr. Goodwin's condition should change."

When Dr. Swartz had departed, Mike said, "Rose, I think this time you should take the doctor's advice. Go home to Jill and get some rest. There's nothing you can accomplish by staying here. Take a sleeping pill if you have to. You'll be a basket case if you don't get some sleep. Are you okay to drive?"

"Yes. I'll be okay?"

"Are you sure? I can drive you if you want."

"No, Mike, I'm good."

CHAPTER 50

Mike had just pulled into his parking spot when the alert sounded on his cell phone. The suspect was on the move. He watched as O'Connor's car drove past him on the way to the exit. McMahon waited until the vehicle had left the building before starting his engine. He plugged in his cell phone, placing it in the holder on the dash. Once on the street, he made a right turn following the moving red dot on the screen.

His cell phone rang—it was Bowman.

"Hey, Jack."

"Hey, Mike, O'Connor's on the move."

"Yeah, I know. I'm following his car as we speak."

"I'm leaving right now. I'll catch up as soon as I can."

"Don't bother. I can handle it."

"Are you sure?"

"Yeah. I don't think O'Connor's on his way to kill anyone. He's probably going to get groceries or buy gas."

"I'll call if I need you."

"Okay. Be careful."

The GPS tracking device allowed McMahon to follow at a safe distance. After twenty minutes, O'Connor's car pulled into the parking lot of Music City Lanes. Mike parked a few rows away and watched as O'Connor struggled to stand on one foot while removing his crutches from the back seat. The support boot was on his left foot.

Once O'Connor had entered the building, Mike cautiously approached the entrance and peered inside. It took a few seconds to spot O'Connor. He was sitting with his bowling team members, Joe Carson, Steve Larkin, and Fred Thomas, and another unidentified man—his sub. The men were drinking beer and laughing.

McMahon went back to his car and made a phone call.

"What's happening?" Bowman asked.

"I don't think O'Connor is going to kill anyone tonight. It's Wednesday. He's at Music City Lanes drinking beer with his bowling team. Oh, and he's wearing his boot on his left foot."

"Interesting," Bowman said. "What are you gonna do?"

"Just to be sure he doesn't have any other plans, I'll wait here until O'Connor leaves and follow him. I'll be glad when I get home. I'm looking forward to a hot shower and a stiff drink. See you in the morning."

"Okay. See you tomorrow."

Shortly after ten, Joe Carson held the door as O'Connor came out on his crutches. They said goodbye, and O'Connor headed to his car. McMahon was relieved when O'Connor drove straight home.

After his shower, Mike felt relaxed and human again. He went into the kitchen, poured a double whiskey on the rocks, and headed to his recliner. McMahon decided to forgo watching TV and read the newspaper instead. As he picked up the *Nashville Star Daily,* the headline jumped out at him.

GOLF CLUB KILLER STRIKES AGAIN!

By Jeff Stone, Investigative Reporter

On Monday evening, the Golf Club Killer struck again. This time his target was prominent Nashville criminal attorney Paul Robert Goodwin. The attack took place in the parking lot behind Goodwin's office building. Fortunately, he survived the attack and is in critical condition at Vanderbilt University Medical Center.

My source informed me that a homeless man saved Goodwin's life. When the man saw the attack, he yelled just as the killer struck his first blow. That caused the attacker to stop, drop his weapon, the golf club, and flee the scene.

Paul Goodwin is the ex-husband of Detective Sergeant Rose Goodwin, one of the two detectives initially assigned to the Golf Club Killer case. The other detective is Mike McMahon.

Detective Jack Bowman, formerly with narcotics, has recently joined the Homicide Unit under Lieutenant Robert Foster's command. He will work the case as Detective McMahon's interim partner. Detective Sergeant Goodwin is currently on leave without any explanation. I'm guessing, with the attack on her ex-husband, the case is now too personal?

Why was Paul Goodwin targeted? Is it because he represented scumbags like Bruce Daniel Morton, alleged killer of six gay men, the man he recently murdered. Only the Golf Club Killer knows the real reason.

McMahon quickly reviewed the paper to see if he could find any stories that might provide the GCK with a new victim. Nothing caught his attention, so he turned on the TV to catch the eleven o'clock news. The lead story was about a ten car pile-up on Interstate 65 near Brentwood. Nothing else caught his attention, so Mike decided to call it a night.

Mike downed one more double before crashing and was out for the count as soon as his head hit the pillow. It seemed like he had just fallen asleep when, at 5:00 a.m., the beeping from the digital bedside alarm woke him with a start.

Still half asleep, McMahon crawled out of bed and headed to the kitchen. After drinking two cups of black coffee, his foggy head began to clear. Mike headed back to the bedroom, changed his attire, and went down to the gym. He was determined to get back into shape.

CHAPTER 51

At eight-forty, carrying a coffee and a bagel, McMahon entered the squad room and was surprised to see Jack Bowman at Rose's desk.

"Good morning, interim partner. You're here early. What did you do, shit the bed?"

Laughing, Bowman countered with, "Good afternoon, McMahon. Sleep in, did we?"

"I was up at five and worked out before you rolled out of the fart sack, smartass."

From the sound of their back-and-forth ribbing, anyone who was unaware of the two detectives' animosity would assume they were good friends.

What time did O'Connor leave the bowling alley?" Bowman asked.

"He left just after ten and drove straight home."

"Well, at least we know your GPS idea works."

"Did you read the article by Jeff Stone?" Mike asked.

"Yeah, I did. Even Stone calls me your interim partner."

Mike laughed. "That's because you are my IP."

"Do you have abbreviations for everything, McMahon?"

"No, not everything. I still call you, asshole, not AH. I was just kidding."

Bowman smiled and said, "You'd better be, or I might have to pound the shit out of you."

"You and whose army?" McMahon said, giving Bowman a soft punch on his bicep.

"Are you two at it again?" Lieutenant Foster barked as he walked up behind them.

"No, sir," Bowman said, startled, "We were just clowning around."

"I'd like you clowns to join me in my office. Now, please!"

After McMahon and Bowman were seated, before Foster could speak, his phone rang. He glanced at the screen and smiled. "Sorry, dear, I can't talk now. I've got two clowns in my office. I'll call you later."

Foster held up the *Nashville Star Daily* and asked, "Have you read Jeff Stone's latest article?"

"Yes, we have, Lieutenant," Mike said while Bowman nodded.

"I can never figure out where Stone gets all his facts. He always seems to be one step ahead of every other reporter. Does he have someone in the MNPD on his payroll? That's the only thing that makes sense. Any suggestions as to who that person could be, gentlemen?"

"No, Lieutenant," McMahon said. "I've got a few ideas, but I don't have any proof. I always thought it was someone in forensics, but they probably wouldn't know about Jack replacing Rose."

"As the new kid on the block, I don't have a clue," Bowman said.

"By the way, Detective McMahon, what's the latest news on Paul Goodwin?"

"I'm sorry to say he had a relapse and is in a coma. His condition is critical."

"Damn. That's too bad. I'm sure Rose is going through hell right now. Please tell her my thoughts and prayers are with her, Paul, and her little girl. What's her name?"

"I will, Lieutenant. Her name is Jill."

"The last time we met with Chief Cummings, he asked you to come up with a plan to catch the Golf Cub Killer. Have you come up with anything?"

Bowman and McMahon both spoke at the same time.

"We've got a plan," Bowman said, letting the cat out of the bag.

"We're working on it, " McMahon said.

Confused, Foster asked, "Do you have a plan, or don't you have a plan?"

Before Bowman could screw things up further, Mike said, "We're using a tracking device to follow a suspect. We tested it last night, and it worked perfectly."

"A tracking device? Do you mean on a suspect's vehicle?"

Bowman jumped in and said, "Yes, sir."

"And who the hell is your suspect? Does he have a name?"

"Yes, Lieutenant. His name is Patrick O'Connor," Mike said, waiting for the shit to it the fan.

"Patrick O'Connor?" Foster snapped. "Our Patrick O'Connor?"

"Yes, sir," McMahon confirmed.

"And how did you clowns come to that conclusion?"

Mike went on to tell Foster the story about the support boot and that O'Connor had a motive to kill Tyron Parker, his wife's killer. He also mentioned that O'Connor was away on vacation for a month during the time the killings stopped. When he had finished, the boss leaned back in his chair, scratched his head, and took a deep breath. Suddenly Foster shot forward and glared at McMahon.

"You do realize that what you just told me, Detective, is all conjecture."

"Yes, sir, I do. That's why we planted the tracking device on his car. We plan to catch him in the act."

"You do know that what you did is illegal, don't you? Placing a tracking device without obtaining a warrant won't stand up in a court of law. Any evidence you find will be inadmissible."

"Yes, sir, we are aware of that," Bowman interjected. "We won't be looking for evidence in his vehicle."

"We did it to save countless hours of sitting in a car waiting for the suspect to make a move. By placing the tracking device on his vehicle, an alert will sound on our cell phones as soon as he starts his engine. When he decides to kill again, he`ll lead us to his intended victim. We'll stop him and arrest him before anyone gets killed," McMahon said.

"Or we can do it the old-fashioned way if you can spare several uniforms to help with the surveillance, Lieutenant," Bowman said.

"With all the budget cuts, we don't have enough officers to cover regular duty, let alone what you would require. I don`t like it, but carry on with your plan and see where it leads. Sometimes we have to color outside the lines. For now, let's keep what you two are doing in this room. I don't think it would be wise to inform Chief Cummings of what you're up to. If he asks, I'll tell him you're working on it. That's it for now."

As they sat down at their desks, Mike said, "What the hell were you thinking? I didn't want to tell Foster about our plan just yet."

"I know, I know, it just slipped out. I'm sorry."

"In the future, you'd better think long and hard before you speak when dealing with Foster, especially when it comes to Patrick O'Connor. For some reason, Foster and Cummings have placed O'Connor on a pedestal. In their eyes, he can do no wrong."

"It won`t happen again."

"Make sure it doesn't. In the meantime, let's take a little trip."

"A trip? Where?" Bowman asked.

"To Nashville General."

"Nashville General?"

"I want to check out O'Connor's story. He told me the day he hurt his foot; a fellow jogger drove him to the hospital. Based on what we now know, I think that was a bullshit story. If he told the truth, there should be a record of his visit."

At the emergency department reception desk, Mike presented his badge to the receptionist. "Hello, I'm Detective McMahon of the MNPD, and this is my partner, Detective Bowman. We're working on a case and need to confirm some information."

"What kind of information do you require, Detective?"

"A week or so ago, your emergency department treated a man with a foot injury. I need to find out if that's correct."

"Do you know the man's name?"

"Yes, his name is Patrick O'Connor."

"I believe Ms. Tucker in our records department will be able to help you." She picked up the phone and dialed an extension number. "Molly, this is Joan in emergency reception. I have two detectives who need your help. Okay, I'll tell them. She's on her way."

In her mid-thirties, a trim lady with long, dark hair and a friendly smile approached them in less than one minute.

"Good day, Detectives. I'm Molly Tucker. How may I help you?"

Mike introduced himself and Bowman. After explaining what they required, she asked them to follow her to the records room.

Molly typed Patrick O'Connor's name on her keyboard and waited a few seconds.

"According to our records, the last time Mr. O'Connor visited us was just over three years ago. Due to privacy restrictions, I'm sure you understand, I can't go into details."

"No problem, we understand," Bowman said.

"Are you sure your records don't show that Patrick O'Connor came to the hospital recently? Like a week or so ago," McMahon asked.

"If he did, it would be in our records."

"Here's my card, Ms. Tucker. Thanks for your help," Mike said.

On their way to the car, McMahon turned to Bowman and said, "It's obvious that O'Connor lied about the injury and about going to the hospital. He probably knew I would pay him a visit when Tyron Parker turned up dead. The fake foot injury is his alibi. The day we visited him, in his haste, he put the boot on the wrong foot."

"You're right. It looks like O'Connor could be the GCK."

CHAPTER 52

Six days and five false alarms later, McMahon and Bowman were becoming frustrated. They had followed O'Connor to the grocery store twice, to a service station where he purchased gas, to a barbershop where he had his hair cut, and to Music City Lanes, where he spent an hour with his bowling buddies. During all these trips, the fake cast remained on his left foot.

On the night of O'Connor's last trip to the bowling alley, Mike arrived home shortly before eleven. He poured a double shot of whiskey on the rocks and retired to the living room. Picking up the remote, McMahon turned on the TV just as the eleven o'clock news came on.

"Good evening, I'm Harvey Stewart, and this is Channel 4 late edition news."

The words BREAKING NEWS scrolled across the screen.

"Earlier today, the MNPD arrested forty-two-year-old Ralph Henderson at his residence for possession of over 100 images of child pornography. Henderson was convicted and served eight-year concurrent sentences for child porn and sexual battery cases against a young girl. He is currently being held on a $100,000 bail bond."

"Holy shit!" Mike said out loud. "I think I just found the GCK's next victim."

Feeling optimistic about the case once more, he watched the rest of the news. McMahon downed his drink and went back to the kitchen for a refill.

Mike was still in good spirits the next morning when he arrived at the squad room. When Bowman walked in and sat down at Rose's desk McMahon greeted him cheerfully. "Good morning, IP."

"What's got into you, McMahon? Did you take some happy pills for breakfast?"

"Better than that, Bowman, I think I've found the GCKs next victim."

"What are you talking about?"

"I presume you didn't watch the late news last night."

"Nope. I was too exhausted. I didn't even have the energy to make love to my wife. I went to bed at nine and slept like a log until six."

After Mike told the story about Ralph Henderson, Bowman said, "No shit. I agree; Henderson could be the killer's next target. Good work, partner."

"Correction. IP."

Bowman laughed. "Right. IP."

"What's so funny?" Lieutenant Foster asked.

"God, Lieutenant," Mike said, "you've gotta stop sneaking up on us like that. I swear one of these days; you'll give me a heart attack."

"One of these days, the chief is going to give me a heart attack. He keeps calling, looking for your plan to catch the Golf Club Killer. I can't stall any longer. You'd better come to my office. We've got to discuss what I'm going to tell him."

Once everyone was seated, Nancy Allman appeared at the door carrying a tray containing three mugs of coffee and a plate with three jelly doughnuts. Without saying a word, she placed the tray on Foster's desk and left, closing the door behind her.

While they sipped coffee and munched on their doughnuts, Foster's phone rang.

"Good morning, Chief. Sorry, I haven't talked to them yet. I'll call you back with an update after our meeting. Goodbye, Chief."

"Okay, gentlemen, what do I tell the boss?"

"Tell the chief we have a suspect under surveillance that we believe could be the Golf Club Killer. We plan to catch him red-handed when he goes after his next victim," Mike said.

"If I tell the chief that, he's bound to ask the name of the suspect. I can't lie. I'll have to inform him it's Patrick O'Connor. He'll probably go through the roof when he hears O'Connor's name."

"Not if you say why we suspect O'Connor. Tell the chief about the fake boot story and that O'Connor lied about going to the hospital."

"Okay, but I still think the chief won't be happy when he hears your suspect is O'Connor."

Fifteen minutes later, after calling Chief Cummings, Lieutenant Foster went back to the squad room.

"I just got off the phone with Chief Cummings. At first, he was upset when I told him your suspect was Patrick O'Connor. However, he calmed down when I gave him the reasons you suspect him. For now, continue with your plan. Keep me posted."

After Foster had left, Mike said, "Now that the brass knows what we're up to, let's pray that O'Connor is our killer. If not, we'll be in deep shit for chasing an MNPD legend."

"Yeah, or we'll be up the creek without a fuckin' paddle," Bowman said, forcing a weak laugh.

CHAPTER 53

That evening, when McMahon arrived home, Suzanne popped into his head. It had been a few weeks since he had visited her at the Ormond residence. He wondered how she was doing. There was only one way to find out. Mike picked up the phone and dialed her cell number.

After two rings, Suzanne's cheery voice said, "Hi, Mike, I was wondering if you were ever going to call."

"Hey, Suzanne. It's nice to hear you sounding so upbeat. Is everything going okay?"

"Things are great. I've seen Dr. Hamilton five times since you were here. He says I'm making excellent progress. And I haven't had any nightmares lately."

"Wow! That's great news. Keep it up, girl, and you'll be back on stage in no time."

"I'd love that, but we're gonna take things slowly. I'm hoping in a month or so, I'll be back on tour."

"Be careful. You don't want to rush back and have a relapse. Are you still staying at Bill and Joyce's?"

"Yes, I am. With all this time on my hands, I've been doing a lot of thinking."

"What have you been thinking about?"

"My life, my career, and you and me."

"What about you and me?"

"I realize I was too hasty in breaking our engagement. Mike, I—" Suzanne broke down and began to cry softly.

"Are you okay?"

Finally, Suzanne composed herself and whispered, "What I'm trying to say is, I still love you, Mike. Would you be willing to take me back and try again? I know that's a lot to ask after what I put you through. I'm not asking for the ring back."

"Suzanne, I told you I still love you, and I always will. Why don't we go out for dinner one night soon and talk things over?"

"Sure, Mike, whenever you're ready."

"How about this Saturday evening?"

"Saturday is fine."

"Okay, then. I'll make reservations someplace nice where we can talk without loud music. I'll pick you up at seven."

"Okay. See you Saturday."

After hanging up, McMahon sat staring into space. *Am I doing the right thing?*

Mike arrived at the Ormond residence at five to seven. When he rang the bell, Joyce opened the door.

"Hi, Mike. How are you this evening?"

"I'm fine, Joyce, and you?"

"I'm as excited as Suzanne. She's pacing in the living room and can't sit still. She's like a teenager waiting to go on her first date."

Before Mike could say another word, Suzanne appeared looking as pretty as ever, a radiant glow on her face.

"Have a good evening. See you guys later," Joyce said as she turned and walked away.

"Hey, babe, you look stunning."

"And you're as handsome as ever, Detective McMahon."

When they were in the car, Suzanne asked, "Where are we going?"

"It's a surprise. You'll see when we get there."

As soon as Mike pulled into the parking lot, Suzanne's eyes lit up.

"Great choice, Detective. The last time we were here was on Valentine's Day, the day we got engaged."

"I'm glad you approve. The food is excellent, and we can talk without having to shout."

By nine-thirty, the main course over, they were sipping wine and contemplating dessert when Mike's cell phone vibrated in his belt holder. He checked the screen and winced. It was dispatch.

"Detective McMahon."

"Hey, Detective, it's Sergeant Harding. Sorry to spoil your Saturday evening. We have another murder. The Golf Club Killer has struck again."

CHAPTER 54

Mike wrote down the address, then gave Suzanne a brief explanation of what had happened. On his way to the crime scene, McMahon dropped Suzanne off at his condo to save time. She had decided to stay overnight in the guest room.

After dropping Suzanne off, Mike's mind went into overdrive. *How did O'Connor elude us? There was no alert on my cell phone. Maybe he found the tracker and removed it. Or perhaps O'Connor isn't the GCK after all.* If that was the case, they were back at square one with no suspects and in deep shit with Foster and Cummings.

By the time McMahon arrived at the cream-colored stucco house on Duke Street, the crime scene was a beehive of activity. He parked behind one of three patrol cars on the street, logged in, and headed toward the crowd.

Mike recognized the face of the man lying on the walkway from the picture on TV a few nights ago. The dead man was Ralph Henderson. There was a golf club driver in Henderson's right hand, a red golf ball in his mouth, and a sad-looking beagle sitting next to the body. ME Tony Capino conversed with one of his tech support guys while Jack Bowman spoke with an older woman on the lawn next door. McMahon strolled over and stood next to Bowman.

"This is my partner, Detective McMahon. Mrs. Truman found the body and called it in. I was just about to take her statement. Would you like to do the honors, Detective?"

"No, Jack, you go right ahead."

"Okay. Mrs. Truman, how did you come to discover Mr. Henderson's body?"

"I was watching TV. Shortly after eight, I heard this mournful howling. I came out to take a look and saw Mr. Henderson lying on the ground and poor little Jiggs wailing away. Every few seconds, he would stop his howling and lick his master's face. It was so sad seeing that poor dog in distress. It made me cry. Next, I noticed a man dressed in black standing across the street looking right at me. He gave me a little wave, turned around, jumped on a motorcycle, and took off. That man scared the hell out of me. I ran into the house and called 911."

When Bowman finished writing in his notebook, he asked, "Mrs. Truman, did you see the man's face?"

"No, I didn't because he wore a helmet with a dark shield."

"What about his height and build? Can you describe him to me?"

"I'd say he was at least six feet, maybe a little taller, with an average build. Not fat and not skinny."

"Mrs. Truman, do you remember what he was wearing?"

"All his clothing was black."

"Did you notice if he wore gloves?"

"He may have, but I'm not sure. My eyes aren't too good anymore."

"Here's my card. If you think of anything else, please call me. Thank you, Mrs. Truman, you've been extremely helpful," Bowman said.

"I didn't know Mr. Henderson very well, but he seemed to be a nice man. He was renting the house next door and hadn't lived here long. I saw on the news that Mr. Henderson was a pedophile. Do you think that's why that man killed him?"

"Sorry, Mrs. Truman, we can't comment on that," Mike said.

Mrs. Truman turned toward her front door, mumbling that she wouldn't be able to sleep all night.

"Well," McMahon said, "this is a real shocker. We picked the right victim, but maybe we picked the wrong killer."

"Yeah, this is weird. My tracking alert didn't go off, did yours?"

"Not a peep," Mike said. "If O'Connor is our killer, he didn't use his car. Does he own a motorcycle? If not, then someone else is the GCK."

"If we've been wasting our time on O'Connor, and he's not the killer, we're in deep shit. Foster and Cummings will have our nuts roasted."

"Ouch. That's not a pretty picture," McMahon said. He began to sing off-key. "Chestnuts roasting on an open fire, and Foster nipping at our asses."

Bowman cracked up laughing.

"What's so funny?" Capino asked.

"Just a little warped cop humor," Mike said.

"We'll be wrapping up shortly. In case you wish to attend, I'll be performing the autopsy tomorrow at two."

"We'll be there," Mike said.

"As you can see, the crime scene is staged the same as all the others. And we didn't find any fingerprints or DNA."

"What else is new?" McMahon said.

After parking his car, Mike decided to look for a motorcycle before going up to his condo. As he toured the garage, he spotted a gleaming black Harley at the far end nestled between two cars.

"Bingo," McMahon said aloud. He pulled out a pen and his notebook and wrote down the plate number. On his way to the elevator, Mike stopped at O'Connor's car and checked. The tracking device was still in place.

When he walked through the door, the sound of an action movie playing on the TV caught his attention. Entering the living room, he found Suzanne sound asleep on the couch. Oliver was curled up at her feet, purring contentedly.

Mike glanced at his watch and saw that it was a few minutes after one. He turned off the TV but wasn't sure what to do. *Should I wake Suzanne? Maybe I should get a blanket, cover her, and let her sleep on the couch.* He decided to carry her into the guest room. As he lifted Suzanne and cradled her in his arms, she awoke with a start.

"What...what's going on?"

"Sorry to wake you, babe. You fell asleep on the couch, and I was trying to carry you to the guest room without waking you."

"What time is it?"

"It's a little after one."

"I must've fallen asleep during the movie. I guess I was tired, and the film wasn't that good."

"Do you want me to carry you, or would you prefer to walk?"

Now wide awake, Suzanne gave a seductive smile and said, "I'd like you to carry me into your bedroom. I don't think I'm quite ready to fall asleep in the guest room."

Mike smiled. "What do you have in mind, Ms. Taylor.?"

"Do I have to draw you a picture, Detective? For God's sake, use your imagination."

CHAPTER 55

It felt like old times, waking up with Suzanne snuggled in his arms. McMahon checked the clock on the night table—10:21 a.m. He couldn't believe it was that late. Quietly Mike slipped out of bed and tip-toed into the living room. He sat down at his desk and turned on his computer. On the DMV website, he punched in the plate number, and a few seconds later, he printed off the information. Smiling, McMahon picked up the phone and dialed Bowman's cell.

After two rings, he heard, "What's up, interim partner?"

"Would you do me a favor and attend Henderson's autopsy without me? I've got company and won't be able to make it." He went on to tell Bowman about his date with Suzanne that got cut short by the GCK.

"Okay, McMahon, but you owe me one."

"Yeah, yeah! Oh, by the way, when I got home last night, I checked the parking garage. Guess what I found?"

"Let me take a wild guess. Santa's sleigh? An ice cream truck? I know, I bet you found a motorcycle."

"Bang on. I just checked the plate number on the DMV site. Guess who owns the bike?"

"Do I have three guesses? If I get it right, do I win a prize?"

"Yeah, you get to stay my interim partner a little longer."

"Is the owner Santa Claus?"

"No."

"Am I getting close?"

"No."

"Is it Mary Poppins?"

"No."

"Is it Patrick O'Connor?"

"Bingo! You win the prize and get to keep your job as my IP a little longer."

"Whew. Thank God."

"Goodbye, Bowman, see you and your warped sense of humor Monday morning."

"Goodbye, IP."

McMahon was starting to enjoy Bowman's weird sense of humor. *Maybe he wasn't such a bad guy after all. Nah, Bowman is still an asshole.*

As Mike was making breakfast, he heard the shower running in the master bedroom bathroom.

Ten minutes later, Suzanne walked into the kitchen wearing Mike's Predators jersey.

"Hey, babe, you ready for some bacon and eggs?"

"I sure am. Smells good."

Mike poured Suzanne a coffee and placed it on the table.

"Thanks, Mike. Hope you don't mind me wearing your jersey?"

"You look sexy as hell, Ms. Taylor. After breakfast, I'd like to use my imagination again."

"Sounds good to me, Detective."

Monday morning, Mike dropped Suzanne off at the Ormond's, and by the time he got to the squad room, Bowman was waiting for him.

"Good morning, IP," McMahon said with a broad smile.

"What makes you so happy this morning? Oh, I know you got your oil changed."

Mike's good mood ended abruptly when Lieutenant Foster stormed into the room.

"Into my office, now!" Foster demanded, his face red and the vein on his forehead pulsing a mile a minute.

As they followed the lieutenant, Mike whispered, "It looks like the shit's about to hit the fan."

Bowman whispered back, "You're right. I think it's nut-roasting time."

Once they were seated, and the door closed behind them, Foster got down to business.

"What the hell happened Saturday night? I go away for the weekend with my wife to relax and celebrate our anniversary, and I come back to another mess. How did the Golf Club Killer strike again when you were tracking him. Have you two clowns been wasting time watching Patrick O'Connor when the real killer is someone else?"

Bowman glanced at McMahon and nodded, indicating that he wanted him to answer the questions.

"No, Lieutenant, I believe we've been tracking the right suspect," Mike said.

"It sure doesn't look that way to me."

"Please, Lieutenant, let me explain."

"Okay, Detective, you've got the floor."

"It turns out that O'Connor didn't use his car. A witness at the crime scene saw the killer take off on a motorcycle. When I checked the parking garage at our condo building, where O'Connor lives, I found a black Harley-Davidson. It's registered to O'Connor. I suspect he rides his motorcycle when he goes out to commit his murders. I checked his car last night, and the device is still attached. It looks as if we'll have to put a tracking device on his bike. Do you remember after the Smoke murder, I got a call from someone who said he saw a man on a motorcycle leave the crime scene. The caller wouldn't identify himself or come in and give us a statement. At the time, we assumed it was the killer toying with us. Maybe that call was legit."

"That's quite a story, Detective. Do you truly believe that O'Connor is the Golf Club Killer?"

"Yes, sir, I do."

"What about you, Detective Bowman. Do you believe Patrick O'Connor is the Golf Club Killer?"

"Yes, boss, I do."

Foster paused to swallow an antacid tablet, then calmly said, "To tell the truth, I don't know what to believe anymore. I'll give you one more chance to prove you're right about O'Connor. Attach a tracking device to his motorcycle and see where it leads. When I tell your story to the chief, you'd better hope he believes me. Dismissed."

Back in the squad room, Bowman said, "That went better than I thought it would."

"I agree, but we're on thin ice. If we're wrong about O'Connor, we'll probably be taken off the case and be put back walking the beat or in a patrol car."

"That thought makes me sick to my stomach. Maybe narcotics wasn't so bad after all," Bowman grumbled.

"By the way, how did Henderson's autopsy go?" McMahon asked.

"Fine. There were no surprises. Capino said he's way behind, and the report could take a week or more."

Bowman and McMahon spent the rest of the morning and half the afternoon writing reports and updating the murder book. At four, Mike headed home armed with a tracking device for O'Connor's motorcycle. Seeing no one in sight, he placed the magnetic tracker under the front fender and headed toward the elevator. Just as the door opened, Mike was surprised to see Patrick O'Connor about to get off. The fake cast was on his left foot, and he was still using crutches. Both men appeared surprised to see one another. McMahon stepped back to let him off.

"Hey, Mike, home a little early, are we?"

"Yeah, I'm wiped. I didn't get much sleep last night."

"Is the Golf Club Killer case keeping you awake? The TV news said he killed some low-life pedophile Saturday night."

"Yeah, he's keeping me awake a lot these days," Mike replied. The real reason was his marathon lovemaking session with Suzanne.

"I'm surprised you haven't caught that bastard yet."

"I'm not. The killer, whoever he is, is one smart cookie. Do you have any suggestions?"

"Just keep at it. Sooner or later, your luck will change."

"I hope so. I've got a feeling we're getting close. I see you're still hobbling around on crutches. How is your heel coming along?"

"Slowly, but surely."

"Where are you going?"

"I'm heading out to pick up a few groceries."

"Next time. if you let me know what you need, I'd be happy to do some shopping for you."

"Thanks, Mike, but I manage all right. I'm lucky it was my left heel and not my right; I can still drive okay. It's good for me to get out. It helps keep me sane. Nice to see you. Why don't you drop in for a drink sometime?"

"I just might surprise you and do that, Pat."

"Good. I look forward to it. See you around, Mike."

"See you, Pat."

As soon as McMahon walked into his unit, he picked up the phone. When Bowman answered, he said, "Ignore the alert on your cell phone. I just bumped into O'Connor. He's on his way to buy groceries."

Are you sure?"

"That's what he told me."

"Okay. Thanks for the heads up, but I think I'll follow him anyway."

"Suit yourself."

CHAPTER 56

Rose was dozing in the chair next to Paul's bed. She wasn't sure if she was dreaming or if the voice in her head was real.

"Rose, wake up, Wake up, Rose."

As her eyes fluttered open and began to focus, the same voice repeated, "Rose, wake up. Wake up, Rose."

She turned her head, and her eyes locked on a familiar smiling face.

"Paul, oh, my God, you're awake."

"Where am I? Have I been asleep long?" he asked, sounding weak and confused.

"You're still at Vanderbilt, and you've been in a coma for a few days."

"How long have I been here?"

"A few weeks. Do you remember what happened?"

"No, I don't."

"You were attacked by the Golf Club Killer as you were leaving your office. It happened in the parking lot behind your building."

"The Golf Club Killer? Why would he want to attack me?"

"I'm sorry, Paul, I have no idea."

After a brief visit to the nursing station, the nurse assigned to Goodwin's room returned and was astonished to see Rose and Paul carrying on a conversation.

"Mr. Goodwin, what a pleasant surprise. You're awake. How are you feeling?"

"I've got a slight headache, and I'm as hungry as a grizzly bear who just came out of hibernation."

The nurse laughed. "That's a good sign, Mr. Goodwin. Before we try to feed you, it's best if Dr. Swartz examines you first. Excuse me while I check to see if he's still at the nursing station."

Within a few minutes, Dr. Swartz walked into the room. He smiled and said, "Mr. Goodwin, welcome back to the land of the living. I hear you're as hungry as a grizzly bear."

"Yes, Doctor, I could eat a horse."

Dr. Swartz chuckled at Paul Goodwin's sense of humor.

"I'm sorry, we're all out of horse meat, but I'm sure we'll find something suitable. Mrs. Goodwin, would you mind going to the waiting room while I examine Mr. Goodwin? It won't take long."

"Certainly, Doctor."

Mike had just finished eating when his cell phone rang.

"Hi, Rose, what's up?"

"I'm at the hospital, and I wanted to share some good news with you. Paul came out of his coma less than thirty minutes ago, and so far, he's speaking well, and his memory seems to be intact. I'm in the waiting room while Dr. Swartz examines him."

"That's excellent news, partner. It sounds like our prayers are working."

"It's a true miracle, Mike. I didn't expect him to pull through. Dr. Swartz just walked in. I'll call you back."

"Okay."

Five minutes later, McMahon's cell phone rang again.

"That was fast. Is everything all right?"

"Dr. Swartz said that Paul's examination went well, but he's sending him for another scan to make sure he's on the mend. As soon as Dr. Swartz has the results, he'll give me an update. I'll let you know when I know."

"Try not to worry; I'm sure it will turn out okay."

Less than an hour later, Rose called back. She was finding it hard to contain her excitement. "Dr. Swartz said the scan looks good. Paul's injury is healing nicely, and he's optimistic that Paul will make a full recovery."

"That's amazing, Rose. I'm sure you're relieved to hear that."

"If Paul continues to improve, it won't be long until I can come back to work."

"Don't rush it. You might want to wait a while to see how Paul's recovery goes. Plus, you'll be able to spend more time with Jill."

Rose laughed. "Gee, Mike, it sounds like you don't want me back. You and Bowman must be getting along. Have you two become buddies?"

"I wouldn't say that. We tolerate one another, and for now, we've put our differences aside. As far as I'm concerned, Bowman is still a jerk, but I must admit he has a weird sense of humor."

"Weird sense of humor?"

"Yeah, he cracked me up a few times with some of his remarks."

"By the way, how's the case coming along?"

"I think we're getting close. Bowman and I believe that Patrick O'Connor is the Golf Club Killer."

Mike gave Rose an update on what they were doing to try to catch him.

McMahon had no sooner finished his conversation with Goodwin than his home phone rang. It was Suzanne.

"Hey, beautiful, what's happening?"

"I was sitting here thinking about this past weekend. I want to thank you. I had a great time."

"So did I. Maybe we could do it again sometime soon."

"I'd like that. But let's take it slow until I get my head straightened out. Dr. Hamilton is pleased with the progress I'm making. I'm sleeping well and haven't had any nightmares lately. He says that's a positive sign. "

"That's good to hear. Why don't you give me a call when you're feeling up to it, and we can go from there. I agree we shouldn't rush things."

"Thanks, Mike. I'm glad you understand. I'll be in touch. Goodbye."

"Goodbye, Suzanne."

After hanging up, McMahon sat in his recliner, pondering his conversation with Suzanne. He enjoyed the two nights they had spent together. It felt like old times. However, he didn't want to jump from the frying pan into the fire. He still had deep feelings for her, but he'd rather err on the side of caution. He didn't want to get hurt again, nor did he want to hurt Suzanne in her fragile state of mind.

To get his thoughts off of Suzanne, McMahon picked up the remote and turned on the TV. *Top Gun* was just about to start on the movie channel. He went to the fridge, retrieved another beer, and returned to his recliner. Halfway through the film, Mike's cell phone rang.

"What's up, IP?"

"I followed O'Connor. Just like you said, he went to a grocery store and then returned home."

"Okay, Jack, thanks for letting me know. See you in the morning."

"Yeah, see you, IP."

When the movie ended at eleven, McMahon switched to the news channel.

"I'm Winston Hoover, and this is Channel 4 late-night news. Our lead story this evening comes to us from Nashville, where a white police officer shot and killed an unarmed black man. The details are still sketchy, but a reporter with CNN said the suspect was gunned down during a chase after an altercation in front of a liquor store. This shooting marks the fourth killing of an unarmed black man by police in the past two months. The other shootings took place in Minneapolis, Atlanta, and Los Angeles. Protesters with Black Lives Matter signs have been vocal after all these incidents, calling for murder charges against several police officers. After tonight's shooting, rioting and looting broke out on Broadway Avenue in downtown Nashville. Police in riot gear are trying to stop the civil unrest with tear gas, rubber bullets, and pepper spray. We will keep you updated as this story unfolds. In other new—"

"What's the fuck's going on in this crazy world?" Mike muttered, turning off the TV.

CHAPTER 57

At ten the next morning, in the city hall council chamber, Chief Bradley Cummings and Mayor Tyler Hardy held a press conference to address the previous night's shooting, protest, and riot. Reporters from local media, Fox News, and CNN packed the room, waiting impatiently to ask their questions.

A hush fell over the crowd as Chief Cummings stepped up to the podium.

"Good morning, ladies and gentlemen. Before we get to your questions, I have a few opening remarks. I ask for your patience." The chief took a sip of water and cleared his throat. "Last evening, we had an unfortunate situation in which a young African-American, Bernard Fleming, twenty-two, was shot and killed by an officer of the MNPD."

Chief Cummings went on to tell a similar version of the story as described by Channel 4 TV news anchor Winston Hoover the night before. When he had finished, he said, "I will now take your questions one at a time in an orderly fashion. Please raise your hand, and when I point to you, identify yourself and the media you represent."

Hands shot up like birds taking flight. The chief pointed to a middle-aged man in the front row.

"I'm Drake Benning from CNN. Chief, has the officer who shot the unarmed man been charged with murder?"

"The officer is currently suspended from active duty pending a full investigation of the incident. Our investigators will need time to interview the officer and review any security video in the area to determine what happened. Once that is completed, a decision, if charges are appropriate, will be decided at that time."

The next question came from Tressa Walker from Channel 4 news.

"The killing of unarmed African-American men by white police officers is becoming an epidemic in this country. Do you have any comments about this situation?"

"Systemic racism is a part of everyday life in this country and throughout the world. Unless we can eliminate racism, bigotry, and prejudice from all police forces, the problem will never go away. Better screening and training are needed to remove racial profiling from law enforcement. Community leaders and police forces must work together to find solutions to these problems. It will not be an easy task, but we've got to try. To serve and protect all citizens regardless of their skin color should be every law enforcement officer's goal. If they cannot do that, they have no business wearing the uniform."

The next question came from Jeff Stone of *Nashville Star Daily*. "Chief, what do you have to say to the family of Bernard Fleming? They believe your officer murdered their son in cold blood."

"I plan to visit the parents of Bernard Fleming this afternoon to personally extend my heartfelt sympathy and condolences for the loss of their son. I'm sure you know, Mr. Stone, that all police officers put their lives on the line every day. Sometimes they must make split-second decisions that, unfortunately, can take a life or cause them to lose their own life. As I mentioned, the officer is currently suspended pending a review by the Office of Professional Accountability. Until the OPA reaches a decision, I have nothing more to say at this time."

The chief pointed to an attractive female reporter in the back row.

"I'm Mary Anne Martin with Fox News. "Chief, as an African-American, have you experienced racism in the MNPD?"

"I would like to say no, Mary Anne, but that would not be true. Over the years, I have experienced my share of racism inside and outside of the MNPD."

"Would you care to elaborate?"

"No, Mary Anne, I have nothing further to say on that subject at this time."

After several more questions were asked and answered, Chief Cummings, said, "I will now turn the podium over to Mayor Hardy."

As the mayor stepped to the podium, Jeff Stone yelled out, "Mr. Mayor, have you and Chief Cummings considered my suggestion to bring Homicide Detective Patrick O'Connor out of retirement to consult on the Golf Club Killer case?"

Not prepared for the question, the mayor hesitated for a moment. "Mr. Stone, your suggestion is under consideration, but we have decided to let the detectives working the case handle it for now."

"But Mr. Mayor—"

"That's enough, Mr. Stone. Chief Cummings and I would like to thank you all for attending. Have a good day."

Mayor Hardy stepped away from the podium, leaving Jeff Stone with his mouth wide open without uttering another word.

The day after the press conference, the OPA began their investigation into the shooting death of Bernard Fleming. Since MNPD officers didn't wear body cameras, the OPA panel viewed video from area security cameras. The footage showed Bernard Fleming running away from Officer Brian Moody. Five times, Moody ordered Fleming to stop. Suddenly he turned to face Moody, dropping to his knees, panting and out of breath. Reaching into his jacket pocket, Fleming pulled out an asthma inhaler. When interviewed, Officer Moody said he mistook the inhaler for a gun. Thinking he was about to be shot, Moody said he fired three rounds. After several hours of deliberation, the panel ruled that in the darkness of night Officer Moody had to make a split-second life-or-death decision. The OPA panel unanimously agreed that Officer Moody believed he acted in self-defense. They ruled the Bernard Fleming shooting was a good shooting and reinstated Officer Moody to active duty.

As soon as the OPA ruling hit the media, protests broke out on the streets of Nashville. Protesters chanted for murder charges to be laid against Officer Moody and for Chief Cummings to resign. For the most part, the marches were peaceful. The protests lasted for several days before gradually petering out.

CHAPTER 58

Two weeks went by without any alerts from O'Connor's motorcycle tracker. Every day or two, his car's signal would lead McMahon and Bowman on a wild goose chase to grocery stores, a dentist's office, a service station, and the bowling alley. O'Connor's boot remained on his left foot, and he was now using a cane instead of crutches.

With the case stalled, McMahon's and Bowman's frustration level was at an all-time high. Their search for potential GCK victims on TV and in the newspapers had dried up. Once again, Lieutenant Foster and Chief Cummings were becoming impatient by the Golf Club Killer case's lack of progress.

The next Wednesday evening, after following O'Connor to the bowling alley and back home again, Mike was unwinding with a drink when his cell phone rang.

"Hey, Rose, what's up?"

"Mike, I'm so excited. I just had to call to tell you that Paul came home today. His mind is as sharp as a knife, and he hasn't skipped a beat. Jill is thrilled to see her father again."

"That's excellent news, partner. I'm sure Paul will enjoy recuperating at home instead of in the hospital."

"I can't believe he wants to go back to work next week. Paul plans on working half days at first, but knowing him, that won't last long. I've told him to take more time to make sure he's fully recovered, but Paul won't listen. That man is as stubborn as a mule."

"Didn't he take on an associate recently?"

"Yes. Three months ago, Paul hired a bright young lawyer who graduated from Yale a few years ago but was having a tough time making ends meet independently. The workload was getting more than he could handle by himself. Paul plans to retire in five years. That will give him enough time to groom his associate to take over his practice."

You and Paul have a lot in common. Neither of you can sit around and do nothing."

"I suppose you're right. I can hardly wait to get back to work again."

"Have you talked with Foster about returning?"

"I plan to do that tomorrow. Sorry, Mike, I've got to go. My sister Marilyn is on call waiting."

"Okay. Take care. I'm looking forward to you coming back."

The following morning, when Mike arrived at his desk, he opened up the *Nashville Star Daily* and noticed a new article by Jeff Stone.

GOLF CLUB KILLER SURVIVOR RETURNS HOME
By Jeff Stone, Investigative Reporter

After surviving a vicious attack by the Golf Club Killer, criminal defense attorney Paul Goodwin came home from Vanderbilt University Medical Center yesterday. Mr. Goodwin underwent surgery for a brain injury caused by the attack several weeks ago. For a time, it appeared as if Goodwin would be another notch on the killer's golf club, but miraculously he pulled through.

As he left the hospital, Mr. Goodwin said, "I'm planning on going back to work next Monday. To start, I'll work part-time from 5-9 p.m. when it is quiet, and my staff has left for the day."

When I asked him for his thoughts on why the Golf Club Killer attacked him, Goodwin said, "In our justice system, everyone is innocent until proven guilty in a court of law. Every accused person is entitled to a fair trial and to be represented by counsel. I guess the Golf Club Killer doesn't appreciate the clientele I defend. I believe that's why he attacked me."

I asked Mr. Goodwin if he had a message for the Golf Club Killer. "I sure do," he said. "As far as I'm concerned, Mr. Golf Club Killer, I hope you burn in hell because that's where you belong."

As I mentioned in a previous article, Paul Goodwin's former wife, Detective Sergeant Rose Goodwin, and Detective Mike McMahon are the lead detectives assigned to the Golf Club Killer case. When Paul Goodwin was injured, Sergeant Goodwin was placed on leave, and Detective Jack Bowman took over as Detective McMahon's interim partner. So far, the Golf Club Killer has eluded capture and recently killed again.

I strongly recommend that Chief Cummings and Mayor Hardy consider bringing legendary Detective Patrick O'Connor out of retirement and making him a consultant on the Golf Club Killer case.

What do you think, Nashville?

Just as Mike finished reading the article, Jack Bowman returned from the men's room.

"Hey, Bowman, did you read the latest article by our friend Jeff Stone?"

"No. What's it about?"

McMahon handed him the paper and said, "Read it for yourself."

A few minutes later, "Wow," Bowman said, "Stone sure knows how to stir the pot."

"Tell me about it. Stone does that every time we have a case that doesn't get solved overnight. He's a relentless bastard."

"I can see why you and Rose don't like the man."

"Stone's suggestion to bring O'Connor in as a consultant on the case is like putting a mouse in charge of the cheese. Can you imagine the irony if the GCK is advising us on how to collar himself?"

Bowman chuckled. "That's a good one. I'm sure O'Connor would enjoy doing that."

Mike began to laugh. "Yeah, I'm sure he would."

"What's so funny, Detectives?" Lieutenant Foster said, walking up behind them.

"Jeff Stone's article. He's suggesting Chief Cummings and Mayor Hardy bring Patrick O'Connor out of retirement to consult on the Golf Club Killer case. That would be like putting a monkey in charge of guarding the bananas," Bowman said.

"Yeah, that would be hilarious if O'Connor was the Golf Club Killer, but it wouldn't be funny if the killer were someone else? That would make monkies out of you two. Get your asses into my office. We need to talk."

Once the door was closed, and everyone had taken a seat, Lieutenant Foster said, "The chief called this morning. He and the mayor are seriously considering Jeff Stone's idea of bringing in Patrick O'Connor as a consultant on the Golf Club Killer case."

"Why would the chief do that? I'm sure he's aware that O'Connor is our number one suspect," Mike said.

"Although we may believe that, the chief has never been convinced that O'Connor is the killer. I told him you were getting close to making an arrest and asked him to hold off for a few weeks to give you a chance to prove your suspicions."

"What did he say?" asked Bowman.

"He said you have two weeks from today. If you haven't collared the killer by then, he'll bring in O'Connor."

"Damn," McMahon said, "that doesn't give us much time."

"It's two weeks longer than you would've had if I hadn't intervened."

After the meeting, McMahon and Bowman decided to go to the break room for a caffeine fix. As they sipped their coffee, Mike said,

"I've been thinking. It's time to do some fishing. We need to bait a hook to get O'Connor to strike."

"Easier said than done. What do you have in mind?"

"I'm going to call Rose and see if she and Paul will agree to help."

"Help? How?"

McMahon went on to explain his plan. When he had finished, Bowman said, "It just might work."

That evening, Mike sipped on a beer while he worked on the pizza he had picked up on the way home. When he had finished eating, McMahon grabbed another beer and retreated to his recliner. He picked up the phone and dialed Rose. After the third ring, she answered.

"Hi, Mike, what's up?"

"Hey partner, how's Paul doing?"

"Fine. Paul was relieved and delighted to get home to Jill and familiar surroundings. At the moment, he's taking a nap."

"And how are you feeling?"

"I feel great, but I'm chomping at the bit to return to work."

"Did you talk to Foster about coming back?"

"Yeah, I did, but he wants me to stay on leave a while longer. Foster told me, if I did come back, I wouldn't be working the Golf Club Killer case due to a conflict of interest. That sucks. After what happened to Paul, I've got even more incentive to collar that psycho."

"I understand how you feel. Would you be interested in working on the case unofficially?"

"What do you have in mind?"

Mike outlined his plan.

"Sounds interesting. Let me sleep on it. I'll talk to Paul and call you tomorrow."

"Okay, but the clock is ticking."

CHAPTER 59

Saturday morning at ten, Mike made up a list and headed out to buy a few groceries. As he was getting off the elevator, his cell phone began to beep. He checked the parking garage and noticed O'Connor's car heading for the exit. McMahon trotted to his car, fired up the engine, placed the phone into the dash holder, and followed the moving red dot. Less than five minutes later, Bowman called.

"Hey, Jack."

"I see O'Connor's on the move."

"Yeah, I'll handle it. I'm on O'Connor's ass right now. I'll call you later."

"Okay."

Not wanting to be spotted, Mike stayed a safe distance behind O'Connor's vehicle. In less than thirty minutes, the car pulled into the Nashville Family Medical Clinic's parking lot. Patrick O'Connor got out of the car, still wearing the boot. Without using a cane, he hobbled into the building. Twenty minutes later, O'Connor came out of the clinic carrying the boot and walking normally.

Instead of going home, McMahon followed him to Hendersonville. Watching from a block away, Mike saw O'Connor pull into the driveway of a two-story home in a newer middle-class neighborhood. Three Harley-Davidson motorcycles, similar to the one owned by Patrick O'Connor, sat in the driveway.

"What the hell?" McMahon said to the empty car.

Mike's thoughts were interrupted by the ringing of his cell phone. He was expecting a call from Rose, but the screen showed Nashville General Hospital.

"Detective, McMahon."

"Good morning, Detective, it's Molly Tucker from Nashville General. Do you remember me?"

"Yes, Molly, I remember you. What's up?"

"I would like to apologize for giving you incorrect information when you and your partner were here inquiring about Mr. O'Connor."

"Incorrect information? I don't understand."

"Mr. O'Connor did visit the hospital recently. I was away the day he came in, and a part-time girl took my place. Somehow she forgot to enter the information into the computer. I just found the form in the wrong file folder. I'm updating Mr. O'Connor's record now. Sorry about that."

"No problem, Molly. Thanks for letting me know."

After hanging up, Mike couldn't believe what he had just heard. *Shit, shit, shit! Does this mean Patrick O'Connor is not the GCK? His injury must've been legit. Was I mistaken about him placing the boot on the wrong foot? I'm gonna look like the bungling idiot Inspector Clouseau in the eyes of Lieutenant Foster and Chief Cummings.*

Just as O'Connor opened the car door, three men came out of the house to greet him. They were all drinking beer and laughing.

Pulling out his binoculars from the glove box, McMahon recognized them as Joe Carson, Steve Larkin, and Fred Thomas. They all wore black leather jackets with the name OLD FARTS MC in bold white lettering on the back.

"Holy shit," Mike said aloud. "The bowling team are members of a biker's club."

As he continued to watch, Joe Carson went inside the house and returned with a beer for O'Connor. They all clinked bottles, then O'Connor reached into the back seat and grabbed the boot. He tossed it into the air, and when it hit the ground, the men all cheered. Patrick O'Connor kicked up his heels, began clapping his hands, and danced an Irish jig around the boot. McMahon laughed as he watched O'Connor's three friends start to dance along with him.

Fifteen minutes later, Larkin and Thomas started their motorcycles, waved goodbye, and took off while O'Connor and Carson continued their conversation.

Mike decided since O'Connor was no longer a suspect, it would not be necessary to continue to follow him. Disappointed, he called Bowman.

"Hi, I.P. What's up."

"Meet me at the station in thirty minutes."

"Why? What's up?"

"I'll tell you when I get there."

CHAPTER 60

When McMahon arrived in the squad room, Bowman was on the phone carrying on a conversation and laughing. As soon as Mike sat down, Bowman said, "I've got to go, my dear. See you later. What's up, IP?"

"Brace yourself, Jack, have I got news for you."

After Mike filled Bowman in on the phone call from Molly Tucker and what he had witnessed in Joe Carson's driveway, Bowman sat silently, trying to absorb what he had just heard. Finally, he said, "Based on what you witnessed, it looks like O'Connor isn't the GCK after all."

"I hate to admit it, Jack, but I was wrong. Patrick O'Connor, Steve Larkin, and Fred Thomas all had airtight alibis the night of Tyron Parker's murder. That leaves Joe Carson as the only possible suspect. Since he didn't have anyone who could confirm, he was home with a migraine headache, Carson could be the GCK."

"Do you really believe Carson's our man?"

"It's getting to the point where I don't know what the hell to believe."

"Okay, let's assume Carson is the GCK. How do we collar him?"

"We use the same plan as we did with O'Connor. We attach a tracking device to Carson's motorcycle and vehicle."

"How do we do that?"

"Now that I know where he lives, I'll do it tonight after dark."

"Do you want me to come with you?"

"No, I'll do it myself."

"What about Foster? Should we give him an update Monday morning?"

"I don't think that's a good idea at this time. If we tell Foster the latest news, he'll probably go ballistic and pull us off the case. The chief gave us two weeks to catch the GCK. He won't give a shit who the killer is as long as we collar the right person."

Just then, McMahon's cell phone rang.

"Hey, Rose."

"Hey, Mike. I discussed your plan with Paul, and he agreed."

"Good. I'd like to set up a meeting with the two of you as soon as possible to discuss the details."

"Can you pop by this afternoon?"

"No problem. Is three okay?"

"That's fine. See you then."

"Oh, by the way, Joe Carson and not Patrick O'Connor is now our prime suspect." Mike went on to explain why.

McMahon arrived at the Goodwin residence at five minutes to three. Maria, the nanny, answered the door and escorted him into the spacious living room where Paul and Rose awaited his arrival.

"Thanks for coming, Mike," Paul said, extending his hand.

After the men shook hands, and McMahon took a seat, Paul asked, "Would you like a coffee, Mike?"

"That would be great if you have some?"

"Maria, would you please bring coffee and some of those delicious cookies you baked?" Paul called out.

A few minutes later, as they sipped coffee and nibbled on oatmeal cookies, Mike said, "You're looking good, Paul. How do you feel?"

"I feel pretty damn good. As I said in the article written by Jeff Stone, I'm going back to work on a part-time basis starting on Monday. I plan to go in from 5-9 p.m. after my secretary and associate go home for the day. That way, I can catch up without any interruptions. My new associate has been a busy beaver while I've been in the hospital. She added four new cases that I need to become familiar with."

"I'm glad you won't be defending that scumbag, Morton, now that he's dead," Rose said. "Morton murdered six gay men and was guilty as sin."

"Guilty or not, everyone, including Bruce Morton, is considered innocent until proven guilty in a court of law. You know that."

"I know, but I still don't like the clients you represent."

"Like it or not, someone has to represent them. After all, I am a defense attorney. And besides, I make a lot of money doing it."

Sensing the discussion between Paul and Rose was starting to get heated, Mike interrupted. "Getting back to why I'm here, Your hours should work perfectly with the plan I've devised. I'm sure the Golf Club Killer has read the Jeff Stone article and will be wanting to finish the job he started. Especially after you said, you hope he burns in hell."

"Yeah, I bet my comments pissed him off. I'm sure he'll be looking for another opportunity to finish me off."

"That's what I'm counting on. When that maniac comes looking for you, we'll be ready and waiting."

McMahon went on to explain the details. When he had concluded, Rose said, "It could be risky, Paul. Do you still want to go through with it?"

"I'm sure I'll be safe. Your plan sounds good to me, Mike. I can't wait for you to catch that psycho."

That evening, dressed in dark clothing, Mike took the elevator to the parking garage. Before he went to his car, he removed the tracking devices from O'Connor's vehicle and motorcycle.

A light rain began to fall as Mike parked on a side street a few blocks from Carson's house. When he reached Carson's address, the home was entirely in darkness. McMahon did a quick three-sixty to make sure no one was around before creeping to the back door of the attached double garage. Cupping his hands, he peered through the small window and spotted the motorcycle. The vehicle was missing, indicating that Carson must have gone out. McMahon turned the doorknob and was surprised to find the door unlocked.

Just as he placed the device under the motorcycle's front fender, the metal garage door began to creak open. Mike made a quick exit, crouching low behind the rear entrance. A vehicle entered the garage, the motor died, and the garage door started to descend. A door slammed, and thirty seconds later, the lights on the garage door opener switched off. Mike waited until he was sure the coast was clear before reentering the garage. He attached the tracker to Carson's pickup truck and left.

Monday morning, when Mike sat down at his desk, Bowman asked, "How did it go Saturday night?"

"Smooth as silk," Mike replied.

"What's smooth as silk?" Foster asked.

"Nothing important," McMahon said. "God, Lieutenant, you've got to stop sneaking up on us like that. You almost scared the shit out of me."

"Would you like me to clear my throat as I approach?"

"That would certainly help."

"Sounds like your nerves are shot, Detective. Is the case getting to you?"

Mike ignored Foster's comment and asked, "What's up, Lieutenant?"

"At the moment, Chief Cummings is still dealing with the fallout from the police shooting of a young black man. He asked me to give him an update on the Golf Club Killer case in a few days. Is there anything new to report?"

Bowman glanced at McMahon and gave a slight nod. Mike took that as a cue for him to do the talking.

"Nothing new at the moment, Lieutenant. Tell the chief we're getting close and plan to arrest the killer in a week or so."

"You wouldn't be shittin' me, would you, Detective?"

"I shit you not, Lieutenant."

"Okay, but you'd better deliver. All our asses are on the line."

After Foster disappeared, Bowman turned to Mike and said, "I hope you know what you're doing, McMahon."

"I guess we'll soon find out."

CHAPTER 61

At four that afternoon, as part of Mike's plan to collar the GCK, a brand new 6-yard dumpster measuring 5 feet by 6 feet by 6 feet high replaced the old 5-yard model in the parking lot behind Paul Goodwin's law office. Bowman and McMahon drilled tiny peepholes through the metal on all sides and placed two folding metal chairs with padded seats inside. A security firm that Paul Goodwin hired installed two hidden digital cameras that covered the entire parking lot.

At seven o'clock, Mike and Rose used a small step ladder to enter the dumpster. Once they were inside and seated on their chairs, Jack Bowman removed the ladder and handed it to Mike.

"I hope you two are comfy. I'm heading back to the car. I'll let you know if Carson leaves his house. Have fun."

Shortly before eight, Mike received a call from Bowman.

"My phone just started to beep."

"Yeah, mine, too."

"Carson has left the house in his truck. It's too early to tell where he's heading. I'll call back with an update as soon as I know."

"Roger that," Mike said.

Twenty minutes later, Bowman called again.

"It looks like Carson is coming in our direction."

"It looks that way," Mike agreed.

"Since he's driving his truck and not his motorcycle, he's probably on a surveillance mission, but be prepared just in case."

"Copy that."

At eight-thirty, Bowman watched as Carson parked his truck a block from Goodwin's building and walked to an area where he could view the parking lot without being seen.

Once more, Mike's phone vibrated.

"What's up, Jack?"

"It looks like Carson is watching to see if Paul Goodwin leaves the building around nine," Bowman said. "He's not carrying a golf club."

"It would appear he's just casing the place to make sure Goodwin is at the office," Mike said.

"That would be my guess," Bowman replied.

At five minutes past nine, carrying a briefcase, Paul Goodwin came out of the building. After locking the door, he walked directly to his car and left the parking lot.

Carson went back to his truck and drove off.

Tuesday evening at seven, Mike and Rose were seated in the dumpster while Bowman relaxed in his car a block away. Shortly after eight, the alert sounded on Bowman's and McMahon's cell phones. This time the signal came from the tracker on Carson's motorcycle. Once Bowman knew Carson was heading in their direction, he called McMahon.

"Get ready," he said when Mike answered. "The motorcycle is on its way. I estimate Carson will arrive in about thirty minutes."

"I've been tracking him, too, Jack. We'll be ready."

"Roger that, IP," Bowman said and hung up.

McMahon turned to Rose and said, "Game on,"

Drawing her Glock, Rose replied, "I can't wait to play."

A short time later, the distinct rumble of a Harley-Davidson entered the parking lot and stopped behind the dumpster. As the motor died, Mike and Rose watched through the peepholes. A man dressed in black leather wearing a tinted motorcycle helmet deployed the kickstand. He dismounted and slipped what appeared to be a homemade cylindrical carrying tube from his back, pulling out a shiny new golf club driver. Crouching low, the man peeked around the dumpster, zeroing in on the back door. At six minutes after nine, Paul Goodwin came out of the building. Just as he turned to lock the door, the Golf Club Killer sprang to his feet and crept toward Goodwin.

That's when Mike and Rose jumped up and pointed their pistols over the top of the dumpster.

"MNPD! Hold it right there, or I'll shoot," McMahon yelled.

"Stop, or you're a dead man," Rose shouted.

Hearing the commotion behind him, Paul Goodwin unlocked the door and quickly disappeared back inside the building.

A split second after the detectives called out, the man wheeled around, discarded the golf club, and reached behind his back, pulling a handgun from under his jacket. That's when several shots rang out. Mike, Rose, and Jack Bowman fired simultaneously. The Golf Club Killer crumpled to the ground like a ragdoll.

At the body, slipping on latex gloves, McMahon knelt and lifted the visor. As expected—the Golf Club Killer was Joe Carson.

"It looks like Carson preferred suicide by cops instead of capture and trial," Mike said.

"It appears that way," Rose agreed.

Within fifty minutes, the CSU team arrived on the scene. When ME Tony Capino removed the helmet from the killer's head, he stared in disbelief when he realized that the Golf Club Killer was Joe Carson.

Lieutenant Foster was all smiles as Goodwin, McMahon, and Bowman sat down in his office the following morning. Before he could say a word, Chief Cummings rapped on the door, entered, and took a seat next to Foster.

"Congratulations, detectives," the chief said. "I'm happy to hear the Golf Club Killer case is finally solved. However, I'm distraught and baffled to find out the serial killer was Joe Carson, one of our own."

"I wish to add my congratulations as well, Detectives. Well done," Lieutenant Foster said. "As of now, you're in limbo for a few days. Once the OPA committee reviews the security video and completes your interviews, it shouldn't take long before you're back on active duty."

The chief checked his watch and said, "Sorry, gentlemen, I have to leave. I'm meeting with Mayor Hardy in thirty minutes to plan a press conference. He told me to add his congratulations as well."

As soon as the chief walked out the door, Lieutenant Foster turned to Rose and scolded, "Detective Sergeant Goodwin, I'm not pleased that you disregarded my orders to stay off the case. However, I understand your enthusiasm to catch your ex-husband's attacker. Once OPA clears you, you will be back on the job with Detective McMahon."

"Thank you, Lieutenant."

"It was my fault, Lieutenant," Mike said, "I asked Sergeant Goodwin to help."

Ignoring McMahon, Foster focused on Bowman. "As for you, Detective Bowman, once reactivated, I'm assigning you a new partner. Her name is Melody Smylski. You can all go home until you are called to appear at the OPA hearing. Enjoy your time off."

As they left Foster's office, Rose turned to Mike and said, "I guess we'll have to postpone our trip to Timbuktu."

Mike grinned. "Damn. I was really looking forward to an extended vacation."

That evening, all the local TV channels carried the Golf Club Killer story. At eleven, Mike tuned in to Channel 4 just as Winston Hoover came on screen.

"Good evening. I'm Winston Hoover, and this is Channel 4 news at eleven. Our lead story comes from Nashville, where, last night, MNPD detectives took down the Golf Club Killer, the vigilante who has been terrorizing the streets of our city the past several months. We were shocked to learn the killer is a retired cop. He has been identified as retired Homicide Detective Joe Carson, the former partner of legendary Homicide Detective Patrick O'Connor."

Hoover went on to explain the circumstances that led to the shooting of Carson.

"We now switch to a live report from our field reporter, Rhonda Wright."

"Thank you, Winston. Good evening. I'm here outside of Tootsies with Homicide Detective Jack Bowman and his wife, Shirley. They have been out celebrating the closure of the Golf Club Killer case. I understand you were one of the detectives who took down the Golf Club Killer last evening. Is that correct, Detective?"

"Yes, Rhonda, that's right."

"Can you tell the audience what happened?"

"The case was going nowhere until I joined the team and came up with a plan to lure the killer into action again."

McMahon couldn't believe Bowman was taking credit for his plan. He went on to describe in great detail how Carson was shot and killed after drawing a gun.

When the interview ended, Mike turned off the TV and screamed into the silent room. "That fucking Bowman hasn't changed. He's still an asshole and a glory hound. I feel sorry for his new partner."

CHAPTER 62

Two days later, after interviewing the three detectives and watching a video recording of the incident, the OPA panel ruled Joe Carson's death was a good shooting. The detectives were cleared of any wrongdoing and reinstated to active duty.

McMahon saw Bowman sitting in the break room the first morning back on the job, carrying on a conversation with his new partner. For a split second, the two men locked eyes, but neither man spoke. Mike was about to confront Bowman about the TV interview but decided to bite his tongue and get the hell out of there before they came to blows.

As Rose sat down, McMahon asked, "Did you see Bowman on TV the other night?"

"I did. Bowman'hasn't changed. He's still the same smug jerk he's always been. I hope that douchebag gets transferred to a precinct on the far side of town so I won't have to look at his ugly, arrogant face anymore."

"Amen to that, partner. By the way, are you and Paul still thinking about getting back together?"

"Paul suggested that I move in with him and Jill on a trial basis to see how things go. I told him I'm not ready to do that just yet. I don't want to get Jill's hopes up. She'll be disappointed again if it doesn't work out."

"I agree. It's better not to rush things unless you're sure that it's the right move."

"What about you and Suzanne?"

"We're taking it one day at a time."

"Good idea."

After walking through the door that evening, McMahon fixed himself a stiff drink. He popped a meat pie into the oven, set the timer, and headed to his recliner. While Mike sat sipping his whiskey, his mind focused on Jack Bowman and the TV interview. Somehow he would find a way to get even with that backstabbing bastard.

His thoughts were interrupted by the ringing of his cell phone. The ID on the screen showed Suzanne Taylor.

"Hey, beautiful, what's up?"

"Hey, handsome. I just wanted to give you a call before I go on stage to tell you that we'll be finishing the concert with your song 'As Cold As Snow.' I'll call you after the show to let you know the reaction from the audience."

"Okay, that's great. I'm sorry, I forgot, where are you?"

"I'm in Detroit. We're playing the Joe Louis arena."

"Oh, yeah, now I remember. It's your first gig since you've been cleared to go back on the road. Break a leg."

Suzanne laughed. "I hope you don't mean that literally. Have to go. Call you later."

Mike had just finished eating and was pouring another drink when the doorbell chimed. When he opened the door, he was not surprised to see Patrick O'Connor.

"Pat, what a pleasant surprise."

"Hey, Mike, I hope I didn't catch you at a bad time?"

"Hell, no. I just poured a drink. Come in, and I'll pour you one. Or would you prefer a beer?"

"A beer would be good."

"Okay, a beer it is."

Mike went to the fridge, grabbed a beer, and handed it to O'Connor.

"Let's go to the living room," Mike said.

"Okay, Mike. Lead the way."

When they were seated, McMahon asked, "What's on your mind, Pat?"

"I'd like to congratulate you on solving the Golf Club Killer case. I was shocked when I watched the TV news and found out the killer was my former partner, Joe Carson. I couldn't figure out why he didn't answer his phone that night. I tried several times, and I kept getting his leave a message recording. How did you find out it was Joe?"

McMahon decided not to tell O'Connor he was their first suspect. He said they zeroed in on Carson because of his weak alibi the night of Tyron Parker's murder. And Mike didn't say anything about planting tracking devices on Carson's truck and motorcycle.

"We figured sooner or later the killer would want to finish the job on Paul Goodwin, so we devised a plan, and it worked. We didn't know who the killer was until we lifted the visor at the scene. We were all surprised when the Golf Club Killer turned out to be Joe Carson."

"Come to think of it; looking back, I found it unusual that whenever we discussed the Golf Club Killer case, Joe always agreed with what the vigilante was doing. When we were partners, he always got so damn angry every time a criminal slipped through the cracks in the justice system. After his wife, Eileen, died of cancer, Joe took her death hard. He went into a shell and became anti-social. It took a lot of work and coaxing to get him back into the real world. I never suspected he would go off the deep end the way he did."

"I guess we'll never know why Carson did what he did. Sometimes people just snap."

"You're right. It's a mystery that may never be solved."

"Would you care for another beer, Pat?"

"No, thanks, Mike. I've taken up enough of your time. I'd better get going. Six a.m. comes early."

"Six a.m.?"

"Now that my injury has healed, I'm back to my early morning jogging routine."

"Good for you, Pat. How is your heel?"

"Like new. It feels great."

"Glad to hear that."

After O'Connor had gone, Mike stretched out on his recliner and fell sound asleep. Shortly after eleven, he awoke to the ringing of the phone. It was Suzanne.

"Hey, babe. How did your concert go?"

"You sound drowsy, Mike. Were you sleeping? Have you been drinking?"

"I nodded off in my recliner. I've had a few to celebrate solving the Golf Club Killer case."

"You solved the case? Congratulations! That must be a weight off your shoulders."

"Yeah, it is. It was a tough one."

Without warning, Suzanne said, "I hope you're not becoming an alcoholic, Mike."

"No, Suzanne, I'm not becoming an alcoholic. I just like to drink a lot," Mike joked.

"Hilarious, McMahon. Anyway, I'm excited to tell you about the concert. We had a full house. More than half the crowd came across the border from Canada. I would like to think they came to see me, but I suspect they came to see their fellow Canadian, Marven Jones. At the end of Marven's opening set, the Canadian fans gave him a standing ovation while chanting Marven, Marven, Marven. Then they began to sing O'Canada. I could swear Marven had tears in his eyes. During my set, when I brought him back on stage, we received a standing ovation after we sang, 'Don't Throw Our Love Away.'"

"That's wonderful, babe."

"We finished the concert with your song, 'As Cold As Snow.' When the song ended, everyone stood, clapped, cheered, and whistled. I couldn't believe the response. It's going to be the first single release on my next album. And Mike, I love the song, 'Broken Dreams,' your homeless friend, Matt Hatter, wrote. Tell him I want to meet him and that I'd like to record his song. Oh, and Bill and Dave were blown away by his other songs and want to sign him to a songwriter contract."

"Glad to hear the crowd liked my song, and I can't wait to tell Matt the terrific news. Maybe this is the break he needs to get him off the street."

"I'll be coming home in two weeks. Would you be open to me moving back in on a trial basis? We can take it slow and see where it leads."

"Are you sure that's what you want to do?"

"Only if you want me to."

"Okay, I'm good with that."

"By the way, Mike, have you heard about a deadly virus killing people in China?"

"Yeah, it sounds scary. I hope it doesn't come here."

"So do I. It's getting late, my dear Michael John. I'd better go and let you get some sleep. Talk soon. Love you."

"Love you, too."

After hanging up, Mike poured another drink. Just as he was about to take a sip, Suzanne's words echoed in his head. Feeling guilty, McMahon walked to the sink, poured it down the drain, and went straight to bed.

As he slept, little did Detective McMahon know that a deadly killer named COVID-19 would soon go on a killing spree throughout the world—a killer that he would not want to catch.

———•+•———

Manufactured by Amazon.ca
Bolton, ON